LOST WORLD II
SAVAGE PATAGONIA

DANE HATCHELL

SEVERED PRESS
HOBART TASMANIA

LOST WORLD II SAVAGE PATAGONIA

ISBN: 978-1-925342-76-5

CHAPTER 1

SKEER-AK! The cry of the pterodactyl electrified the air as the shadow of the thirty-foot leathery wings passed in front of the cave's entrance.

"Not this shit again," Gerald Hawkins said. He had been daydreaming—thinking how good a cool margarita would taste right now. The memory of the tartness of lime had his mouth moist. What he wouldn't give for the tangy beverage and a bowl of chips and salsa.

"Why would today be different than any other day?" Will Prescott sat with his back pressed against the cave wall and continued to rub the edge of a smooth, knife-shaped stone with a coarse black rock.

"Because we're not in the movie *Ground Hog Day*. We aren't living the same day over and over again. Every day is new. As long as we stay alive there's hope someone will find and rescue us. There's no way Ace Corporation is going to ignore the cache of red diamonds Patagonia has to offer. You know how greedy Henry Lear is. He wants to grow Ace Corp into the most profitable outfit in the world. I'm sure once Perkins showed him the diamonds I put on the drone, Lear picked up the phone and started gathering an army to come out here."

"We didn't stay alive the *first* time," Will said, and carefully rubbed his thumb across the stone's sharpened edge. "What makes you think we need to stay alive? If we die again, we'll just end up back over at the volcano. Right by that vortex. I don't know who was more surprised that day, me or you."

"I was more surprised. I watched that pterodactyl grab your ass and haul you off. I knew you were as good as dead. When I walked out of that vortex light show, the last thing I expected was seeing you alive. You were just in shock when you saw me arrive."

SKEER-AK!

"Shut the fuck up, motherfucker," Gerald said as he peered from the mouth of the cave into the sky above. The cave had only one access. It was a good fifteen feet wide inside and about as deep. The walls were solid too. He and Will didn't have to worry about some nasty creature finding a way in through a tunnel or crevasse looking for food—like before.

The cave's entrance had rows of bamboo spears strategically embedded into the ground. The spears' sharp points reached about ten feet high and were spaced enough for a grown man to snake his way around, but discouraged a flying predator from swooping down for an aerial attack.

"I was also in shock from being divided and fed to the pterodactyl hatchlings. The mother held me down, digging a talon into my gut, and then plucked off an arm and fed it to one of the babies. Then she ripped off the other arm and a leg, and then the other leg. I blacked out not long after, but that *shit* hurt." Will closed his eyes, gritted his teeth, and shook his head. "If I think about it too much, I can still feel the pain."

"I didn't have such a fun time dying either. Those two dinosaurs, hell, I don't know what they were. They were a little taller than me, walked on two legs, and played tug-of-war with my arms. I remember one of them swallowing an arm up to the elbow and stripping the meat off the bone like a hungry man in a chicken wing eating contest. And if that wasn't bad enough, one of them ripped open my bowels, and I watched my own intestines pop out."

"Just like Mel Gibson in *Brave Heart* at the end," Will said.

"Hey! Don't you make fun of my death."

"I wasn't making fun. I was just saying." Will had let his words die toward the end.

Gerald cast his gaze toward the ground. "This is bullshit. All *fucking* bullshit. We shouldn't be here—alive again. Patagonia shouldn't be here either—crawling with dinosaurs that have been extinct for millions of years. I do have to wonder, though. If we get killed again, will we be reborn in the vortex by the volcano or was that a onetime thing?"

"I don't know, and I don't want to find out. I'm mentally fucked up enough over dying the first time. Can you imagine the physiological problems you'd have faced with multiple deaths haunting you?" Will's jaw dropped, and his eyes stared into an unseen void. He shook his head and looked over at Gerald. "As far as Patagonia goes, I think it's scientifically feasible to exist. The area's been walled off by mountains for millions and millions of years. The living conditions have remained the same, so I guess there was no other outside forces of nature to mess with evolution. One thing we don't know, is how many or what other dinosaurs exists other than pterodactyls and those other two legged lizard types you told me about, and the smaller ones we've been surviving on. There might be T-rexes or Velociraptors, like in *Jurassic Park*."

"Yeah, and I wouldn't want to meet up with anything like that. You know, it just occurred to me that you and I relate to things in life to movies. How pathetic is that? Modern life is so fucked up that we spend more time identifying our lives with fiction than real events."

"Hmm, I see your point. But dinosaurs only existed in movies, until now. It might be a while before we go out for dinner and a movie again. If we *do* survive this thing and make it back to civilization, I don't know if I'll ever be able to fit back in like before. I bet we'll be changed forever."

Gerald rubbed the hairs on his chin. He thought they would have grown more by now. How long had they been in Patagonia? There was no way to know. The time between their deaths and waking by the volcano was a complete unknown. The marks he had made on the wall counted six weeks, but there was a day or two or three that he hadn't bothered to count. His heart just wasn't in it. Living day to day was enough of a struggle. If he died, what difference would it make how many days it took for that to happen?

The air *whooshed* with the flapping wings of the air dragon as it hovered above the spears. Gerald watched as the taloned claws of the pterodactyl reached toward his face, stopping just short of meeting the business end of the sharpened bamboo only a few feet away. "Damn, this one just won't give up. It's either real pissed that it can see us but can't get us, or food's been kinda hard to come by, and it's desperate."

Will pressed his hands tightly over his ears. "I wish it would just go away. It's getting harder for me to go through this. I'm going to reach my breaking point one day."

"Go on, get!" Gerald yelled, and then reached down and picked up a rock a little smaller than a baseball. He held the rock at waist level and waited for the claws to pull up, before he hurled the projectile and hit the brown colored beast in the chest. The giant flying reptile squawked once and raised its triangular shaped beak into the air before leaving from sight. "Asshole. Don't come back."

Will had removed his hands from his ears and had his arms wrapped around his knees. He gently rocked back and forth, again focused on an unseen void. "You know what I think about sometimes?"

"Pussy?"

Will stopped rocking, and his mouth formed a slight grin. "No," he followed with an incredulous giggle. "I haven't thought about *that* for a while." He turned his gaze to Gerald. "I think about getting caught again by that flying devil. It picks me up and takes me to the nest—just like before. And it slowly tears me in pieces, relishing in the agony that it's putting me through, as if my suffering itself will strengthen its offspring in a better way. And then I die and appear again out of the vortex. But then I'm caught again, and my torture begins anew. Divided and fed to hatchlings. And the next day the same, and the next day the same. Until one day the hatchlings are large enough to leave the nest. And the next time I wake from the vortex, one of the grown hatchlings catches me up and brings me to its nest where I'm used as food again. Every time I'm reborn, I'm eaten. Over, and over, and over again. Throughout time. Throughout eternity."

Gerald listened to Will's words cooled by the inner terror that held an evil grip on his friend's soul. The sharing had grabbed his spine with icy fingers and held any words of rebuttal or consolation that he had might want to offer. As if things weren't bad enough, he had to worry about Will's sanity. There wasn't any

Prozac available in Patagonia, and he doubted a slap in the face would do much to cure a mental issue.

SKEER-AK!

The winged wonder was back. Right now Gerald was only catching a good case of *red ass*. How long would it take before this constant harassment reduced his fortitude to jelly?

"Will, we're going to have to build a fire and shoot some flaming arrows at it. Maybe that new bow you made will have enough pull to penetrate skin. I'd love to see that thing catch an arrow and smoke all the way to the ground."

Before his partner had a chance to respond, the pterodactyl flew low, just beyond the fence of spears leading to the cave's entrance. Instead of making a passing swoop and squawking a few reptilian cuss words as usual, it rapidly flapped its wings until it slowed and hovered above the ground. Its legs lowered, and its feet rested on terra firma. With its wings drawn in close to its body, it moved its head, as if looking for a way past the spears.

"Uh oh. Pretty bird is thinking outside the box. It's never been brave enough to land on the ground before. You better hurry up with that fire. We need to teach it a lesson," Gerald said.

"I'll try." Will crawled over to the pile of branches and began layering wood. He scooped up a handful of kindling and a hand sized rock with a flat surface on one side. He placed some kindling on the flat part of the rock and used another rock in the other hand to strike the edge of the other, creating sparks.

The pterosaur stretched it wings wide to its sides and flapped them a bit in frustration.

"You're not going to scare the bamboo away, big boy."

With some caution, the reptile advanced toward the spears. When it got close enough, it reached out a tiny little hand attached to a tip of its wing and pushed against one of the bamboo spears.

"It's not going to be as easy as you think," Gerald said.

"What?"

"I wasn't talking to you. I was talking to big bird. He's testing the bamboo defense. How's that fire coming?"

"It's coming. You know how long this shit takes."

Yes, Gerald knew. He was getting worried about the pterosaur snooping around but didn't want to excite Will any more than necessary. That bamboo was some pretty strong stuff. The spears were nearly three inches in diameter, and the ends sunk four feet into the ground. Will had scoffed at the thought of burying the bamboo. Gerald knew how to do it, though. It was easy—a hell of a lot easier than cutting the bamboo with those stone knives. Boy Scout training had come in handy many times since his resurrection. All that was needed was some water on the ground where the bamboo would go, and then someone had to hold the shaft upright and twist it back and forth. In this case, both he and Will had to work together because the fourteen-foot shaft was awkward to handle. As the end of the bamboo sank into the ground, he'd add a little more water, and continued the twisting motion. It took less than five minutes to sink a shaft.

The pterosaur pushed at the spear fence with one of its wings. The bamboo leaned a bit but not enough to encourage the beast to put more effort into it. It spread its wings again and squawked.

"The big, bad wolf is getting pissed," Gerald said to Will. He turned his gaze back outside the cave. "These two little piggies didn't build their house with straw. You better *get* while the getting's good, or we're going to fuck you up in a major way."

The reptile stared through the fence, twisting its head back and forth like a curious bird looking through a cage. It slowly stretched out its neck, turned its head to the side, and closed its beak on one of the spears. It tugged on it a few times without any success and let go.

"See, I told you." The metallic smell of flint mixed with smoldering moss let Gerald know that fire was soon on the way.

Undeterred, the pterosaur's beak latched onto another spear, and this time it used its body weight and leaned backward as it tried to pluck the bamboo from the ground.

Gerald's eyes widened as the shaft slowly lifted out the earth until the end was completely out. "Oh, that's not good."

"What?" Will said. He was hunched over blowing the smoldering kindling. Tiny flames popped up heating the sticks. "Got the fire going."

"Good, and not too soon."

"What?" There was no need for Will to wait for an answer. He turned and saw the pterosaur's beak latch onto a spear and pull it out the ground.

"Big bird learned a new trick. Now it's time to make him pay for not listening to his superiors. C'mon, let's fire up a few arrows."

Gerald went to the weapons cache and gathered the six arrows they had made. They were crude, to say the least, and flew about as straight as a one winged pigeon in a hurricane. Still, at short distances they were accurate enough to skewer some of the small two legged dinosaurs. He didn't want to wait to see the white or yellow or what-the-hell-ever color of its eyes were before taking a shot. They need to scare the beast away as soon as possible. It needed to be afraid of mankind. Humans might be the new kid on the block, but if he and Will had any chance of surviving, it was time to start establishing some territorial boundaries. "Or get eaten. Whichever comes first," Gerald said only loud enough for him to hear.

Will had some plant material and wrapped it near the arrowhead while Gerald held it. He used some thin, coarse vine to secure it to the shaft. "I wish we had fuel to dip this in. This stuff won't light a fire big enough to do any real damage. Hopefully, it will be enough to scare it away."

Once Will tied the knot, Gerald brought the arrow by the fire, and held the shaft near the arrowhead until the plant material caught fire. Will was already by the cave's entrance with the bow in hand. Will's tight jaw and wide eyes told Gerald the pterosaur was making good progress.

"Here, it's ready to go," Gerald said has he handed Will the arrow. He looked up to see the predator had made its way halfway home. "Shit."

"It's hard to get a bead on him. The bamboo's in the way, and I can't get a straight shot," Will said.

"You're going to have to do the best you can. That fire won't last long. Take your shot. Show it we mean business."

With a sign of frustration and moving his aim from side to side, Will let the arrow fly.

The arrow ricocheted off two spears before finding its target. It hit the pterosaur in the left wing, but didn't penetrate it, and fell harmlessly to the ground. The flame of the arrow, as small as it was, did take the beast aback for a fleeting moment. But the flame quickly dimmed until it smoldered out, and the reptile went back to work edging his way closer to dinner.

"Let's try again," Gerald shouted.

"We don't have time to make another fire arrow. He'll be on us in no time."

"At least shoot some regular arrows at it. I'll get my spear." Gerald ran to the weapon cache and grabbed a long spear, while Will scooped up the remaining arrows. "Try to hit that thing where it counts. In the head, or the eye, or something."

"I'll be lucky if I hit it at all. It moves its head around too much."

"Just shut up and shoot." Gerald had the long spear by his side and thrust the end past the few remaining pieces of sharpened bamboo fencing. The stone spearhead challenged the pterodactyl's beak in a duel for the next picket. It wasn't much of a fight, as the spear's tip bounced off the rock-hard beak.

Will's first arrow whizzed by the predator's head. The second arrow hit it square in the chest. The arrowhead penetrated enough to embed into the flesh, but not by much. The arrow hung limply toward the ground as blood trickled down. "That thing's tough!"

With another piece of fence uprooted, the saw-toothed maw of the flying reptile had reached the cave opening.

"Look out!" Gerald dove to the side as the massive head shoved past two bamboo pickets into the entrance.

Will backpedaled, tripped over his own feet, and fell on his ass. The reptile's beak snapped empty air mere molecules from his right foot.

In the reptile's haste, its strategy for removing the bamboo defense made it vulnerable to attack. Instead of removing a layer of pickets at a time and allowing all of its body to advance, it essentially carved out a wedge shaped passage. Its head advanced farther than its body. While the head was the deadliest weapon, the rest of the body didn't pose a threat, at least for now.

The pterosaur's neck was extended as it made a move for Will. Gerald seized the opportunity and ran the long spear through its neck. At first the stone head came to an abrupt stop as it entered flesh, but adrenaline had made him numb to mortal limitations. Red blood spurted from the wound, wetting his chest, as the spear's shaft pushed deeper.

The beast shrieked and jutted its head to the side, knocking Gerald away, and slamming him against the cave wall. As it tried to pull its head back, the spear prevented an escape from the cave's mouth as it hung up on the remaining bamboo pickets. It shrieked again, sounding more pissed off than hurt.

Will was up on his feet, and though Gerald saw the weight of terror pulling the skin on Will's face downward, Will pulled back on the bow as the pterosaur's beak flew forward for another attack. The predator's head stopped just short of the poised archer. Will let the arrow loose.

At that short distance, direct hit. The arrow went straight through the eye, and the stone tip stuck out the back of its head. The beasts went berserk, thrashing its head about. There was no telling how much the head weighed. If it connected with either of them, the results might prove deadly.

Gerald scampered to the back of the cave by Will. "Good shot," he said amongst the turmoil.

"Yeah, but why isn't it dead?"

"I don't know. They say dinosaurs have brains the size of marbles. Maybe you missed the brain?"

"The cranium's not that big to begin with. The arrow went right through it. There's no way I missed the brain."

"I don't know. Maybe it's dead and just doesn't know it."

The head flopped around a few more times, sometimes hitting the ground and kicking up dust. The movements did suggest an automatic response, with no effort to pull back and flee. Longer than Gerald thought it should take, the beast finally gave up the ghost, and the head stopped moving, the body relaxed.

"Son-of-a-bitch, we beat it," Will said with a bit of disbelief in his voice. He looked over at Gerald. "*We*, beat it." It was obvious an epiphany he hadn't really considered before.

"We sure did. And you made the kill. *You*, Will Prescott. *You*."

"I did, didn't I? This changes everything." He looked at Gerald, with a calm, confident gaze. "Things are going to be different from now on."

"Whoa, there. We survived this one, but who knows what tomorrow will bring? Let's not get too big for our britches here."

"That's not what I mean. I'm not thinking we're some great dinosaur hunters. I've been living scared ever since our resurrection. It's clouded everything. My fear has been a monster controlling me. It had me held in a *victim mentality*—like my only option was to lose. Well, I now know that's not true. So I'm not going to let my fear have that control any more. I'm going to man-up and push past that fear—take things head on—regardless of the consequences. I may be torn in half tomorrow by God-knows-what, but I'm not going to live in fear any longer."

"Sounds reasonable. We both need as few distractions as possible in order to survive."

"Well, at least we know what's for dinner tonight," Will said, and rubbed a knuckle under his chin.

"How about I cook and you clean?"

"I don't know. That's a big beast to clean. I'm not even sure what parts are the best to eat."

"Wings and feet are a no-go for me. Not much meat on the arms and legs either. You can't go wrong with ribs. We'll gut it and figure it out," Gerald said.

"You know, that head would look good as a trophy hung on the wall."

"Or as a Halloween mask."

"Ha. I don't know about that. Might be too heavy and break your neck to wear it."

"I wonder if we can make some clothing out of the wings. I'm tired of looking at your junk."

"Really. And *why* were you looking at my junk? It's because it's three times bigger than yours, isn't it?"

"Hey, I'm a grower not a shower," Gerald said, throwing his arms up into the air.

"That's *not* what she said," Will said with the seriousness of a declaration in a court of law.

The banter unleashed an avalanche of suppressed tension and purged it to the wind. The two roared in laughter until both gasped for air. This was the first time Gerald could remember a happy moment since the time they awoke from the strange vortex by the volcano.

CHAPTER 2

Perpetual clouds enveloped the massive land of Patagonia, an uncharted area in the south-eastern portion of South America. The cover was a timeless weather phenomena generated by the freezing air of the surrounding mountains and the hot rivers of magma that hid not far below the Earth's surface.

The horizon to the north offered the eleven survivors a spectacular view that evoked both awe and anxiety. A mighty volcano poked through the earth like Satan's horn piercing flesh. The mountain's jagged mouth opened as if a massive finger flicked off the peak. The vent hole of Hell burped black smoke and rank gases into the orange sky directly above as streams of lava bled down its sides.

"Meat. Shut the fuck up," Vince Cooper, a geologist employed by Ace Corporation and leader of the expedition, said to Clint Perry, a large block of a man of Samoan descent, otherwise known as *Meat*. "We all just found ourselves here with a lot of questions, for sure. The last thing we need is some nut-ball mystic religious bullshit to confuse the situation." Coop pointed a crooked index finger bent by the onset of arthritis. "*Brahma creates and Shiva destroys*," he said in a mocking tone, repeating one of Meat's earlier rants. "You almost had me for a moment. I've had time to think about it, and I'm sticking to what I know is real. In my over sixty years of existence, I've learned that science has, or will find, the answer to any question. There is a scientific answer as to what happened to us." He redirected his index finger over to the smoke-like spiral churning like a slow moving pinwheel. The interior of the vortex danced with ethereal flashes of blues, greens, and reds. "That thing over there is what's responsible for our situation. I don't know what it is, but it's more than likely a product of nature."

"If it was a product of nature, then why aren't there others like this around the Earth? You'd think by now we'd have stumbled upon another," Alex Klasse said, a Professor of Zoology by profession, Cryptozoologist by passion. As leader of the group from Southwood University, he had failed miserably fulfilling his duties as the keeper of his crew's welfare. "You all know my background, exploring the fringe of science. I've read a lot of strange books and listened to a lot of kooks on late night radio. Never has something like this come up. This...this *thing* has the ability to bring us back to life."

Coop slowly passed his gaze over the group, trying to come up with an answer. Chief, lead member of the seven member Redwater security team, had his head hung low and appeared to be in deep thought. Henry Hunter—*Suge,* the only African American with the security team, looked about as if his head was on a swivel; no doubt expecting the unexpected. Tim Colter, who had earned the nickname *Bats* for being bat-shit crazy, had his eyes shut and looked as if he were trying to *will* the situation away. Unfortunately, the only medicine that seemed to keep Bats in emotional check was to kill something every few days. John Jones, known as *Caveman* for his outdoorsman prowess, pushed a rock around with his big toe. If Curly of *The Three Stooges* had a twin, it was Caveman. Ron and Don Bartel, the twins who were also the oldest of the whole bunch, just stared at each other in disbelief. *Well, doesn't look like anyone else has a suggestion,* Coop thought.

Coop turned his gaze over to the college crew. Ace Corporation had to use Alex and his associates as cover for entering Patagonia. Authorities in Chile didn't have a problem accepting bribes for a *dinosaur hunting* expedition. Had the authorities known the truth, that the main purpose was to locate and bring back a horde of rare red diamonds, well, things wouldn't have gone as smoothly. Susan Klasse stood by Chief, and not her husband, Alex. She had realized Alex sent her in anaphylactic shock by putting peanuts in a canteen and giving it to her to drink, not long after her rebirth. The situation would only add to complications the group currently faced. Natasha Kamdar was Alex's student and probably the reason Alex killed his wife. Coop had thought Alex and Natasha spoke to each other with a familiarity that went beyond teacher-student before Susan died. Natasha certainly was a beauty, and her bronze East Indian skin tone added to her allure. Natasha was nearly young enough to be Coop's grandchild, though, and he wasn't one of those lecherous old men who fantasised over younger women. Alex was around fifty-years-old, and Coop thought the age difference between Alex and Natasha was creepy enough.

Natasha caught Coop's gaze and held it for a moment, and then said, "How do we know that this isn't something God made?"

"Because when you shave this thing with *Occam's Razor*, you eliminate God from the equation. Saying *God did it* because we don't understand it has been a hindrance to mankind for centuries," Coop said.

The rock under Caveman's toe stopped. The rotund man asked, "What the hell is Occam's Razor?"

"When you have two competing theories that offer the same results, the simpler one is usually better. You have to discount the unobserved. That alone cuts out any mystical force responsible for our rebirths," Coop said.

"Okay, then. The question is, *what are we observing*?" Natasha said.

Everyone turned toward the vortex. The fog-like spirals reached some fifty feet in the air, and the colors danced like in the Aurora Borealis.

"Let's talk this out," Coop said. "What does it most resemble?"

"It reminds me a satellite shot of a hurricane," Suge said.

"Yeah, I see that. It resembles a weather pattern, so it might be a force of nature," Coop said.

"But," Alex said, "notice the rotation. It's spinning counterclockwise like a hurricane would do in the Northern Hemisphere. We're in the Southern Hemisphere. If it was affected by nature as weather, then it would rotate clockwise."

"Point noted. So, if it's not a force of nature, then it's something manmade," Coop said.

"Or alien," Alex said.

"Don't jump the gun, Alex. Let's keep this to what we can observe. If you get right down to it, there is zero evidence that life exists anywhere in the universe except Earth."

"Yeah, but—" Natasha started.

"But nothing. Despite the odds that life of some sort exists outside of Earth due to the magnitude of the universe, we still have not one shred of evidence that it's so," Coop said.

"What about the Pyramids?" Meat asked.

"What about them? There's no evidence anything other than man built the Pyramids," Coop said.

"True, there're engineers today who claim they could recreate the building process using only human labor if someone would fund it," Alex said.

"Let's stay with this. We have a machine that does what? Returns people to life after they die. How could it do that? Does it revive a dead body? I doubt that. I was torn to shreds and eaten by a Spinosaurus. Would it use our DNA to reconstruct the body? How would we get our minds, personalities, and our memories back?" Coop asked.

Alex rubbed a finger on his bottom lip and then raised his hand in the air. "Because it's not a machine that resurrects the dead," Alex said. "It's a time machine."

Coop went to speak a rebuff, but something inside held him in check. "Go on."

Alex cleared his throat and let his gaze drift over at Susan for a brief moment, then turned it toward Natasha, and then back to Coop. "The best explanation for how we live again is that somehow we were snatched back from a previous time before we were harmed."

"Playing on that, what about our memories? I remember a lot of pain I felt before I died. The rest of you?" Coop asked.

The others nodded, except for Bats, who just shrugged his shoulders. Bats died a quick death due to a head injury when an attacking Spinosaurus knock over his vehicle.

"How can our memories be explained?" Coop asked.

"I've done a lot of reading on the subject of time. Not only from crackpots, but I've studied hard physics too. Maybe it works like this: we live in a world made of three dimensions. Length, width, and height. We travel past these three dimensions through the dimension of time. But—and try follow me here—if we went up into a higher dimension, the fifth dimension let's call it, then you could see the entire timeline stretched out like a snake, seeing the beginning and the end. As if everything in the future that will happen has already happened. But in our normal lives we aren't above the timeline, so we have to travel through time past these three dimensions in order to experience it. But, if we are transported from a time earlier than our death, we move up to a *higher place* on the timeline—let's call it *now*, we have access to any memories experienced on the timeline at any time—including the memories of our previous death," Alex said.

"Huh?" Caveman said.

"I don't know, Alex. That's a lot to swallow. Some of that sounds like religious predestination speak," Coop said.

"No, not in the least. I'm not saying our lives are predestined by God. I'm saying that using the laws of physics, it's possible to see from the beginning of time until the end. We were moved from a time we were alive to now, another point on the timeline," Alex said. "I may not have it right how we have retained our memories, but what difference does it make? We have them, and that's that."

"Alex is right," Meat said.

All eyes turned toward the Samoan.

"What do you mean?" Natasha asked.

"My arm. Look at it." Meat lifted up his left arm and pointed to the inside of his forearm. "I tattooed my arm the day before I was killed. It was of Natasha's face. Remember?"

Natasha gasped. "You're right. It's gone. Wait," she said, and twisted her left leg to the side and looked down at her heel. "I still have my tattoo." She felt her left elbow and then looked at her forearm. "I had skinned my elbow on the trip across the mountains—when the Warthog went sideways and I hit the floor. That wound's still there. But the day I was killed, I scraped my left forearm on a tree. That cut isn't there. So it doesn't look like we're rebuilt from DNA. My body is from a time between the two events."

Coop ran his fingers through his graying hair, and said, "Let's say the vortex *is* a time machine. Why would it be here?"

"I think it's obvious," Alex said. "It's here ensuring that prehistoric creatures don't go extinct. Whoever did this wanted to preserve dinosaurs from the past."

"So you're suggesting that dinosaurs, or anything that dies in Patagonia, are reborn by the vortex," Susan said, her tone more civil than Coop had expected.

"Yeah. It looks that way. That vortex isn't some creation of a God or Gods intending to play some type of game throughout eternity. It's a machine put here to preserve the most magnificent life that's ever roamed the planet. We just happened to be caught up in the process because we invaded the land," Alex said.

"Aw, hell," Ron said, and looked at his twin brother, Don.

"You was thinking what I was thinking, weren't you?" Don asked Ron.

"Guys, what are you two talking about?" Coop asked.

"When Alex was saying this here was a time machine, well…" Ron hesitated and cleared his throat. "I was thinking, and I was thinking Don was thinking it, too, that we could use the time machine to bring back The Bear, Coach Bryant."

"Yeah. Wouldn't that be a hoot," Don said. "I bet that man could have led Alabama over Ohio State in that playoff game and won the National Championship to boot."

"Now, we ain't saying we don't like Coach Saban," Ron said.

"No, we ain't saying that," Don said.

"But he just ain't *The Bear*. Right, Don?" Ron said.

"Right, Ron," Don said.

"Roll Tide!" both brothers said at the same time.

Coop closed his eyes and shook his head. "Seriously, guys. There is a time and place for football—"

"But it's *Alabama* football," Ron said.

"This isn't time for any kind of football. *Can it* for now," Coop said.

"So if this is a machine placed here to preserve dinosaurs, that means we aren't trapped in some pocket universe in a different dimension. We have another chance in our world if we can escape," Chief said. He brought his right hand up and gently placed it on Susan's shoulder. She leaned her body closer to the rugged leader.

"If there's a way out of this mess, I'll find it," Caveman said.

Bats lifted his head as if coming out of a daze, and said, "I don't think it's going to be that simple."

"So Alex," Suge started, "you said *whoever* made the time machine. Who do you think made it?"

"Aliens," Alex said, and with a closed eye, cast a gaze at Coop as if expecting a verbal slap down.

"Alex, Occam's Razor. There are no aliens," Coop said.

"What then?" Meat asked.

"Could be mankind—from the future. What if in the future it was decided to go back to prehistoric times and set up a machine that kept a select group of dinosaurs alive?" Coop said.

"You mean like a habitat of sorts?" Susan asked.

"I guess so. Just think, by doing so mankind in the future will be able to see, study, marvel, and enjoy these great creatures," Coop said.

"Yeah, just one big fucking petting zoo," Bats said. He then coughed up some phlegm and spit it in a puddle of molten lava. The spit hissed like a fast burning firecracker fuse.

"Well, if man went back in time to preserve dinosaurs to one day introduce them back into the world, that means the future is *now*," Alex said.

"That's right. It does. Because we found them *now*. Guys, it's a hunch, but the very fact that we found prehistoric life and are still alive to talk about it, just may mean that we will succeed in getting out of here and reintroducing dinosaurs to the world," Coop said. "That may also suggest that the time machine put here was built some time in our near future."

"It's hard to imagine this advanced technology coming from anything in this century, but you never know what advances science may bring," Alex said.

"Science output doubles every nine years. So I guess anything is possible," Coop said.

"Okay, what's the plan?" Suge asked.

The dead, rocky land in this area was too harsh of an environment to support even one blade of grass. The volcano was on the opposite side, to the north-west, of where the All-Terrain Tracked Carrier, known as the *Warthog*, carried the expedition into the heart of Patagonia. That vehicle, along with a Humvee-like truck affectionately called the *Mule*, were essential for travel and protection in the hostile lost world. "Survival first. Escape second," Coop said.

"Yeah. We's need to eat," Caveman said. "I'm hungry enough to eat the ass out of a low flying duck."

Coop never found a limit to the imagery of what Caveman's observations painted in his mind.

"We will have to find food—water too. It's going to be tough out here without our guns," Chief said. "As far as escape goes, what do we do? Try to go back the same way we came in? We still have those mountains to cross. That's going to be a long and dangerous journey. A cold one too. We won't survive the hike without warm clothing and plenty of calories in our bellies to burn."

"We're a long way from the Warthog's entrance point," Chief said. "If we're lucky enough to make it to that location, the odds might be even worse trying to cross the mountains. Those mountains have kept mankind out of Patagonia for centuries."

"There's that major river we're going to have to cross too. The drone's video showed us there was every imaginable dinosaur at that one location it circled. If there's that much life all up and down the river, I don't know how we can make it across alive," Natasha said.

"We have no choice. We're going to have to cross the river at some point, unless we head west from here, and hope to find a suitable passage between the mountains," Coop said. "But even if we make it out the west side, there's no camp for us to take refuge. There's no civilization to the west for miles and miles. If we're going to try to leave, we at least have go somewhere close to where we can find people."

"The Mule. It has a satellite phone on board. If the nuclear engine is still good, we can call for help," Suge said.

"Yeah, but not only that. That far south is where Hawkins and Prescott crossed over on foot. An earthquake opened a path big enough for them to make it through. I know they left their cold gear somewhere this side of the mountains, because they wouldn't have carried it with them on their expedition to the cave. If worse comes to worst, and the Mule's phone doesn't work, a couple of us can use the cold gear to cross over and get help," Coop said.

"As far as a plan goes, I think this is about as good as it gets," Chief said, stepping away from Susan, and slightly away from the group. With a hand on one hip, and the other pointing in the general direction of the others, he said, "People. For this thing to work, we're going to have to be disciplined. We need to keep the same order as before. Coop will be in charge. I'm still head of security, and the rest of my Redwater guys know their duties. Alex, we'll need you as a consultant. But I want you to know, I've got my eye on you. The past may be the past, and it looks like we all have a new lease on life. Just stay in line, and there won't be any problems."

If Alex had an issue with the warning, his lowered gaze to the ground hid it. He nodded slightly.

"Natasha and Susan. You may not have the physical strength to hold your own out here, but you two are just as important as the rest of us," Chief said. "Just be there to help any way you can when needed. That'll offer our best chances for survival."

Before Coop could utter another word, the vortex lights went into overdrive. Emerging from the swirling mist, an infant T-rex around the size of a Great Dane waddled out.

"Looks like we got company," Suge said.

The theropod acted as if in autopilot and ignored the group. It walked away from the vortex and headed south.

"Motherfucker," Meat said, his mouth then fell slightly open.

"What?" Coop said.

"The T-rex. Did you see that? Meat asked.

"I saw it, but what are you talking about?" Coop asked.

"I saw it!" Natasha said. "The ears. They were deformed. Just like the T-rex that attacked me, Logan, and Meat." A micro flash of anger showed on her face as she gritted her teeth. "Logan..." she said almost in a growl.

"That little bastard stopped our chances of getting back to the Warthog. I outsmarted it and took it over the edge of the cliff, but not before pulling the pins on two grenades and going over with it," Meat said.

"The time vortex brought it back to life from infancy. I think we're getting an idea how the process works here," Coop said.

"Is there a chance an older—and I mean bigger and more of a threat dinosaur—could come through that thing and attack us?" Susan asked.

"Can't say for sure, but I doubt it. We should leave as soon as we can, though. But first, we might want to take advantage and put a little protein in our stomachs," Coop said.

Heads nodded, and a few voices mingled in agreement.

"Well, what are we waiting for? Our dinner is walkin' away from us," Caveman said. The man looked about and picked up a stone too big to carry with one hand and sped off for the kill.

CHAPTER 3

"We made it!" Matt King, Associate Professor at Southwest University and colleague of Alex Klasse, cried out. He still had his hands braced against the Warthog's dash in expectance of the worst. The nuclear powered engine purred at an idle, showing no sign of stress from the All-Terrain Tracked Carrier's journey of careening through the narrow passageway leading through the mountains from the Lost World of Patagonia.

Ben Wilson, one of Alex Klasse's students, was in the driver's seat. He leaned his body forward but still clutched the steering wheel in a death grip. "That was one furious ride. I don't know how we made it. That earthquake brought a shit-ton of stuff down on us. There were times I couldn't even see. I figured it was better to keep moving and have a chance than stop and be buried under rock."

"You figured right," Logan Sandler said, another of Alex's students. He had been strapped in the back of the Warthog and kept a watchful eye on the rear camera. Now he was up and standing behind his two friends in the cab. "That took a lot of courage to maintain control. I'm not so sure I could have kept my cool the whole way."

"Yeah. What he said." Matt finally let his arms fall in his lap, leaned back, and sighed deeply. "I was so freaked out, I caught myself repeating the *Our Father* prayer. It's been years—I was a kid since I remember praying that. I guess when it comes down to life and death, we find out what we truly believe. I didn't realize I still defaulted to a belief in God." Matt turned his gaze toward Ben. "What about you? What do you do for inspiration?"

Ben thought a minute, lowered his head, bit his bottom lip, and then said, "I...I have a confession to make. It's a little embarrassing, so bear with me a second." He held up a hand and then brought his gaze up. "As you know, I'm a big X-Men fan. And The Beast is my adopted totem. But whenever I face a challenge, I try to push everything else in my mind aside, and ask, *What would Nick Fury do?*"

"You ass!" Logan slapped Ben's shoulder. "Matt's sharing an emotional moment, and you go back to your wisecracking self. Can't you ever be serious?"

"Lighten up, *Francis*. I am serious. Nick Fury is one cool dude. Especially now that he's black. He has to think his way out of messes, because he doesn't have superpowers. Some people say I look like a younger version of Samuel L. Jackson," Ben said.

"Really, I'd have said you favor *Laurence Fishburne* better," Logan said, and then suppressed a smile.

"Yeah, well, that doesn't surprise me. You white people get the two confused all the time," Ben said. "I expected a little keener eye from a gay man."

"What? You think we're born with some discerning *queer eye* that makes us special over heteros?" Logan put a hand on his hip and held out a limp wrist with the other. He slowly turned the hand upward to Ben's face, extending his middle finger in a display of defiance.

"Really, you two. We almost die, and you're cutting up. We might be alive, but our problems aren't over. We're still trapped here until help arrives and..." Matt looked away, "and there're the others. The others we lost back there."

The sadness in Matt's voice was palpable. Logan knew Natasha's death would weigh on his friend's soul. His mind drifted back to the day before when he, Natasha, and Meat were by the cliff about to change direction and head to the Warthog, which was only minutes away. Meat had proved himself to be a hero, luring the deformed T-rex to the cliff's edge, and using the grenades and the weight of the theropod to send the two some sixty feet downward as the ground gave way beneath them. Logan doubted that Meat would have made that sacrifice if Natasha hadn't been there. It was obvious she had captured the large man's fancy to some degree.

What Logan did next came from some dark place deep inside he didn't know existed. Thinking back now, it seemed like someone else took control of his body and pushed Natasha over the edge of the cliff as they looked at Meat's twisted body by the riverbed. Logan's jealously had gone supernova when Natasha wished aloud for Matt's comfort. Who did that girl think she was?

She had been in an illicit relationship with Alex, and then after his death, *what*? Just move on to the next guy waiting in line? She had evaded Matt's advances for the most part, but really put him on his ass after Susan Klasse died. There was no reason for Alex and Natasha to keep their relationship a secret then.

But that wasn't fair. Not after Logan spent all that time getting closer to Matt. Their relationship had entered a new level. Logan had so hoped that Matt would see him in a different way than before. To see him as something more than a friend. Logan wanted to be there for Matt. To care for him. He wanted Matt to fall in love with the person Logan was inside. Once that happened, then he hoped to push aside the stigma of social norms and for the two to become true soulmates. That couldn't happen if Natasha had returned with him to the Warthog.

The memory was clear. Logan had his arms wrapped around Natasha as she cried over Meat's death. He was mired, too, in sorrow, but when she said *Matt, I need Matt*, a switch flipped in his head, and he knew what he had to do. A devious ruse emerged, and when he told her he saw Meat moving below, she spun around to see. One small push to the small of her back sent her screaming over the edge.

"You know guys, I feel guilty I wasn't out there with you when the pack of Troodons attacked," Ben said. "I mean, it just wasn't right I got a pass."

"You're feeling survivor guilt. A lot of soldiers returning from war who have lost men in their platoon feel that way. I have a cousin going through a lot of that since he got back from Afghanistan," Matt said. "You didn't do anything wrong, Ben. There were too many of those man-eating lizards. You would have died too. Besides, your ankle. You think you could have taken on the Troodons by whacking them with your crutches? Trust me, there was more automatic gunfire, grenades flying through the air, and RPGs exploding than you can imagine."

"I'm not saying I could have beaten them. Just maybe…" Ben shook his head. "Just maybe I could have been there to save someone. You survived in the tree, Matt. If I had been up there with you and Alex, maybe I would have been close enough to hold onto him before he fell. If I could have saved one life, it would have been the least that I could have done."

Matt's eyes widened, and he quickly turned his gaze away from Ben.

Logan couldn't help but notice. It was possible Matt was feeling a bit of survivor guilt too. After all, Matt and Alex had taken refuge in a tree during the attack, as commanded by Chief. Alex had been frantic, calling for Natasha, and trying his best to see if she was still alive. And then Alex fell to the ground, and the Troodons were on him in an instant. Strange, though; Logan remembered the two in the tree, and they weren't all that far apart. If Matt had seen Alex start to fall and had made an attempt to save him, then that was a secret that Matt had kept to himself. But what if Matt did see Alex about to fall and intentionally did nothing? That way Matt could have had Natasha all to himself. This was the first time that possibility had crossed Logan's mind.

"That's just so weird that Alex fell like that. You'd think he'd have been holding on for dear life," Ben said.

"Uh, yeah, well…" Matt raised his hands in the air. "There was a lot of commotion, you know. Guns rattling, explosions, and unnerving cries as men were eaten alive. I…I guess Alex was trying to get a better view of Natasha through the tree limbs to make sure she was all right. He got careless, slipped. There…there was nothing *I* could have done to save him," Matt said, his tone defensive.

Logan noticed the strange shift in demeanor. Matt sounded at best unsure. Something had Logan suspecting Matt was hiding something. Something that held his friend in fear.

"Hey, man. I'm not saying that. I'm sure you would have if possible. But had I been up there, we all would have been closer. Maybe I could have grabbed an arm when he slipped and kept him from falling," Ben said.

"Guys, please. We have to stop beating ourselves up over this. I know how you feel. It was by sheer luck when that T-rex charged I wasn't taken over the side with Natasha and Meat." That had been Logan's version of the event, and the only version anyone else needed to know. "Matt was in the tree with Alex. Alex fell, Matt didn't. Ben, you twisted your ankle and couldn't go on the expedition. That was by chance too. We all are here right now by chance. So rather than questioning the *why* of it all, we should just accept this blessing, and move forward in our lives." He placed a hand on one shoulder of each.

"Yeah. You're right. The camp's only a couple of miles from here. I don't know if the rescue party's arrived or not," Ben said. He placed the Warthog in gear and started forward.

"Matt, we haven't called Ace Corp since before we started crossing the mountain range. Why don't you let them know we made it?" Logan asked.

"Sure. Give them time to line up the mariachi band and dancing girls," Ben said.

"I guess we need to give them a heads up even if help hasn't arrived. Might move things faster if they know we're alive," Matt said. He picked up his satellite phone and pushed a hotkey. It rang twice before someone picked up on the other end. He pushed the phone to speaker.

"Olá," a male voice came through.

"This is Matt King. I'm here to report the Warthog's made it over the mountain range, and me, Sandler, and Wilson are safe. We're about ten minutes away from camp."

"Hold," the voice said in English.

A few seconds later, a different voice came over the speaker, "This is Captain Diaz."

"Diaz, we've been reporting to Waterman from Ace Corp for the last few days. Are you aware of our situation?" Matt said.

"Yes, Mr. King. My crew and I arrived at the campsite just a few hours ago. We are fully informed of the situation," Diaz said. He had a slight foreign accent, but spoke clearer English than most Americans in the U.S.

Matt turned to his friends and lifted a thumb into the air. "You don't know how glad we are to hear this. Keep a light on. We'll be there in minutes."

"We will be waiting. There is someone very special that wants to meet you," Diaz said, and the called ended.

"I wonder who wants to meet us?" Matt said. "I wonder who that Captain Diaz is too. He was definitely foreign. All the Redwater bunch were from the U.S. I hope the Chilean officials didn't get wind of our expedition and now their military is involved."

"Man, I hope that didn't happen," Ben said. "Can you imagine the red tape we'll have to go through before we get to go home?"

"You mean *if* we get to go home. I don't like this. You know how these third world governments can act. They might want to charge us with some type of crime—hold us here for months or longer until someone gives them enough bribe money to bail us out. I sure hope a representative from Ace Corp is here to cover our asses and not leave us here holding the bag," Logan said.

"That's some imagination you have there, Logan," Ben said. "Hang on, the camp's just around the turn." The Warthog tracked to the east, and the area opened up to the campsite. "Looks like they were expecting us."

The fog of early morning still hung above the ground. A tandem rotor Chinook set off to the side, and personnel were in the process of unloading supplies. Six military members dressed in black waited next to an aging man in a well-fitted business suit. His hands gripped either side of his lapel, and he had a huge cigar stuck in one corner of his mouth as he puffed away. Behind the camp, two bulldozers set unmanned.

"What do you think about that?" Ben asked.

"I hope the guy in the suit is from Ace Corp. I don't like the look of those mercenaries," Logan said.

"Well, if you're still worried we could go to jail, I could just open up on the whole bunch with the Warthog's gun. We could fly the Chinook out of here," Ben said.

"Really? Is that what *Nick* Fury would do? You couldn't fly a Chinook anyway," Logan said, doing his best to match Ben's B.S.

"I could figure it out…eventually," Ben said.

"You two, stop. This is serious. Let me do the talking at first. Let's be calm and not confuse the situation. I'm only going to give brief answers. Let's not embellish the story. Only go with what we know," Matt said.

"What the hell? It's not our fault the mission is a bust," Ben said.

"No, it's not our fault, and we aren't going to give them any reason to think it is. We're a long way from home, and there's no

American Embassy here to protect our rights. Ace Corp put up a lot of money for this expedition. When money's involved, things can really get serious. Life and death serious, if you catch my drift."

"You're right, Matt. Leave it to you to think of the best way to handle a situation. It's one of the many reasons I admire you so much," Logan said, finding it difficult to hold back from expressing deeper feeling toward the associate professor.

Ben brought the Warthog in slowly and parked the massive vehicle parallel to the receiving entourage.

"Let me go first. I'll get the ladder," Logan said. He unhooked the short step ladder from a wall and opened the Warthog's door. His heart beat faster in his chest, more from the uncertainty of the situation than the physical exertion. After stepping on the tracks, being careful not to slip on any of the caked-in mud, he placed the ladder on the ground, and stepped from the tracks down to the ground.

Matt's head popped out the door, and he stepped onto the tracks and moved to the side.

Ben's crutches lowered to the tracks, and he maneuvered his feet down next. With a supporting hand from Matt, he took the ladder down, and stood next to Logan.

The two waited as Matt descended and continued over to the man in the business suit, and then they followed.

Logan couldn't help but feel like he was walking into a courtroom and about to go on trial. The seven men waiting remained ridged in position. No greeting offered; only blank stares ahead from five of the black-clad mercenaries. The other mercenary, the one standing next to the man in the business suit, wore a red beret instead of black. His nametag sewn on his uniform read *Diaz*. The old guy in the suit had his head cocked back slightly as he looked down his nose. He reminded Logan of a vulture waiting for a wounded animal to die.

Matt stopped in front of the old man and Diaz, waited for Logan and Ben to arrive next to him, and said, "I'm Matt King. That's Ben Wilson. Logan Sandler's on the end."

The old man let go of his right lapel and plucked the cigar from the corner of his mouth. "We know who you are. We knew you had made it over the mountains before you called in—real time satellite imagery." He flicked his cigar, sending a half inch of ash to the ground. "My name is Henry Lear. I own Ace Corporation."

"Mr. Lear," Matt said, obvious surprise in his voice. "Coop mentioned your name from time to time. I...we know how important this expedition was to you."

"I've achieved a fair amount of greatness in my time on this Earth. As successful as I've built Ace Corporation, this venture was to be my pinnacle achievement. But you must realize, you haven't just disappointed me, you have disappointed a host of investors."

Ben stiffened, and for a moment, Logan thought his friend was going to unleash a verbal tongue lashing.

Matt's gaze narrowed, and he turned his head slightly to the side. "I fail to see how I've done, or we've done, anything wrong."

"I'm disappointed, Mr. King. I don't like failure. Who would you like me to express my disappointment to? Coop? He's not here. Chief or any of the other Redwater crew? Can't happen. You're all I've got," Lear said.

"That doesn't seem fair," Matt said.

"I'm Henry Lear. I don't have to be fair."

Matt raised upturned palms in front of his chest. "We just want to go home."

"I'm sure you do. But first you'll have to be debriefed by Captain Diaz. Diaz is the leader of a Brazilian taskforce I hurriedly put together. I highly recommend you give him your full cooperation."

"A *brazillion*? I don't see a brazillion. I only see six," Ben said.

"Fuck me," Logan said only loud enough for him to hear. Ben just had to take a poke at authority.

Diaz broke down in laughter. The contrived mirth towered over the silence. He eventually composed himself, and said to his crew, *"Ele confunde Brazilian com bilhões, como seu Presidente Bush."*

Laughter roared from the mercenaries. Lear was content looking lazy eyed toward the three survivors and blowing smoke from the side of his mouth.

"You Americans. You are so funny," Diaz said, and turned to his men. "*Equipe*, if this man or the other two disrespect Mr. Lear again, shoot them."

CHAPTER 4

"So, what do you want to do today?" Will Prescott asked.

"I was thinking we could take a drive downtown. Spend the day at the art museum and grab some cocktails at Olive-R-Twist afterward. I'm dying for a martini with blue cheese stuffed olives," Gerard Hawkins said.

"Not today. The car's in for repairs."

"Think we can saddle up a few dinosaurs? I'm getting tired of walking everywhere we go."

"At least we have some shoes for our feet now." Will pointed to four shoe-sized wads of pterodactyl wing by the cave's wall. Vines had been woven into the top to act as laces.

"Yep. And some dinosaur underwear to maintain our dignity. I wish it would breathe better. It makes my ass sweat. Doesn't do much to support the nads, though. I'm going to have to figure out how to make a jockstrap."

"You know, if we make it out of here, we might be able to sell our clothing on EBay. We could make a fortune."

Gerald pulled off a piece of meat skewered by a stick above a now extinguished cooking fire. "More pterodactyl?"

"Thanks, but I've stomached as much as I can for one morning. Plus, it gives me gas." Will lifted a leg, made a path for escape, and let one rip.

"I'm *eating*," Gerald said, sounding offended. "Have some manners."

"What for? It's just me and you. We're not bound by any of society's rules. We can make our own. Think about it. We were brought up a certain way—had rules imposed on us by others. We think there's a proper way to do things, but there's nothing genetic in mankind to make it so."

"Yeah, but rules are what sets us apart from animals," Gerald said after swallowing a bite of meat.

"But we *are* animals."

"Okay. We're animals with rules. That's what makes us human and superior to other animals," Gerald said, and then ran a fingernail between his front teeth to remove a trapped piece of meat.

"What makes us superior to animals, is *might*. If we couldn't have found ways to beat them, then they would have the rule of the world. Not us."

"You know, for us to be having this discussion is a sign that we're adapting. You remember how it was after the resurrection. We hardly said a word that didn't deal with survival."

"I guess as long as we have shelter and plenty of food we'll be able to maintain our humanity. We'll revert back to animals if resources dry up. Then it'll come down to just me and you. The strongest would survive."

"Or the smartest," Gerald said.

"Animals have smarts too. Some animals are smarter than others. The strongest, though, has the advantage."

"I didn't say animals weren't smart. I think having smarts is more of an advantage than strength."

"Who would win in a fight? A T-rex or a human."

"In a surprise attack the T-rex. But give the human some time, he could set a trap and win. Intelligence will beat out strength if enough time is allowed for the plan to develop."

"But life's not scripted. You'll never know what's around the corner until you turn down it."

"Dude, I agree. Why are we arguing about this silly shit? We sound like an old married couple fighting over which way the toilet paper should face," Gerald said.

Will ran his finger through the dust on the cave's floor and picked up a rock. "I don't know...I guess I'm just bored."

"You go from scared every second of your life to bored in less than twenty-four hours? I didn't realize how high-strung you were."

"Sorry. I guess I need a change of scenery."

"Water supply is getting low. We'll have to make a trip by the river. I hope that pterodactyl's friends and family aren't around in these parts." Gerald rose and wiped his fingers on the backside of his loincloth. "You ready to head out?"

"Yeah. Let's go risk our lives getting water. You know, I used to be a thrill seeker back in my teens. I rode motorcycles, bungee jumped, and even skydived a few times. None of that comes close to the adrenaline rush of fighting for your life. We do that on a routine basis now. I don't think any man-made activity will ever top that." Will stepped over to the weapons cache, picked up his bow, and put it over his shoulder. A crude quiver made from pterosaur wing contained eight arrows, and it went over the other shoulder.

"Hey, we could go into business. We can offer people the thrill of a lifetime. All we have to do is buy a large ranch somewhere and put some wild animals on it. You know, tigers, pumas, wolves, buffalo. I hear buffalo can be some mean son-of-a-bitches. Let them pay us to *run through the jungle* for the ultimate survival experience." Gerald gathered sections of bamboo they used as water containers. He had woven a crude backpack of sorts from an indigenous plant with fan-like leaves. The leaves were nearly as tough as leather. What made it usable was that the fibers in the leaves tore easily, vertically, by hand. Cutting it crossways took much effort, but that quality is what gave it strength. The bamboo went in the backpack, and then Gerald snaked his arms through the straps.

"If we get out of here, I'm going to spend some time alone. This place, dying and coming back, it's done a number on my head. I have to rethink what my life is really all about. Do some real soul searching. Maybe meditation and shit," Will said, and then picked up two long spears.

"Are we talking about going to the top of a mountain and speaking with a Guru or hanging out in a cabin by the lake smoking weed?" Gerald asked.

Will handed Gerald a long spear. "Both."

***

A humid breeze blew as the sun rose in the clouded sky. Gerald looked overhead at the bright spot remembering the glowing orb he used to take for granted. Would he ever see a sunrise or sunset again? The most spectacular sunrise he'd seen was in Tanzania when he visited the Serengeti National Park. The stars at night looked like someone had spilled a bucketful of diamonds on the deepest black velvet. As morning approached, the stars faded, and the brightest orange fire peaked the horizon. Before long, the terrain warmed to life revealing green grass and acacia trees peppering the landscape. The faint sweet smell of acacias flowers mixed with the earthy musk of the wild. As the sun rose, the clouds above glowed with its reflection. For a brief moment, the horizon looked like it raged on fire. The sun continued its journey, and its light dried the mists and dreams of night.

No time for Memory Lane now. He needed to put all his senses on full alert. Trees offered cover from a dive-bomb attack from the giant pterosaurs. A few of the smaller varieties of the flying reptiles hung out in the treetops now. For the most part, they weren't any concern. One time, though, a pterosaur decided to relieve itself and baptized Gerald across his back as he walked underneath.

They had traveled enough times to the stream to form a path. The groundcover was some type of grass that grew less than a foot high. Stickers hadn't been a problem. There were a variety of bushes that grew long thorns and they had to be careful of those. The thorns were as useful as they were a hazard, as they made excellent needles.

Will stopped and stared off to the west side of the path.

Instinctually, Gerald froze in his tracks and lowered his body, bringing the spear up in two hands, preparing for the worst. He listened carefully and spied in the direction of what had Will's attention. After several seconds passed without any clues, he stepped over to his companion's side.

"What is it?" Gerald whispered, keeping his body low.

"I wonder what's over there? We haven't explored that area yet."

"We're not here to explore. We're here to get water, remember?"

"Yeah, but I think we should venture forth a bit—look for other stuff to eat. I mean, a man can't live on dinosaur alone. We need some fruits and vegetables—some roughage."

"Some roughage might help you with your gas problem," Gerald said.

"I'm serious. Let's branch off here and look around a bit."

"Don't you want to get water first and think about it?"

"No. If we get water you'll use that as an excuse not to explore and want to go back to the cave."

"You've got me figured out. Okay, we'll take a quick tour. If we find anything that looks edible, it's your turn to be the guinea pig and eat a little." Gerald gritted his teeth and widened his mouth. "I can still taste that blueberry thing I tried a week ago. That was the bitterest tasting shit I ever put in my mouth."

"Deal," Will said. "C'mon, I'll lead the way."

The two slinked through the jungle, careful to watch where they stepped. So far they hadn't encountered any snakes but weren't sure if any were in Patagonia.

After a good half hour had passed without coming upon anything new, Gerald was about to suggest they call it quits when Will stopped and pointed.

"Look, over there. Those trees. They look different."

Gerald turned his gaze and tried to focus in the distance. "They *do* look different. Look in the tops, there something orange and red in there."

"Might be something we can eat," Will said.

"You know, I think I've seen trees like that before. Yeah, I think that's a wild date palm."

"Dates? We can eat that."

"They're edible, for sure. It'll be good to eat something sweet for a change. I think dates have enough roughage to do you some good, too," Gerald said.

Fifteen minutes later, the two arrived at the nearest date palm. The palm leaves crowned the top and arched toward the ground—in some way reminding Gerald of an exploding skyrocket. The clusters of mostly orange and red dates hung in large bunch to the base of the tree's crown. Three tiny theropods dined on some of the fallen fruit below. The dinosaurs scampered away as soon as they saw the humans approach.

"I wonder what those dinos would taste like," Gerald said.

"They'd taste like the same kind of lizard we've eaten before."

"Not necessarily. They had a diet containing fruit. What an animal eats can affect the taste. I had a gator farmer tell me if you fed a gator chicken, it tasted like chicken. If you fed it fish, it'd taste like fish. Those little critters might make some good eating," Gerald said.

"We'll just make a sauce out of the dates and mop on them while they're cooking."

"Yeah, if we can get any. Those date clusters are pretty high up there." Will turned his gaze downward. "These on the ground look rotten."

"You smell that?" Will asked.

"Yeah, these rotten dates stink."

"They may stink, but they're fermenting. You know what that means?"

Gerald laughed. "I sure do. We'll be eating dinosaur on a stick and washing it down with date wine."

"The trees on down look smaller. We might be able to reach those clusters with our spears—especially if we tie the ends together and make it longer. Let's go," Will said and trotted off.

In the excitement, Gerald caught himself ignoring his surroundings. He turned on his heels and did a quick 360, and then sped up to catch Will. The date palms had more space between them than the other trees, so an attack from above wasn't out of the question.

"Hey, look over there." Will slowed to a walk, but didn't stop at a tree with fruit low enough for them to reach with a single spear.

"Where're you going?"

"Look, you see that?"

Gerald turned his gaze away from the low hanging prize, and said, "The mountains are pretty. We've seen mountains before. Let's get some dates."

"Look how low they are. We're on a cliff. Let's go see." Will didn't wait for Gerald to respond and headed off.

Will's curiosity might prove to be the death of them, Gerald thought. Still, if not for Will they would have missed finding the date trees.

The terrain rose slightly uphill, and then when the two came to the crest, they saw a magnificent sight. The terrain came to an abrupt halt, and a valley full of trees covered the expanse all the way to the mountain range.

The two looked at each other and then slowly walked over to the land's edge. The valley was at least a hundred feet below. The only way down was also the quickest, but there would be no chance of surviving that jump.

"It's so beau—look over there!" Will exclaimed.

Gerald followed Will's pointed finger and saw what had his buddy so excited. In an open area between some trees stood a giant gray colored, bipedal dinosaur feeding on another slightly smaller animal. The large head went down for another mouthful of the unfortunate creature and came back up with a hunk in jaws filled with rows of sharp looking teeth. Part of the meat hung out the side of its mouth and flapped in the wind as it chewed. Its legs had to be powerful to support the dinosaur, as its tail was so large it probably matched the upper body's weight. The underside of the dinosaur was pale in color. "This answers our question about other dinosaurs in Patagonia."

"It sure does. It was bad enough dealing with those giant pterodactyls and those other man-sized two legged lizards that got you before. That's a fucking T-rex down there."

Gerald didn't know many dinosaur names, but T-rex was one dinosaur practically everyone in the world knew of. "Yeah, and it's eating something too. Can't really tell from this angle. It's got four legs. Only thing I can think of right now is that it could be a Triceratops or Stegosaurs. We've got the belly side to us, so I don't know."

"I wouldn't want to meet up with either one," Will said, and cast a quick glance behind him. "I hope nothing that big is up here. Maybe all the large dinosaurs live in the valley."

"Let's hope so."

The T-rex hesitated on the way going down for another bite and lifted its nose into the air. It turned its head in a few different directions and resumed eating.

"Something's shaking the tree limbs in front of the T-rex," Will said.

"I see a head…looks like another T-rex wants in on the action."

"The head looks smaller."

"Maybe it's Junior coming to supper."

"No, its head is shaped different than the T-rex's. There's its neck—it's pale green, not gray," Will said.

The second dinosaur wasn't quite as tall as the T-rex, and its body didn't match in mass either. It was slightly sleeker, and the three fingered claws posed more of a threat than those of the T-rex.

"That might be an Allosaurus," Gerald said. "I had some plastic dinosaurs as a kid, and the Allosaurus looked a lot like a Tyrannosaurus. It was smaller, though, like that one."

T-rex gulped down another mouthful and let out a screeching warning to the approaching interloper.

Cold chills ran down Gerald's back. He nervously laughed. "Oh, fuck. The shit's about to get real."

The Allosaurus matched the battle cry with its own and inched its way closer.

T-rex went back to eating, showing the prize was his and his alone.

The Allosaurus lowered its head and stepped toward the dead dinosaur. The T-rex roared and jutted its head back before the thief could steal a bite. But the threat didn't distract the Allosaurus for long; it leaned its neck forward and bit off a mouthful of back.

"Brazen thing. I'll say that much for it," Will said.

T-rex watched the intruder eat and then lowered its head toward the dead animal, with no intention of eating. As the Allosaurus went for bite number two, T-rex snapped the air between them.

The Allosaurus rose on its legs and lifted its claws in the air. A challenge was made, and the challenge accepted. The two prehistoric beasts squared off for a fight to the finish.

"This is going to get good. I wish I was on my easy-chair eating some popcorn and drinking a Bloody Mary right now," Will said.

"I'd settle for a handful of dates. We don't have any of those either." Gerald took a quick look around and then sat cross legged on the ground.

Will followed his lead, and said, "Might as well sit and enjoy the show."

T-rex made the first move; it bounded forth and snapped at the Allosaurus' neck. The slightly smaller dinosaur proved to be more agile as it made a quick sidestep and raked its claws across the T-rex's chest. The claws slashed deep enough to plough three deep ditches into flesh, which quickly filled with red blood, and spilled down to the earth. T-rex's hiss rang with primordial anger but only seemed to strengthen the Allosaurus' resolve.

With a quick move of its own, the Allosaurus dipped low and sprang upward, catching the T-rex off-guard, and biting down on the T-rex's neck. The T-rex thrashed about, but not enough to free itself. The Allosaurus struggled to maintain its hold, but maintain it, it did.

"See, the Allosaurus outsmarted the bigger, stronger T-rex," Gerald said. "Give me smarts over brawn any day."

With no sign of succumbing, the T-rex twisted its body, and brought its tail flinging to the side like a tennis racket striking a short lob ball with a smash hit. The tail hit the Allosaurus with enough force for the T-rex to break free of its grip.

The T-rex roared again into the sky.

"*Godzirra* is *mucho* pissed," Gerald said.

"*Tadzirra* isn't down and out yet," Will countered.

The Allosaurus sidestepped to where the dead dinosaur was between it and the T-rex. For a moment, the two walked in a circle pursuing each other. It was obvious the Allosaurus was biding its time, but from the looks of things, the T-rex was ready for it to end.

Faster than Gerald thought possible for a thing as big as T-rex to move, it double-timed its pursuit and caught the Allosaurus. Before the Allosaurus could react, the T-rex came down with a foot and buried the Allosaurus' tail into the ground. The Allosaurus fell forward, and its face crashed into the earth.

"Man, he's going to have a tough time getting his ass off the ground. Those short arms aren't going to help him to get up at all," Will said.

The T-rex removed its foot from the Allosaurus' tail and lurched forward with an open maw. The Allosaurus tried to right itself back on its feet, but stopped abruptly when the T-rex's bear trap-like jaws clamped down on its neck. The Allosaurus let out a cry that sounded like a wounded bird. Its body squirmed about, and its tail repeatedly hit the T-rex in the side. The mighty T-rex held its own; its feet remained firmly planted to the ground.

"Look at that. The Rex is going to win. I wonder why the Allosaurus wasn't able to kill the Rex when it grabbed it by the throat," Will said.

"Must be the strength of the jaws. Look at the way the Rex's jaws are shaped. I bet there's a lot more muscle for crunching bone."

"Looks like the Allosaurus just about shot its wad. It's limp, and its arms are hanging down from its side."

Will was right, Gerald thought. The mighty animal had taken its last breath. "You know, it was because the Allosaurus wasn't as smart as the T-rex that it lost the fight."

"What? Are you kidding me? You can see the size difference. The Allosaurus lost the fight because the T-rex is bigger and stronger," Will said.

"Nope. It has nothing to do with strength. If the Allosaurus had been smart enough, it would have known better to pick a fight with something bigger and meaner. There, I rest my case," Gerald said, daring his buddy to challenge his logic.

Will went to say something, but held himself in check, and let out a sigh. "Whatever."

A reptilian roar from behind sent goosebumps across Gerald's flesh and weakened his bowels to the point he thought he might shit himself. The two rolled to the side and laid flat on the ground, seeing a new horror had arrived.

"Son-of-a-bitch!" Will cursed. "We should have been paying attention."

"What the hell is that thing? It looks like an Allosaurus with a fin on its back," Gerald said, and then gasped. "What do we do?"

The Spinosaurus stood taller than the wild date palm it was next to. The beast was a good fifty yards away, but that was still far too close. There was no way he or Will could outrun it.

"I don't think my arrows will do much good. These spears will be as effective as tooth picks. I don't think we're going to make it," Will said.

The Spinosaurus sniffed the air and slow stepped forward. The closer it got, Gerald could feel the ground tremble. "There's only one way one of us comes out of this: we split up—you run one way, and I run the other. Whoever lives goes back to the vortex by the volcano and meets the other."

"That means one of us dies a painful death. I've got another idea. Have you ever seen *Butch Cassidy and the Sundance Kid*?" Will asked.

"We're about to die and you're comparing real life to movies again? The answer's *no*."

"How about *Thelma and Louise*, then?"

"Yeah—oh, I get it. You want to take a one way ride to the bottom of the valley," Gerald said. The ground shook harder with each step of the approaching Spinosaurus.

"Yep. Beats the hell out of getting eaten alive again. You know, Brad Pitt got his big break in *Thelma and Louise*," Will said.

"It disturbs me you'd share that factoid with me right before we jump to our deaths. It disturbs me even more you know that," Gerald said.

Will rose and offered Gerald his hand.

The Spinosaurus roared and quickened its pace.

"Let's go, buddy," Will said.

Gerald nodded.

The two stepped off the edge, and yelled in unison, "Shiiiiiiiiiiiiiiiiiiiiiiiiiiiiiiiiiiiiiiiiiit!"

CHAPTER 5

The infant T-rex waddled on its short legs across the volcanic soil toward an expanse of trees toward the south. Coop thought Caveman looked silly as the man attempted to sneak up on the theropod. The area was wide open, not looking different from a Martian landscape. Caveman's bare feet kicked dust and small rocks in the pursuit. There would be no *sneaking up* on the little bastard.

Suge wandered away from the group, looking at various rocks. Coop hoped he wouldn't have problems with people going off to do their own thing. It was important for them to stick together.

Caveman lifted the rock above his head and ran toward the baby T-rex. The critter turned about in a surprised move and hissed like a cat. The warning did nothing to stop Caveman's objective. The rock crashed down on the dinosaur's skull, and the animal dropped to the ground.

"That's rock, *one*. T-rex, *zero*," Caveman said. He tossed the rock to the side and poked the animal in the stomach with his big toe. "This little guy doesn't even look real."

"Be careful. Keep your hands away from its mouth. The salvia may contain deadly bacteria," Alex said.

Bats walked over to help Caveman carry the dinosaur.

Caveman was preoccupied with examining the T-rex's claws. "I'd like to hang one of these things from the rearview mirror on my truck."

"Yeah. I'm sure that would make a great conversation piece with the ladies," Bats said. He went to the left side of the dinosaur and lifted up the arm.

Caveman stopped playing around and grabbed the right arm. "I'm telling you, it would. Ain't nobody else can say they killed a T-rex with his bare hands. I'd hang the claw right next to my other conversation piece."

The two dragged the theropod along the ground toward the group.

"What's the other conversation piece?" Bats asked.

"Dick bone from a 'coon," Caveman said.

"Dick bone from a raccoon? Why would you hang something like that from your rearview mirror?" Bats asked.

"Ladies get in the truck and at some point notice it hanging down. Naturally they's gonna ask me what it is. I tell 'em. Most of them laugh. Some make faces. But see, I use it as a way to start talking about sex."

"Drag it over here, guys. We'll cook it by this lava pool. The rocks surrounding it are hot enough to cook on," Coop said.

"You just a regular Don Juan, aren't you, Caveman?" Bats said.

"Funny how some animals have bones in their dick," Caveman said.

"Only mammals have penis bones, Caveman. It's called a *baculum*. Humans and spider monkeys are the only primates without a penis bone. Most other mammals have them, like dogs and cats. That's why you see dogs get stuck sometimes after having sex," Alex said.

"How the hell do you know so much about animal dicks? You some kind of *prevert*?" Caveman said.

Alex bit his lip, shook his head, and said, "No, I'm not a *pervert*. I'm a Zoologist. A student of mine once wrote a paper on the subject and pointed out the details."

"You know you can make toothpicks out of 'coon dick bones," Caveman said.

"Can we stop talking about raccoon penises?" Susan said. "If we're going to eat, we need to get that thing cooking."

"Yeah, we need to cook it and get on with the plan," Coop said.

"We's need to gut it first. That's going to be tough to do just using my fingernails," Caveman said. He sounded serious.

"Try these," Suge said. He handed Caveman two knife-shaped black rocks. "The stuff's kind of brittle, but the sharp edges cut like glass."

"Obsidian," Coop said. "It's a volcanic glass formed as an extrusive igneous rock. Obsidian can produce a cutting edge sharper than surgical steel. In fact, some surgeons use scalpels with obsidian blades."

Caveman took the two rocks, looked them over, and handed one to Bats. "Hold this." He then grabbed an arm and started sawing it off from the body. "Ain't a whole lot of meat in this thing. Not much more than a chicken wing." The makeshift knife made rough cuts across the flesh but did an adequate job at severing the arm. Red blood stained the black blade as he started cutting the other arm.

"I wonder what it's going to taste like," Natasha said.

"Might taste like gator. You ever eat gator?" Caveman asked as he cut off the other arm. He tossed it aside, and started sawing on the tail. "I like it. Tastes good fried, blacked—hell—I've even had it in a *Sauce Piquante*."

"I've had fried alligator before—at a restaurant. It tasted like chicken. What's a *Sauce Piquante*?" Natasha asked.

"It's a Creole dish. First you make a roux, you know, with flour and oil. Add the trinity—bell pepper, onion, and celery. After that, add your tomatoes and shrimp or chicken stock. You're making a red gravy. Kick it up with some garlic and Cajun seasonings. Slow cook it until done, add your meat, and cook until it's done. Squeeze a little lemon in before serving, and eat it over rice. You know you go the spices right when the pepper makes your nose run." Caveman cut through the tail and handed it to Bats.

Bats laid the tail over the hot rocks. It made a searing sound, and a wisp of smoke rose from the blood oozing from the cut end.

"I left the skin on. If it ain't good to eat we can just peel it off." Caveman went for a leg next, and said, "This thing might be a female. It has a slit between its legs." He pushed the sides of the sex organ with the knife. "There's something in here." The blade carefully went in and lifted out a two-inch shaft. "This thing's got a little pecker. It was hiding up in there."

"Let me see," Alex said, and went over by the dead animal.

"See, you are a prevert," Caveman said, and started laughing. "Ha! Got you."

Alex chuckled and examined the dinosaur. "There's a lot of questions concerning dinosaur sex organs. Sex organs are made from soft tissue, so there's little fossil evidence. The question is, *did dinosaurs have sex organs similar to alligators or birds*? Male and female alligators have vents. That's why the gender is hard to tell apart just by looking at them. The male's penis is hidden in the body and exits the vent when it's time for sex. The testicles never drop, and the penis is always erect."

"The hell you say," Caveman said. "Lucky bastard."

"Anyway," Alex continued, "birds have a cloaca, which is an orifice where urine and feces are excreted, but also serves as the pathway for reproduction. For the T-rex, at least, this proves dinosaur reproduction is more like the modern day alligator."

"This little pee-pee is hard. Must stay hard like the gator's." He pinched the penis with a thumb and forefinger and carved it off the body with the knife. "Souvenir."

Alex went to speak, but must have thought better, because he simply rose and walked off.

Caveman went back to working, cutting off the two legs and the head. When he sliced through the stomach and started gutting it, Natasha gagged and made a mad dash away.

"Ribs won't have much meat, the back either. Legs and tail are the best part," Caveman said.

"We need calories, so we'll cook everything but the head," Coop said. "People, I don't care what it tastes like, we divide it up, and eat our portion. We need fuel to survive, and we don't need anyone holding us back."

***

The T-rex meat didn't take very long to cook. The rocks were so hot it dried the flesh and made it hard to chew. The group sat in a misshapen circle and dined on their portion.

Caveman held an arm bone with the hand still attached. He chewed on the hand like a dog with a new rawhide bone. The small bones creaked as he bit down, and gristle popped between his slurps.

"From the sound of things, Caveman, you must be enjoying your lunch," Coop said.

"I am. It's knuckle sucking good," he said, and then licked his lips.

Coop noticed as he watched the others eat how there was no interaction. Everyone sat staring at the ground, lost in their own thoughts. Not surprising, their minds were sorting out the events from the last couple of hours. He had to chase his own memories of his violent death away in order to concentrate on the business at hand.

For them to act as a team, distractions had to be at a minimum. After swallowing his last portion of meat, he decided now was the time to clear the air.

"I'm glad to see everyone eating," Coop said. "We'll have to find water—and soon. We can't survive without water."

"This would have been easier to choke down if we had something to drink with it," Susan said.

"You know, modern day chickens are actually descendants of the Tyrannosaurs," Alex said, and wiped his fingers on his thighs.

Even though Alex had spoken to the whole group, Susan glared at him as if offended he'd dare speak to her.

"People, there's a storm brewing amongst us. We've all experienced psychological trauma. I've been trying to hold mine in check, but maybe it's better if we all tell a little of our story. Right now our thoughts are trapped inside and building a monster that may destroy us later. Let's not let that happen," Coop said.

Coop turned his gaze to Susan. "Susan, I knew that you had died from some kind of allergic reaction before I was killed. Not long after we found ourselves alive again by the volcano, you accused Alex of murdering you. How do you know this?"

"I'll tell you how I know. The bastard gave me his canteen to drink from, and I tasted the salt and peanuts on my first swallow. The reaction was immediate and closed up my throat. I couldn't talk or breathe. I saw that evil look in his eyes before he put on a sympathy show to fool the others who came to save me." She turned to Chief. "I remember you too, Chief. You tried to save me. You're a good person. A really good person. I can feel it. Thank you for trying. I…funny, I don't even know your real name."

"You're kind, Susan. I don't know how you ended up with that piece of shit for a husband. Don't worry about him now—or ever again. Oh, and my real name is *Inez Magnus Sheldon the third*."

Susan grinned slightly. "You're serious, aren't you?"

"That I am," Chief said.

"Is it true? Alex," Natasha asked, her tone fearful.

"Of course it's true, and you're the reason why," Chief said.

Alex had held his head low the entire conversation. Red splotches brightened his cheeks.

"Alex killed me because of her? A child? He was fucking one of his own students?" She turned her gaze to Alex. "Who *are* you? Answer me!"

Natasha started, "I had no idea...he never said anything...I thought you—"

"Can it! I'm talking to Alex," Susan said.

Alex finally lifted his gaze from the ground but kept his head down. In a low voice, he said, "I admit that I put the peanuts in the canteen."

"Oh, Alex! How could you?" Natasha stared at the Professor with her mouth open and her eyes wide.

"I did it for you. I did it for us," Alex said.

"No, you did it for *you*. Don't bring me into this. If you had done it for me, then I would have been in on the plan. I wasn't. Because you knew if I knew you'd killed her, I'd have nothing to do with you ever again," Natasha said.

"What can I say?" Alex said, and lifted his hands, open palms to the sky. "I was in a bad place. I was trapped in a relationship that has been dead for years. Taking a life had never occurred to be before—ever. Especially not Susan's—despite our issues. Something...something about Patagonia changed my way of thinking. We were no longer in a world run by rules. Patagonia is a world of *might means right*. Something about this place brought out a person in me I didn't know existed. Patagonia has stirred a savage instinct that I gave in to."

"Cry me a fucking river," Susan said.

"I don't expect you to believe me, but I am sorry for killing you. I can't explain the feelings I had that day that led me to do it. It was a driving force, and I gave in to it. I don't expect your forgiveness either. Please just know that I am sorry, and I'll do anything you ask of me from now on to try to make it up to you," Alex said.

"Just stay away from me. You and that cunt of a girlfriend can be happy together. I don't want anything to do with you ever again," Susan said.

"Leave me out of this," Natasha said. "Yes, I was seeing Alex, and I knew he was married. But I knew there was no love in your marriage. I…I was hoping you'd give him a divorce. But you wouldn't, and you threatened to destroy his career if he left you. I'm not proud of what I did with Alex behind your back, but I was in love. Your hatefulness is what led up to this happening." She turned to Alex. "And you, you killed a woman. Your wife. That was a woman who you once loved dearly. What kind of person can do that? I don't want anything to do with you. I wish I didn't even have to look at you again," Natasha's voice cracked, and she broke down in tears.

Suge rose from his spot, sat next to Natasha, and put his arm on her shoulder.

Coop brought a closed hand by his face and flexed his fingers. That was a lot of drama, but at least it was out in the open. He needed to keep the ball running. "Who would like to speak next?"

"I'm not the only murderer on this trip," Alex said.

"What? Please explain yourself," Coop said.

Alex slowly nodded his head, and said, "There was so much going on during the Troodon battle. Chief was already dead. Natasha, Logan, Meat, Caveman, and Ron were off to the side, so I doubt that anyone saw what happened in the tree. I was hanging on, trying to see how the battle was going, and looking to see if Natasha was safe. I didn't just *fall* out the tree. I was pushed— kicked, actually. Matt brought his foot down onto my back and knocked me to the ground."

"Matt wouldn't do that! He was your friend—a close associate. You've known him for years," Natasha said.

"Yeah, I know him well enough to realize he was trying to make time with you," Alex said.

"I always avoided his advances. You know that," Natasha said.

"You did until this trip. We couldn't spend any time together, so you started getting real chummy with him. With Susan out of the way you spent all your time with me and left him out in the cold. I guess jealousy got the best of him. We were in the tree together with a gang of Troodons on the ground. One swift kick, and I was out of the picture. Matt could have had you all to himself. I guess whatever about Patagonia pushed me to kill Susan also pushed Matt to kill me," Alex said.

"As inclined as I am to say *bullshit* to Alex's story, I do find it intriguing," Coop said. One murder was believable. Two added a strangeness which presented other questions.

"Alex and Susan weren't the only ones murdered," Natasha said.

All heads turned Natasha's way.

She removed Suge's hand from her shoulder. "Me, Clint, and Logan had just barely escaped a pack of Velociraptors. Just as we were about to meet up with Matt and Ben in the Warthog, the T-rex that attacked—Clint lured it over by the edge of the cliff. The weight of the Rex and the two grenades Clint set off collapsed the edge and sent them falling to their deaths by the riverbed. Logan and I went over to look, and I saw them both dead. Logan hugged me while I cried. Meat—Clint, saved our lives, and I know he mainly did it for me. I remember saying I needed Matt. Logan's body stiffened when I mentioned Matt's name, which I did think a bit strange at the time. Then Logan said he saw Clint moving by the river. I was shocked that he could live after the fall and turned to look. The next thing I know, I was falling to my death. Logan pushed me over the side."

"Unbelievable," Coop said. "What would possess him to do something like that?"

"The boy's a tutti-frutti, probably had a thing for Matt," Bats said. "Logan's a tough son-of-a-bitch. I like him. I didn't figure he had a mean streak like that, though."

"I'm finding it hard to wrap my mind around how three civilized people could change so drastically at the same time and murder people close to them," Coop said.

"It was the weirdest thing," Alex said. "It's like my jealousy clouded my judgment. There's something in Patagonia affecting us."

"I don't feel any different," Suge said.

"Us either," Ron said, and patted Don on the knee.

"Me neither," Caveman said.

"I'm my same loveable self," Meat said.

"The past is the past. I know it's easy to say, but I hope Alex, Susan, and Natasha—that you can push all the past events aside and concentrate on surviving. If we get out of here somehow, we can deal with the past issues then. Can you three do that for me? Will you do it for us?"

Natasha said *yes* first, followed by Alex. Susan nodded.

"Great," Coop said. "I'll tell my story, but since I was the last to die, I'll bring the others in my group to speak first. Don, you were the first to go. Tell us what happened."

"Well, you know, I just learned from that phone call that Ron was missing. Well, hell, we've been together all our lives. I could feel that he wasn't alive. I was grieving so badly that I didn't see that big *petro-sarus* swooping down to get me. Took me right on off and fed me piece by piece to her chicks. That thing plucked off an arm, and I yelled *Roll Tide!* It yanked off the other arm, and I cried *Roll Tide!* After it took my legs and two more *Roll Tides*, I looked up into the sky, and I swear I could see the Bear's face forming in the clouds. I bet he has the best football team in heaven," Don said.

"You know he does," Ron said.

"*Roll Tide!*" the brothers said in unison.

"Okay…thanks for sharing, Don," Coop said. "Bats, you were giving the Spinosaurus hell with the fifty. I don't know if you know this, but it did eventually die, but not until after its tail knocked over the Mule, with you in it."

"Yeah. I barely remember that. The Mule tipped over, and my face and head hit the windshield at an angle. Things went black after that," Bats said.

"I'm sure you broke your neck," Coop said. "Suge, that other Spinosaurus was on your heels when its companion ran me into the cave. Did it end quickly?"

"Yeah, fortunately, it did. Still hurt like a mutha, though. Those jaws crushed my chest like it was an empty toilet paper roll. I didn't last long after that."

"Long story short, the Spinosaurus that pulled me out of the cave dropped me to the ground and started eating my head first. The fall hurt and broke some bones, but I didn't feel a lot from the bite," Coop said. "Next?"

Meat raised a hand, and said, "You know my story. I danced with the adult version of the T-rex we ate. I set off two grenades before we fell. I don't remember anything after that."

"I had Troodons on me like pit bulls. They tore me apart and ate me alive," Chief said.

"That's my story. *Roll Tide*," Ron said.

"Mine too," Caveman said. "Ain't no sense reliving it. Are we done here? I'm ready to leave."

"I guess this is about as close as we can come together," Coop said. "This will have to be our *Kumbaya* moment. If everyone is ready, let's gather a few more rocks we can use as weapons and head south. Keep your head turning at all times, and say something if you see something. Stay in a group, and don't wander too far off from the pack."

"What happens if one or more of us dies on the trip? Do we come back here for them to be reborn?" Chief asked.

"I've thought about that," Coop said. "I think the best plan is for survivors to continue without the others. Our goal is to reach the Mule and contact help. If just one of us survives, we can tell the story and get help. Remember, though, we all died at different times, but we all came back at the same time. So for whatever reason, that might happen again."

"Yeah, but Bats and I died since our first resurrection. We came back immediately," Alex said.

"Good point. Hell then, I don't know what to expect. If anyone dies and ends up back here, they can make their own choice whether to stay and wait for others or leave. Can't live without food or water very long, so I suspect everyone will try to make it on their own," Coop said.

***

As far as Coop could tell, the beginning of the tree line was a good one thousand yards away. He felt vulnerable, as he was sure the others did, walking on the dirt and volcanic rock terrain with only a rock in each hand for protection. At least they wouldn't be taken by surprise. With no water and no vegetation, except for a green moss-like plant covering some of the rocks, there was no reason for any dinosaur to hunt the land.

"This is not going to be easy," Natasha said. "We're only halfway to the trees, and I already feel blisters on my feet. I wish we at least had shoes."

"Blisters will turn into calluses eventually. You'll just have to find a way to push yourself through the pain," Coop said.

"That's easy for you to say. You men have been conditioned for situations like this. I haven't trained for survival missions," Natasha said.

"I didn't mean to sound so insensitive," Coop said. The onset of osteoarthritis had the joint in his left big toe burning. This wasn't going to be a cakewalk for him either. "We can only move as fast as the slowest member. We'll try to take it easy for the first few days until our bodies adjust."

"I wish I had a pair of drawers. I don't like Mr. Happy swinging in the breeze. One of them flying lizards might think it's a worm and try to peck it off," Caveman said.

"I wouldn't worry about that," Suge said. "It's too small for one of them to see it."

"Yeah, well, you ain't worried because yours looks like a black anaconda. It'll scare the dinosaurs away," Caveman said.

"Why does the conversation always come back to penises?" Susan said. "Don't you men ever talk about anything else?"

"Sure. We talk about women. This just ain't the time or the place," Caveman said.

Alex moved up from the group's rear and walked alongside Coop. "I've got a question for you."

"Go ahead," Coop said.

"The *commodities* you took the Mule and your men to find, where you all died, did you find them?"

Coop chuckled. "Yeah. I found them. I found them moments before I was attacked in a cave by some small theropod and then eaten alive by the Spinosaurus. Kind of ironic."

"Can you tell me what was so goddamn important out there for you to risk your lives like that?" Alex asked.

Coop didn't slow his pace and looked behind to read the faces of his men. A few showed signs of indifference; no one shook their head in disapproval. "Okay, I'll tell you. Diamonds, but not just any diamonds. These are red diamonds—some of the rarest in the world. The value of the ones Hawkins and Prescott found were estimated to be worth over five hundred million dollars. And there may have been more to find in the cave. We just didn't have time to explore. There's no telling what secrets Patagonia is hiding."

"If we all would have stuck together in the Warthog, we would have made it there and back again alive. It wasn't a good plan to split us up like that," Alex said.

"It's easy to armchair quarterback. But the Warthog was too big to take it all the way to the cave, remember? The reason your group was killed is because you were careless. If your group had stayed in the Warthog, you'd all be alive," Coop said.

"Yep, I let the excitement of the trip and others of the group cloud my better judgment. It's my fault we were ambushed by Troodons," Chief said.

"We couldn't come all the way to Patagonia and just spend it cooped up in the Warthog. All of us wanted the adventure. We just underestimated the risk," Natasha said.

"Don't beat yourself up over this, Chief," Coop said. "I had my head up my ass when we got to the cave. I had let my guard down—we all did. We thought the threats were isolated to certain areas. We didn't know every tree had a potential predator behind it." He paused and thought a minute. "Maybe there is something here in Patagonia that affects the way we think."

"Could it be something in that nasty smelling shit the volcano is burping into the air?" Alex asked.

"Don't know. But if there is, we need to be here for each other. If one of us starts coming up with some strange ideas, the others need to try and get them back on track," Coop said.

"I don't know if that'll work," Suge said. "If we're all affected, it might be like a bunch of drunks try to rationalize with another drunk. Right now I feel like I have a sound mind. I hope it stays that way."

"I feel fine. I'll feel better after I kill something, though," Bats said.

"Yep, the man needs his medicine," Caveman said.

Same old Bats, Coop thought. The man had asserted that he needed to kill something every few days in order to maintain his sanity. Taking on dinosaurs with stones and fists, though, seemed like a stretch. Coop hoped killing lizards and other small reptiles would satisfy Bats' need.

The group made it to the tree line without any surprises. The ground had grown cooler and softer, which was welcomed relief. Short grass replaced the harsh tundra that led back to the volcano.

The trees were of the palm variety, tall and branchy, reaching into the Patagonian sky. Having some cover overhead made Coop feel less exposed, although wondering what might be hiding behind the trees negated that minor comfort.

Everyone remained quiet as Coop led them past trees as they snaked their way around large roots. A time or two they heard a nesting pterosaur flap its wings. The flying reptiles were in the trees' canopies, hidden by thick leaves. This confirmed there was life on the western side of Patagonia. Coop just hoped that as on the eastern side near the mountains, this side would only support life of small theropods and other creatures of a lesser threat.

The tree line gave out after fifty yards and opened up again to a flat grassy area. Coop raised his hand when they reached the tree line's edge and surveyed the surroundings. Farther ahead, no more than a couple hundred yards away, another tree line started.

"We good to go or do we need to rest?" Coop asked.

"I'm afraid that if I stop walking my feet will start to hurt too bad for me to go any farther," Natasha said. "We haven't been walking that long anyway."

"We need water," Susan said. "I'm good to go."

Only the two women answered, and really they were his only concerns. He knew his men didn't need the rest, and that Alex would fall in line with the majority.

"Okay, let's go. Like before, I'll lead. Keep the women in the middle. Ron and Don will bring up the rear," Coop said.

"Those trees look a little different up ahead. Different varieties. That may mean there's a water supply nearby," Alex said as the group plodded on.

"If we find water, will it be safe to drink?" Natasha asked. "We don't have any way to filter it. We don't have any way to boil it either."

"You can't drink water out of a stream without puttin' a bunch of critters in your stomach," Caveman said. "Whatcha' do, is go near the water's edge, and dig a hole until you find water. The ground acts like a filter. That water comin' out of the hole is safer to drink. It's better if the ground is sandy. Sand is a better filter than dirt—gives you cleaner water too."

"It's just a chance we'll have to take," Suge said. "Be ready for some explosive diarrhea, though."

"I can hardly wait," Natasha said.

SKEER-AK!

The pterosaur's cry sent invisible, paralyzing tentacles in the air. Coop turned around in time to see the flying reptile skim the tree canopies behind them and swoop down on Don. The pterosaur was huge. It looked as big as a fighter jet. It landed on the ground and had Don trapped under one of its leg claws to the ground.

"Quetzalcoatlus!" Alex yelled, and ran for his life.

The Professor wasn't the only one to flee. The others made a mad dash for the tree line, except for Ron.

Coop only hesitated for a second before following. He had thought about throwing the rocks in his hands but realized such effort was useless.

The beast was a fascinating sight to behold. Anyone taking a first glance would think a strange looking giraffe held Don underneath its back leg. Coop thought it stood at least twenty feet tall. Its front arms served as front legs, and the pointed wing tips folded neatly away from the ground. The neck stretched from its body to its skull by more than ten feet, and the same brownish hair covered the neck as the body. Its stork-like beak didn't appear to have any teeth when it opened its mouth to let out another shriek. The beautiful green crown on its head looked out of place—like it was painted.

As Coop ran for the trees, a dark shadow moved past him. Another Quetzalcoatlus joined the fray and landed in front of the fleeing group. Chief, Susan, and Bats veered to the left while the other six hung right. Both groups were near the trees.

Before the group of six could make it to safety, a third Quetzalcoatlus landed and blocked the way. Suge, Natasha, and Meat split one way and headed to the tree line. Coop, Alex, and Caveman made it past the trees to safety—barely escaping the snapping jaws of the late arriver.

Don screamed for his life.

Ron hurled curses at the pterosaur after the two rocks he'd thrown did nothing to deter it. The reptile's long neck came down and snapped air as Ron ungracefully jutted backward.

Coop, Alex, and Caveman hid behind a large tree trunk and watched, powerless to do anything to save their companions.

As far as Coop knew, the others in the group had made it into the woods. The nearest Quetzalcoatlus that almost got them had turned and stepped over toward Ron. It was the most unusual sight he had ever witnessed—watching the pterosaur walk on land like a four legged beast. The Quetzalcoatlus who split the group went into the tree line where Suge, Natasha, and Meat entered. It was unfortunate the trees weren't thick enough to prevent the reptile from pursuing, but at least the natural blockade would slow it down and give his companions a chance.

"Ron! Run away!" Coop yelled, knowing the warning was useless. There was no way Ron would abandon his brother. He also doubted that Ron's bravery had anything to do with the knowledge that dying in Patagonia was only a temporary condition.

The Quetzalcoatlus shrieked at the one holding Don, an apparent claim to the other human between them.

Ron twisted his body abruptly about, and the Quetzalcoatlus' beak closed across his chest. "*Roll Tide!*" he screamed in horrific pain.

Not willing to share in the spoils of battle, the Quetzalcoatlus holding Don leaned its head down and held onto Ron's legs.

The two flying reptiles played tug-of-war as the unfortunate man howled in agony. The Quetzalcoatlus holding onto the chest had the advantage, and eventually pulled Ron away from the other.

The loser threw its head back and screeched.

The other ignored it and began feeding on the spoils of victory.

The pandemonium gave way to eerie silence. Don must have died sometime during the battle—perhaps from having all that weight on him and not being able to breathe.

The two giant reptiles enjoyed their meal without any further conflict.

Alex turned to Coop, and said, "What do we do now?"

CHAPTER 6

"Ben, these guys are serious. Don't do anything to provoke them," Matt said. It was ironic how moments before salvation seemed so close. Now he, Logan, and Ben found themselves in a tight spot where the only law was held by those with the most effective weapons.

"*Alvarez, Santos, pesquisar o Warthog,*" Diaz commanded two of his men. He turned to Matt, and said, "If you are hiding any contraband, you need to tell me now."

The two men filed out and headed to inspect the Warthog.

"Contraband? You mean souvenirs from Patagonia? We didn't bring anything with us except some grass and rock samples—and not much of that, because the trip was cut short. We do have a lot of pictures." Matt thought the question was ridiculous to begin with. "We're scientists. We didn't go to plunder a pristine environment." In his mind, he could see Ben wearing a shirt imprinted with: I Went To Patagonia And All I Got Was This T-Shirt. *Funny how you could be around another so much that they affect the way you think*, he thought.

"We're particularly interested in minerals. Do any of the rock samples contain anything that look like gemstones?" Diaz asked.

"No. Nothing like that. Coop said there was nothing special about the few rock samples we have. There's nothing of value," Matt said.

"Why do you ask? Were you expecting to find gemstones in Patagonia?" Logan asked. "Are those the *mysterious commodities* Coop mention to us? The real reason Ace Corp wanted to go to Patagonia?"

"I ask the questions, *Senhor* Logan," Diaz said.

"As a matter of fact, it was," Henry Lear said. "Diamonds, of the red variety. Some of the rarest gemstones on the planet. Having those diamonds that we knew about was going to triple my worth. I need that money to secure my control over the resources Patagonia has to offer. Ace Corporation will handle the business investments with the local governments from all the other investors in the world. Scientists backed by big corporations will be elated to study living specimens of dinosaurs. Pharmaceutical outfits will be beating down the doors looking for the next miracle cures found in the plants and trees. Who knows? Maybe the Fountain of Youth does exist in Patagonia. Every country in the world will want their own dinosaur zoo. At some point I'll build a resort, once we get some heavy equipment in to tunnel through the mountains. I'll make that Atlantis resort in the Bahamas look like an ant hill. The ground where you're standing will become an airport."

"You may have some difficulties making your dreams come true. Patagonia is nothing like you may think. The Troodon attack...you can't imagine the savagery I witnessed. You might have to kill most of the dinosaurs before you set up one permanent camp," Matt said, trying to beat the memories of the slaughter back down. "But none of that is any of my business or any of my concern, right now."

"Fine, fine, Mr. King," Lear said. "If you just step this way," Lear fanned his hand holding the cigar toward a large tent used as the mess hall from their previous stay, "we'll start the debriefing."

Matt turned to Ben, who bit his bottom lip and shook his head. Looking over at Logan, he saw uncertainty and a hint of fear in his eyes. But what were they to do? They were at a complete disadvantage. "We'll answer all of your questions and tell you everything we know."

"That you will, Mr. King. That, I'm sure of," Lear said.

***

Inside the tent where they had first met the Redwater crew over a week ago, three chairs sat in the middle of the room next to each other, with a table and two chairs opposite. The table had a handheld propane torch set by the edge.

A table once used to heat pans of food had a cloth hand towel and a gallon jug on one end and two unbuckled straps across the middle. One end of the table was noticeably higher than the other.

Another table on the other side of the room had a revolver, a fish tank with a snake in it marked with bands of red, black, and yellow, and a fish tank with something furry looking inside— about a foot in length and roundish in shape. The lighting wasn't bright enough for Matt to see if the snake was a milk snake or a coral snake—the two most likely candidates. Matt found himself momentarily confused how to identify the two. Was it *red touch yellow, kills a fellow* or *red touch black, kills Jack*?

Lear walked with purpose past the chairs and sat behind the desk. His hand slipped under his jacket over his tie and lingered long enough for Matt to fear Lear was going to pull out a gun. Instead, a Churchill sized Maduro wrapped cigar eased out. Lear's left hand went into his coat pocket and came back with a guillotine cutter. One snip of the cutter cleanly severed the cigar's cap. The cap fell to the table, and Lear brushed it to the floor. Next, he picked up the propane torch and cracked open the valve allowing fuel to the nozzle. A couple of pushes to the igniter, and a cone-shaped, blue and orange flame, brightened the nozzle's end. Lear brought the cigar's foot to the flame and gently puffed on the other end. The foot glowed like hot embers, and aromatic gray smoke huffed from Lear's mouth.

This is all a production, Matt thought. He, Logan, and Ben were held in check behind the chairs by three of the mercenaries. Diaz had remained by the door. The whole tent looked like it had been staged for the three to look curiously about and question just what the debriefing was going to entail. A table had a cloth and a jug on it. What was in the jug? Another table had a snake, a revolver, and something large and furry—what was their purpose? Lear had meticulously cut the end of the cigar with a cutter. What was similar in size and thickness to a cigar? A finger. Lear was a man who enjoyed the finer things in life. Lighting a cigar with a gas torch is something a plumber might do, not a CEO of a major corporation. It wouldn't take long for the torch to make soft flesh smoke like rolled tobacco. The pit in Matt's stomach sank deeper.

"Before we begin, please relieve yourself of anything on your possession," Lear said.

Matt nodded and removed his satellite phone given to him by Ace Corporation for the mission. The phones only connected to the phones issued to the other explorers and Ace Corporation. It had been a shame he couldn't connect with the outside world.

Ben and Logan both unclipped the phones from their belts and handed them to the mercenaries, who put them on the table in front of Lear.

"That's it? Only phones? There's nothing hidden in your pockets...or anywhere else?" Lear asked.

"That's all I have," Matt said.

"Me too," Logan said.

"Phones were the only thing of value in the jungle," Ben said. "It's not like we needed change for bus fare."

Ben is gonna 'Ben' no matter what, Matt thought. The situation would be so much better if Ben had laryngitis instead of a twisted ankle.

Lear offered no reaction to the injured man's comment. "If you don't mind, my friends here will give you a gentle pat down. Please raise your arms..." he waited as the three complied, "and spread your legs."

Matt felt a hand roughly explore his collar, under his arms, between his legs, and down to his ankles. There was nothing gentle to this bodily invasion. He heard Logan utter *ouch* two different times and knew he wasn't getting any better treatment. At least Ben managed to keep his discomfort to himself.

Lear patiently waited for the three mercenaries to finish, and then called out, "Captain Diaz, you may proceed."

A noise like a stretching balloon came from behind. Matt turned his gaze and saw Diaz pull the cuff of a latex glove down by his right wrist, fitting the glove tight around the fingers. He let the cuff go, and the latex snapped against his wrist.

"Please unbuckle your belts and drop your pants," Lear said, his tone as casual as if offering the three men a seat at a conference table.

"Hey! I don't see the rea—" Matt checked his protest when the rifle barrel of the nearest mercenary moved under the left side of his chin.

The mercenary behind Logan racked a bullet in his rifle to let everyone know he was ready for business too.

Matt wasn't sure what was going on with Ben and was too afraid to turn his head and see for himself.

"This isn't a discussion, Mr. King. You and your friends just need to do as you're told," Lear said.

With shaky hands, Matt reached for his belt buckle and pulled the tongue away from the pin, loosening it, and then slid his pants and underwear to his knees.

Logan's buckle rattled, signaling he, too, had complied.

Silence from Ben's end could mean only one thing and it wasn't good. Without any warning, a rifle stock crashed down on the back of Ben's head. The athletic man toppled against the chair in front of him, knocking it to the side, his crutches falling next to him.

"Ben!" Logan cried.

"Stay where you are, *Senhor* Logan," Diaz said. "Your fate may not be as fortunate."

Matt heard Diaz's steps approach and felt the Captain's hand on his back. Matt submitted to a gentle push and leaned over, the latex covered fingers penetrated his rectum and explored. As Matt brought his gaze up, he saw Lear stare him in the eyes, not showing the least bit of compassion or gloating in victory in anyway. Why was Lear subjecting them to this? What was the man's game?

The pressure was so intense at one point, Matt thought he could feel pain up to his throat. On the finger's exit, blood rushed from his face, and his colon spasmed as if it might dump its contents.

The latex glove cried as it stretched and snapped off Diaz's hands. "You may dress, *Senhor* Matt." He tossed the glove in a small bucket and replaced it with another. It was Logan's turn to be probed.

The mercenary no longer had the rifle barrel pressed against Matt's throat, but it was still a couple of feet away and pointed at him. He looked over and saw Ben's *caretaker* had taken the liberty to unbuckle the man's belt and had pulled his pants down. Ben was out cold.

After Logan passed inspection, Diaz told him to dress. A new glove went on, and Matt and Logan watched powerless as Diaz performed his orders on Ben.

"They are not hiding anything, *Senhor* Lear," Diaz said.

"Pity, I was so hoping to find more of the rare jewels. At least these are men true to their word. I admire that," Lear said. "Mr. King, you may help your friend off the floor."

Logan immediately followed Matt over to Ben's side. He ran his hand over the back of Ben's head. "There's a pretty big knot here."

Ben moaned a little and then began to blink.

"You okay, buddy?" Matt asked.

With some obvious effort, Ben said, "Yeah. I think so…but…what happened?"

"Cavity search…they didn't find any diamonds," Logan said, and patted his friend on the shoulder.

"No shit…well, that might be a poor choice of words. I guess I should feel lucky. When I woke, I first thought something *much* worse had happened to my ass while I was out."

The two helped Ben from his undignified position and soon had his pants up, and sitting in a chair.

"Please, join your friend here." Lear waved the air with his cigar toward the two empty chairs in front of him. "It's time for your debriefing."

"Honestly, Mr. Lear. I don't know what we could tell you that you don't already know. I'm sure you've heard all the conversations that went over the phone. With the satellites you have tracking us, you must have some confirmation to our report. The Mule had made it to the cave. It must still be there. All the evidence, all the video the Warthog uploaded, you must know we aren't hiding anything," Matt said.

Lear brought his elbows on the table and pressed his fingertips together. "The interrogation is not for information, Mr. King."

"Then what?" Matt asked.

"It's for my entertainment," Lear said.

A cold blade with a sharp edge bit into Matt's throat right below his Adam's apple. Each of the three mercenaries had taken position behind them with knives in hand, threatening Logan and Ben in the same fashion.

"You see," Lear said, "when I'm disappointed, I need something to lift my spirits. I enjoy rare excitement. Once you're my age and are jaded to the opulent life, stimulation is achieved through divergent measures." Lear nodded toward Diaz.

The Captain moved over to the fish tank housing the snake. He reached behind it and came back with a set of tongs. The tongs went down into the tank and came back gripping the snake behind the head. A few steps over had him by Ben's side. Diaz pulled the neck of Ben's shirt away from his chest and dropped in the serpent.

The room was dead silent, and then Matt heard Ben breathing harder. One errant move and the mercenary would slice Ben's throat. Maybe that was the best way out of this mess—a quick cut across the jugular, and then bleeding out on the floor. How long would it take before the loss of blood ushered in the gift of unconsciousness? Surely less time than enduring the pain of the snake bite. The venom creeping like wildfire through the veins toward the heart. The swelling so bad that skin around the bite would split like a sausage casing on a hot grill. The dizziness, the nausea, and finally the numbness leading to death.

"The coral snake will appreciate the warmth, being a cold blooded reptile. Although if there's something about your smell that it finds the least threatening, I'm sure it's prepared to defend itself," Lear said.

Diaz wasted no time returning to the table and came back with the large brown furry creature in the other fish tank. He had scooped it out on a wooden *spatula* of sorts.

Matt had originally speculated the creature to be a rodent of some type. He couldn't have been more wrong. The spider was so huge it didn't look real. In fact, it was too large to look fake. It looked like a ridiculous joke found at a party supply store.

The spider stepped off the *spatula* and onto Logan's lap. Its legs looked like Chewbacca's fingers, thick with long hairs. Its jaws resembled industrial pliers capable of cracking walnuts. Two large fangs big enough to be wolf's canine teeth radiated an eerie green.

"It's looking for a soft spot, Mr. Sandler. When it finds an area that suits it, it will puncture your flesh with its fangs, and inject an enzyme into your body. This will liquefy your insides so that the spider can later suck the remains through the hairs on its mouth.

The enzyme is also a neurotoxin and will paralyze you. Just think, you'll be able to watch it feed and not feel a thing."

Logan gasped lightly as he breathed. He held his hands by his sides and moved his fingers about as if he didn't know what to do with them. His body began to shake as the spider slowly crawled up his thigh and raised one arm up to his stomach.

"And now for you, Mr. King," Lear said. "I will give you the key to end this now and go free."

Diaz stepped over to the table and took a seat next to Lear—sliding a revolver in front of the CEO.

Lear picked up the revolver, pulled a bullet from his coat pocket, and placed it in the cylinder. "You, Mr. King, can save yourself and one of your companions. I suggest that you make your decision quickly or else chance may decide for you. If that happens, Mr. King, I'll use the bullet on you, and I'll enjoy watching both of your mates die. So, who will it be? Mr. Wilson or Mr. Sandler?"

Only a madman would make that sort of demand, Matt thought. He'd have to be mad himself to make such a choice. There was no way he could do that. He'd be responsible for one of his friend's death. "Me. Kill me, and let them both go."

"Matt, no!" Logan eked out in a fear-fill voice. "I'll do it. Shoot me. Do it now before this thing bites me."

"No, take me," Ben said in a whisper loud enough for all to hear.

"My, chivalry is *not* dead. I'm sorry, but the decision is Mr. King's alone," Lear said. "Time's wasting, and you don't want to ruin the chance of two of you surviving, so I'm going to give you a little push. Have you ever been *waterboarded*, Mr. King? Don't bother answering, it was a rhetorical question. I have, and let me say, every horror you've heard about it is true. It's one of the most effective ways to trick your mind that death is imminent. Waterboarding will reduce the strongest man into a blubbering coward in seconds."

Diaz rose from the table as the mercenary behind Matt grabbed his hair with the other hand, and with knife still held firmly on the throat, escorted his captive to the table, and forced him to lie down. The captain buckled one strap around Matt's chest, securing his arms by his side. The other strap went around Matt's legs.

Lear left his seat and walked over by the torture table; the thumb and forefinger of each hand latched onto his lapels. "I had myself waterboarded for the thrill of nearing death. You will have your turn in order to obey my will." He turned to Diaz, and said, "Begin."

The cloth went over Matt's mouth. Diaz picked up the jug and poured water over his face. With the table elevated by Matt's feet, the water flowed over and into his mouth and nose.

Matt heaved what air he had in his lungs, expelling the invading water. While the act provided a moment of relief, more water poured in filling his cavities.

"Your lungs are empty, Mr. King. You won't be able to blow out any more water," Lear said, and pulled his right hand away from his lapel and made a short slash through the air.

Diaz stopped pouring water.

Matt coughed and sputtered through moans of stealing air into his lungs. There was no doubt this was the worst experience imaginable. No wonder waterboarding had been declared torture and illegal by the President.

"Are you ready to make your decision?" Lear asked. "We can keep you between suffering and drowning for as long as we want. I recommend you give in now."

With a shudder, Matt shook his head, then closed his eyes, and gritted his teeth.

"Interesting," Lear said. "He's willing to endure more torture rather than choose the death of one of his friends. He even risks all their deaths, but he won't allow himself to make the call. That's not the smartest move. Securing two lives is the soundest decision. But that's a choice made with the heart, not the head. Captain Diaz, please release Mr. King. I have another proposal."

With great relief, Matt felt the pressure release as Diaz unbuckled the straps. He quickly lowered his feet to the floor, spit out phlegm, and blew his nose dry of moisture. "Just let us go. Haven't we been through enough?"

"No, no. I haven't finished my entertainment. You proposed earlier to give your life for your companions," Lear said.

"Yeah…I will," Matt said.

Lear spun the revolver's cylinder, moving the bullet into a random location. "Admirable, I should say, to sacrifice yourself for others. Not to be outdone, I will give you a fifty percent chance for you all to walk out of here alive. We will play a little game of Russian roulette. Are you game, Mr. King?"

Now Matt knew Lear was nuts. Had life for him grown so stale that he was willing to risk it for a thrill? What other reason would he do that? Matt looked over at Logan and Ben. Sadness had replaced the earlier fear they had in their eyes, their empathy palpable.

"May I begin?" Lear asked.

Matt nodded, expecting the gun barrel to point his way.

Instead, Lear brought the gun to his own head. Stoically, he gazed into the distance and pulled the trigger.

Click.

Lear earnestly pointed the gun at Matt's head and fired without hesitation.

Click.

Matt swooned a bit and then took a deep breath.

The gun went back to Lear's head.

Click.

Then to Matt's.

Click.

"The moment of truth is almost upon us. If the bullet is in the chamber and I lose this game, I do wish you and your companions a safe trip home," Lear said.

Click.

"Oh no…Matt…no," Logan said, sighing softly at the end of his words.

"Take me instead," Ben said.

"No. A deal's a deal, is that not right, Mr. King?"

Matt turned his gaze to the ground and nodded. He then turned his head toward Logan and Ben. He couldn't find his voice to say goodbye.

"I love you, Matt," Logan said.

Matt braced himself and found the Our Father prayer playing again in the back of his mind, moving to the forefront.

The gun came up. Lear pulled the hammer back with his thumb and squeezed the trigger.

Click.

For a moment Matt thought he had been shot, but was too numb from fear to hear the gunfire or feel the bullet penetrate his skull.

Diaz and the three mercenaries howled with laughter. The two Brazilian soldiers behind Logan and Ben sheathed their knives.

Lear smirked from one side of his mouth and brought his cigar up from his left hand, taking a long draw.

The scene shifted so abruptly Matt found himself held in a daze. What had just happened? The bullet was a fake? This whole thing had been an elaborate hoax? What about the snake and the spider? What the hell was going on?

Diaz stepped over by Ben and reached to unbutton the man's shirt.

"But what—" Ben started.

"It's not a coral snake, *Senhor* Ben. You're keeping a milk snake warm," Diaz said. He unbuttoned two buttons on Ben's shirt, and removed the snake, returning it to its fish tank.

"And this thing…" Logan pointed to the arachnid hanging on his chest, only inches away from his chin.

"It's called a South American Goliath bird eater. It won't bother you unless you do something to hurt it. Even then, its bite isn't very harmful to humans," Lear said, and tapped a section of ash off the cigar.

One of the mercenaries gently picked up the spider and brought it back to its fish tank.

"I can't believe this" Matt said, the buds of anger sprouting into his tone. "This was all a joke? Why…why would you do that to us?"

"I told you, Mr. King. I was disappointed, and I need a little excitement to make me feel better," Lear said. "Sometimes I kill things to brighten my day. Consider yourself lucky."

Logan brushed off his chest and wiped his hands on the back of his pants. He helped Ben with his crutches, and the two stepped over to Matt's side.

"So you'll let us go now?" Matt asked.

"Yes. After the Chinook's unloaded it will be available to bring you to the airport where tickets await you. You will be taken stateside where you'll meet with a group of my lawyers. From there, authorities will be invited to take your statements. You all must remember that you are bound contractually as to what you can discuss of your outing," Lear said.

As bad as Matt wanted to pound his fists into Lear's face, his mind told him to *get while the getting was good*. Lear was too unstable of a man to give him time to change his mind. So far, Ben had managed to keep his mouth shut, a miracle in itself. He could tell by Logan's body language that he couldn't leave the tent fast enough.

One of the phones on the table started ringing. All eyes turned and stared as the phone's screen rapidly blinked.

"What the…" Matt said.

Lear stepped over and picked up the phone. "The call is from Vincent Cooper."

"Coop? That's not possible," Logan said. "He's dead."

Lear placed the phone back on the table and pushed the speaker button.

A voice called from the other end, "Hello? Hello?"

"Who is this?" Lear demanded.

"This is Vincent Cooper."

CHAPTER 7

Watching the giant Quetzalcoatlus lower its head to strip Ron's flesh from bone in a strange way reminded Coop of an old steam shovel scooping up a dipper full of earth. One of his first geological assignments had him deep in South Africa where an early 20th century version of the behemoth had somehow survived the ravages of time and was used to dig the side of a mountain in search for gold, platinum, and other precious metals and minerals. The boom would lower, and the dipper's teeth would sink into the ground—powering its way along until coming up full. The Quetzalcoatlus' feeding motion had s similar mechanical quality.

"Coop, I said *what do we do now*?" Alex repeated.

The leader had heard the Professor the first time, but didn't have a plan then, and certainly didn't want to blurt out the first thing that came to mind. He, Alex, and Caveman were naked, without effective weapons, and split from the other two groups.

A Quetzalcoatlus was on foot in hot pursuit of Suge, Natasha, and Meat. The bugger's desire for human flesh was so intense, it forfeited aerial advantage, and risked its own safety. If it happened to meet a predator in the woods, the tree canopies might prevent an immediate flight to safety.

Thinking about the scenario had him realizing how the group would have to rely on wit for survival. Their strategy would have to include more than hiding and fleeing. They would have to find a way to force the battle to an even field.

"Coop?" Alex said.

"Sorry, Alex. I heard you. My mind's racing in a hundred different directions," Coop said. "We haven't been gone for three hours, and we've lost two men. A pterosaur isn't far off chasing after Suge and the other two, and we haven't a clue what Chief and those with him might be facing. If only there were some way to communicate."

"We should go after Suge's group—see what we can do to help them. We might be able to distract that big lookin' stork," Caveman said.

"We could, but that puts us at risk. With the trees as obstacles, I think it gives them an advantage to escape. We should stick with the plan of heading south and hope to meet up later. I believe that's what Chief will do. We need to do everything we can for at least one of us to make the journey to the Mule and contact help."

"I hear ya," Caveman said. "It just don't seem right."

"We're going to have to start thinking differently. We'll have to do things—selfish things—that we normally wouldn't do. We may not have the fear of death, but getting killed out here sets us back to start. I think we let Suge, Meat, and Natasha go at it alone. Let's keep moving south. We'll mark the path in case we're in the lead and the others come across our way."

SKEER-AK!

Coop and his companions turned their heads in unison toward the two giant pterosaurs. They were no longer feeding and now stood side by side, their heads warily cocked toward each other.

"What's going on with them?" Coop asked.

"Not sure," Alex said. "Thought they might be considering coming after us, but—"

One Quetzalcoatlus uttered a shriek in an ear-piercing pitch and swayed its head side to side.

Alex continued, "It looks to me like the two are assuming an aggressive stance."

Right after the words had left his mouth, one longed neck pterosaur abruptly swung his neck to the side, and crashed his head into the neck of the other. The Quetzalcoatlus had used its head like a spiked ball of a *flail*, an ancient weapon where the deadly sphere connected to a handle by a chain.

The attack did nothing to ward off the victim, and the pterosaur returned a blow—missing its target with its head, but smashed its neck into the other.

"It's on like *Donkey Kong* now," Caveman said with excitement in his voice.

The violent exchange continued, one would sling its head to the side making contact, and the other would counter with a blow of its own.

"Look how that neck can bow," Caveman said. "It bends a whole lot more than I ever thought."

The back legs of the pterosaurs eased nearer to each other. Occasionally, one reptile would swing its head lower and take a body shot. The battle was obviously taking a physical toll, and the two leaned into each other in an attempt to overpower the other.

A decisive head blow to the neck sent a sharp snap into the hot Patagonian air. The missile had found a vulnerable target, and the unfortunate loser of the fight's neck cocked unnaturally to one side.

The victor squawked and rose on its hind legs, with its beak open toward the heavens. The other collapsed to the ground near Ron's remains. It wasn't dead, but there wasn't any chance that it could survive an injury like that.

With its belly full for now, the victor took to the air, spreading its leathery wings wide across the sky in an awesome display of its unparalleled size.

"That was better'n than watching two queer roosters in a cockfight on Saturday night with a belly full of moonshine in me," Caveman said.

Alex turned half-opened eyes toward the man, and said, "I wouldn't know."

"Yeah, but you know about killin' your wife, don't you?" Caveman said.

The Professor deflated and dropped his gaze to the ground.

"Guys, we can't fight among ourselves," Coop said. "Stay focused. There's no sense sticking around here any longer. Let's go," Coop said.

***

The three traveled for an hour without incident. Coop was surprised they never heard the Quetzalcoatlus chasing through the woods after Suge and the other two. There were a few times a distant cry gave them pause, but they agreed the cry sounded more like a common pterosaur than a distressed human. Perhaps the giant reptile tired of dodging trees and the boney sacks of flesh had maneuvered their way to safety. The Quetzalcoatlus' neck was it most vulnerable part, but Coop couldn't think of any weapon they could devise in the wild to deliver enough impact to break one's neck.

As far as current weapons went, Coop had claimed a five-foot branch straight enough to serve as a spear. Alex found a hockey stick shaped branch and would use the curved end at times to chop aside brush and foliage. Caveman had picked up an odd looking piece of wood shaped sort of like a fat baseball bat. When Caveman held the club, the image fit his namesake well.

One thing they all needed as much as a weapon was bug spray. The *no-see-ums* had been feasting on them from the moment they passed through the tree line. Patagonia entomology's timeline differed greatly from its zoological. Insects were more of the modern day variety, which was a major blessing. With all of the horrors the prehistoric animals presented, at least they didn't have to worry about twenty-inch dragonflies, two-foot-long scorpions, eight-foot centipedes, and God only knows what else.

The terrain had become a bit more difficult to travel as the amount of trees thickened and the ground swelled in low rising hills. With treetops blocking the sky, and the perpetual clouds filtering the sun, at times they would veer off direction. The journey was going to be problematic enough not having a compass to point the right way. Travel at night time was also out of the question, with no stars above to guide them.

Coop's mouth had entered a new stage of dry. Each breath stung the back of his throat on its way to his lungs. At one point, he had thought about saving his urine and drinking that, but then realized that he hadn't had the urge to pee since his resurrection. That couldn't be good. There had to be physical consequences from traveling through time. Had he been reconstructed atom by atom from one timeline to another? Speculation was a luxury he could ill afford now. He needed to keep his mind sharp and focus on survival.

"Coop," Alex said in a low voice. "I think I hear something— might be water. It's coming from over there." He pointed to the right from where they were heading.

"I don't hear nothin'," Caveman said.

"Yeah, well, you spent years of your life shooting automatic weapons and were exposed to explosions. I didn't serve in the military. I've spent enough times in remote locations to pick up on signature sounds."

"We can't pass up a chance. Alex, lead the way," Coop said.

The land rose for ten or so yards before flattening out again. A small brook cut across the landscape, over large and small flat stones. Weeds grew sparsely, about waist high. It was a welcome sight indeed.

"Good work, Alex," Coop said.

Caveman bounded off in the brook's direction.

"Wait," Coop called out. "I'm just a thirsty as you, but we need to be careful. Where there's water, there's other animals coming to drink."

"I don't see nothin'," Caveman said.

"I don't either," Coop said. "That's not the point. We should be ready for what we *don't* see."

"I'm always ready," Caveman said, and lifted the club and shook it in the air.

"Great. Keep an eye out," Coop said. "Alex, you stay in the middle, and Caveman and I will be by your side. Let's go get some water."

Alex nodded, and the three cautiously stepped toward the brook some fifty feet away.

Funny, Coop thought he could smell the water as he approached. It was a sweet smell—refreshing—pristine—invigorating. His lips felt like dry-rotting rubber as he rubbed his tongue around the inside of his mouth.

The brook's song increased with each step toward it. Water trickled along, spinning gentle eddies around rocks and down miniature waterfalls. Coop remembered reading about an Army veteran suffering from PTSD so badly that he had taken to living in the woods away from society. In the interview, he said he understood where the term *babbling brook* came from. The small stream of water he camped by was a constant companion. He said the waters at times actually sounded like people talking. Sometimes the voices would speak directly to him. Sometimes he answered back.

The area was clear, and now they were at the water's edge. The crystal clear liquid cried out to be touched.

Alex stooped and dipped his fingers in the water. "Oh, man. This is like sixty degrees or colder. I'm tempted to put my face in it and drink it dry."

The feeling's mutual, Coop thought. Patagonia's temperature between the mountains would rise up to one hundred degrees at times due to the fact that veins of hot magma flowed near the land's surface. "I'm surprised the water's cold. The other waterways we came across were warm. Some were even hot."

"It's an anomaly, for sure," Alex said.

"It's just one of God's many gifts He gives us," Caveman said. "Count your blessings, boy, or God ain't gonna give you none no more." He set his club aside and began digging with his bare hands into the soft earth near the brook.

Coop leaned down and scooped out handfuls of the refreshing liquid, and rubbed his face. Oil mixed with grime slid across his forehead, slightly digging into his skin. It was if all of his sins were washing away, and renewed hope swelled in his chest. "I wish we had a way to boil it."

Alex had put his face in the water, and splashed the cool liquid on the back of his head and neck. "Ahh..." he said as he pulled out. He wiped his hands over his face. "How's it coming, John?"

Hearing Alex call Caveman by his given name was a bit of a surprise. Hell, Coop would have bet good money Alex didn't remember Caveman's name, *John Jones*. Perhaps the Professor had felt the sting of Caveman's comment concerning Alex murdering Susan, and realized that if he wanted forgiveness, it would have to come from every member of the group, not just his wife. How else could Alex hope any of them would ever trust him again?

Caveman was on his knees with a mound of mud piling up next to a hole. The hole slowly filled with muddy looking water. "It's gettin' there." He lifted his large frame off the ground and gingerly stepped over by the brook to wash his hands. "I sure do wish they's would have brought me back from a time when my knees still worked like they should."

"I don't think it works that way," Alex said. "The vortex brings us back from the timeline in the immediate area of Patagonia. That T-rex was born here. So even though it died as an adult, it could be brought back as a child. We could only come back from a time since we passed over the mountains, or else I think we would have come back as infants."

"You gonna run your trap or you gonna drink?" Caveman asked.

"I'll go first, if no one minds," Alex said, waited, and received nods of approval. He dropped to one knee and formed a bowl with his hands and fingers. The water was still muddy. "Looks like a latte I order from Starbucks." He submerged his hands into the mix and brought it up for a taste. "Hmm…it's wet and a little crunchy, but I've tasted worse on some of my cryptid excursions." He drank another handful and got up.

Caveman motioned for Coop to go next, so he did. The best thing about the water was that it *was* wet. The sediment suspended in the water had a bitter sort of taste. He wondered how long it would take for the puddle to settle and the water to clean up.

Fearing that drinking too much of the organic extras might upset his stomach, he stopped after feeling minimally hydrated, and would wait for the sediment to settle.

Caveman took his turn, lowered his face to the puddle, and sipped off the top of the water.

Alex looked toward Coop, who shrugged his shoulders back at him in response. Caveman was a really great guy—the kind of man who would give you the shirt off his back—and not just because he preferred it that way. But the man certainly had a primitiveness about him that put him in a unique lifestyle somewhere between human and animal. John told the story that once he was in a deer stand when the urge to take a dump hit him. His colon was always on the spastic side, and before he could make it down to the ground, he shat himself. Not having any fresh clothing to change into, he climbed up the ladder and returned to his hunt. When his buddy arrived on a four wheeler and picked him up, his buddy exclaimed *Something smells like shit*. John replied, *That would be me*. Coop thought the story told a lot about how John's mind worked. The fact that John *told* the story was even more revealing.

From his peripheral, a small object drifted into Coop's view, up from his side of the brook. A small bird-like dinosaur crept through the weeds heading straight for them.

"Caveman," Coop whispered.

The man stopped slurping and turned his gaze up.

"Something's coming. Come see," Coop said.

Alex stepped by Coop's side. The Geologist pointed, and said, "Over there."

"It's a chicken," Caveman said.

Alex laughed. "That's no chicken. That's a Velociraptor, one of the most efficient hunters of its time."

"It ain't no bigger than a chicken. If they's can call tuna *chicken of the sea*, then we can call that bird *chicken of the woods*," Caveman said.

"It's not a bird. It's a feathered dinosaur," Alex said.

"But that don't look like the raptors we saw by that big river. This-un is too small," John said.

"The others were a larger species. I do believe this guy here is young and will only grow as large as a turkey," Alex said.

"It's a brave little bastard," Coop said.

"Or stupid. There's three of us, and we're a whole lot bigger," Caveman said. "We're gonna find out how good-a-eatin' this thing is."

Caveman moved toward the small dinosaur but tried to keep out of its line of sight. After he moved past it, he motioned to Coop, who knelt by the water, and splashed it with his hands.

Distracted, the Velociraptor tuned its attention toward the turmoil. John made a quick move with the club and crashed it down on the dinosaur. It eked out an anemic death cry. "Got 'im." He reached down and picked it up by its clawed feet.

"Let me see it," Alex said as John arrived.

The creature was just short of two feet in length. It had a brown feather-like body covering and three-clawed feet. Large, curved talons on the inside toes of each foot were deadly weapons. They held the toes off the ground like folded switchblades, which they would use to dig into prey and latch on until achieving victory.

"They's ain't much meat on this tweety-bird," Caveman said.

Alex poked at the raptor's talons while Caveman held it. He stopped suddenly and looked up the river. "You hear that?"

"What?" Caveman said.

"Listen…"

Coop heard a low roar of sorts emerging over the background noise. The sound became more distinct. He could only describe it as a series of hoarse bird-like caws.

As they focused toward the sounds, a Velociraptor appeared on the other side of the brook's bank and crossed the water.

"Uh, oh. Our friend here has a brother," Alex said.

"Good," Caveman said. "Two eats better than one any day."

The commotion was coming from more than one single raptor. "Guys, I think we need to leave."

No sooner as he spoke than other siblings poured through the tall grass and headed across the shallow water.

"Let's go!" Coop yelled, and headed toward the nearest thick of trees. Alex was on his heels, and Caveman churned his thick legs as fast as he could.

"We're not going to make it," Alex cried.

"Shut and run!" Coop said, and noticed that Alex started drifting behind. He looked and saw the Professor had turned, had now passed Caveman, and was running toward the Velociraptors.

"We can't all outrun them. I'll delay them, but you'll have a chance," Alex called.

Coop stopped and cried, "Alex!" but he realized the Professor had made a commitment he wouldn't be turning back from.

Caveman arrived by Coop's side, and before he turned to follow, he saw the first raptor step within the reach of Alex's stick.

Alex held the stick with both hands and reared back his weapon like a hockey player about to smash the puck. He swung it forward and connected the crooked part of the stick under the raptor's head—severing the head from the body.

There was no time for celebration as more than a dozen small menaces careened in for the attack. Alex managed to kill another before one jumped him from the backside—embedding its claws in his left thigh. He instinctually reached around and tried to pull the dinosaur off, and then was covered by the remaining horde.

Coop and Caveman weren't far enough away to save them from hearing Alex's dying screams. The poor man was being shredded one tiny mouthful at a time. The pain would be merciless until salvation by death.

"Oh, no," Coop said. "Looks like the raptors have a mother, and she's coming for us."

"We'll have to stand and fight it," Caveman said.

"I've got an idea," Coop said, both men keep running at the same pace and disappeared into the tree line.

***

The Velociraptor was noticeably larger than her offspring. Alex had said the adults grew to turkey size, which was large enough, but Coop had a plan he hoped would work.

When the raptor came into view, Coop had positioned himself with his back against the trunk of a towering tree. He held his spear at the ready, waiting for the conflict to begin.

"Here it comes," he said softly to Caveman.

The raptor quickened its pace, seeing its intended victim had given up flight. It made a series of hoarse noises and slowed before coming into proximity of Coop's weapon.

Coop jutted his spear forward at the raptor's head. The dinosaur bobbed and weaved like a boxer avoiding punches. Its level of frustration rose to the point that it tried to bite the spear.

"Now," Coop said.

Caveman had hidden behind a tree just to the other side of the Velociraptor. While the dinosaur was distracted, he reached his chubby hand out and grabbed the neck. He then snatched the feet with his other hand, and quickly wrung the raptor's neck— spinning it around and around until tossing it to the side. The dinosaur had no life left in it.

"John, you did it!" Coop said, and ran over to his buddy.

"Weren't nothin' but a thing. Hell, I wrung many-a chicken's necks at my grandma's. I used to set them on the ground afterward and watch them run around a bit."

"I'm glad this one didn't do like that—oh, you're bleeding."

"Claw got me a little. I'll rub some dirt on it. I'll be all right."

"We need to keep moving away from the Velociraptors for a good mile and then head southward."

"Yep. Too bad about Alex. I think he's really sorry for what he did and wanted to make up for it somehow."

"Yeah, he's given us a chance to continue the quest," Coop said. "All right, let's—" Something wet dropped from above Caveman, hit him on the top of his head, and ran down his cheek.

"Is it rainin'?" Caveman said.

Coop lifted his gaze and saw a greenish looking theropod head poking through the thick foliage behind John. In the excitement of the battle with the Velociraptor, neither he nor John had heard the dinosaur's approach.

The Majungasaurus lowered its large, thumb-shaped head. It opened it jaws showing rows of knife-like teeth. In an instant John's head and the right part of his shoulder disappeared in the Majungasaurus' mouth.

Caveman's scream somehow strengthened Coop's resolve. He didn't feel the debilitating fear right now. His friend was attacked, and he was nothing but mad.

Coop used the only weapon available and ran with his puny spear toward the dinosaur, sticking the tip in the eye.

Blood and other liquids squirted out splashing Coop's face and chest. The beast uttered a cry that shook the ground. The Majungasaurus threw its head aside—John hit the ground and rolled.

A quick glance told Coop his friend was dead. The dinosaur's teeth had mashed half of John's face in and nearly severed the right part of his chest from the rest of the body.

The Majungasaurus stomped through the foliage and lowered its head for an attack. Coop thrust the spear up and harmlessly hit its snout before the mighty jaws opened and jagged blades of death snapped shut over his head and upper body, covering him in a blanket of darkness.

CHAPTER 8

"Keep running! I think it's following us," Meat cried. Natasha was in front of him, and he was determined not to let her out of his sight. Suge led the way, directing them which path to take.

The Quetzalcoatlus lumbered after the humans as they entered an expanse of trees. Occasionally it would squawk out its hungry rage, which only inspired its prey's flight.

"We can outrun it. Keep going," Meat said.

"What about the others?" Natasha called back. Her bronze skin glistened with sweat.

In a different situation the sight of a naked woman would have Meat unable to conceal his arousal. The thought dissipated as quickly as a drop of water on a hot griddle. Survival had a way of mastering all other thoughts. "We worry about *us*. Once we get away, we'll try to find them."

"Careful, the ground over here has some leaves that are slick," Suge said.

Meat had seen Suge slide a couple of feet on one foot and was surprised he didn't fall. "That's not good," he said loud enough for only him to hear. In Patagonia, obstacles were only par for the course. Right now, the humans had an advantage over a giant flying reptile, but escape always presented more opportunities for failure.

SKEER-AK!

The Quetzalcoatlus' warning sounded closer—much closer. Meat gazed upward and saw the massive wings blocking out the sky as the giant reptile flew overhead. "It's back in the air."

"Is it leaving?" Natasha asked.

"I don't...No, it's not leaving. It's circling. It's probably going to land and come back after us."

"We might be faster, but it can still take to the air and catch up with us." Meat had slowed his pace upon arriving at the site with the slippery leaves. The leaves had a waxy coating that made them a hazard. Meat remembered taking his mother's wax paper outside, tearing off a piece big enough for him to sit on, and positioned himself on his swing set's slide. The slippery surface set his ass a good foot from the slide's end and bruised his buttocks. The whipping he received later for taking the wax paper increased his discomfort exponentially.

The Quetzalcoatlus proved itself to be a crafty hunter when it landed directly in front of the direction they fled.

"Shit," Suge said.

"Which way do we go? Do we head back?" Natasha asked.

"Can't go back. You want to live, you always go forward. We just might have to take a slight detour first. I see a tree a ways over that might provide some shelter. Come on," Suge said, and bounded off to the right.

The area from where they were to the tree was in more open space than Meat would have liked. He did see why Suge thought it might provide sanctuary. The tree, and a few others like it, stood out from among the other trees. These trees were taller—with fatter trunks. The roots grew up from the ground. It looked like someone had dug up a tree and then set it on top of the ground. The spaces between the roots were large enough for humans to hide in. The Quetzalcoatlus was shit-out-of-luck of getting in there.

Meat knew Suge could have run faster, but it was obvious the man had a concern for Natasha's welfare too. The slight show of concern Suge gave Natasha when he put his arm around her as she cried by the volcano could have just as easily been an open display of affection. What was it about this girl that had Alex, Matt, Suge, and dare he confess, himself, hooked in some way?

"We're almost there," Suge call. He slowed, waited for Natasha to get even with him, and ran by her side.

SKEER-AK! The Quetzalcoatlus was back in the air and streaking right for them.

"Hurry!" Meat called out. The flap of the leathery wings made his feet lighter than air. He still held one of the two rocks he acquired as weapons back at the volcano, but there was nothing that hurling it at the reptile would accomplish other than pissing it further off.

The tree roots were nearly a foot wide and reached as high as eight feet in some places. Natasha had no problem slipping past the gnarly roots that hung down like stalactites in a cave.

"Move! Move! Move!" Suge called out to Meat.

He knew what that meant. The enemy was near, and one second of hesitation might be the difference in living and dying.

The pterosaur glided low and shifted its body, jutting the claws out for the ready.

Suge snaked his way into safety, and cried, "Hurry!"

Meat didn't need the encouragement. Just as soon as he thought he was close enough, he dove to the ground with his arms stretched out like he was Superman. He felt the air of the claws snapping empty behind his back, and hit the ground sliding up to his waist, past large roots.

The Quetzalcoatlus had to pull up to avoid crashing into the tree. It hovered in the air a few feet from the ground, shrieked in frustration, and flew off.

Meat crawled on his belly, and in no time had his whole body secured behind the wooden fence.

"You okay?" Suge asked from a few feet away. The roots formed a maze of sorts, and some were too close together to fit past.

"Yeah. It's not the first time I've belly flopped to the ground. I might have skinned up my private parts a bit, but I'll be okay," Meat said. "Natasha? You made it all right?"

"Yeah. My feet are killing me, though, and all those bug bites itch. I need hot shower and a bowl of *Rajma Chawal*," Natasha said.

"*Ramja* what?" Meat asked.

"*Rajma Chawal*," is a red bean and rice dish. It's one of my favorite comfort foods," Natasha said.

Suge sighed. "Man, I could go for some red beans and rice. Put a big hunk of pork sausage on top next to hot corn bread with butter—oh."

"What's that noise?" Natasha asked.

"My stomach growling," Meat said. "You people sure are stereotyping yourself."

"What would you pick to eat right now?" Suge asked.

"Hmm, kalua pig with a side of spam and a fried egg on top."

"Pot, meet kettle," Suge said.

"So what now?" Natasha asked.

SKEER-AK! The Quetzalcoatlus landed several yards from the sanctuary. It brought its arms to the ground and folded the wing tips upward before walking toward them.

"He's *baa-ack*," Meat sang. "That thing reminds me of a toy I had. There was this glass bird with a felt head. The neck and body pivoted on its legs, so like it could lower its head. You'd put a glass of water in front of it and dip its beak in the water. There was this red liquid in its bottom that would work its way up the neck until the beak lowered back into the water. As long as the felt beak had water, it would keep going and going. I'm not sure how it worked."

"It reminds me of an evil version of Big Bird," Natasha said.

"Guys, we need to move—it's coming straight for us, and that beak might be able to get past these roots," Suge said.

Maneuvering around the roots was easy for Natasha, and more so for Suge than Meat. They tried moving to the other side—out of the reptile's vision, but it only followed them around.

"It's not giving up," Natasha said.

"Watch it! It's sticking its neck out. Look out for the beak," Surge said, and then backed up as much as he could.

The narrow beak was a good six feet in length, but it's first attempt at fishing for humans came up short as it became wedged between two close hanging roots. It pulled its head back and looked for another passage to try.

"Look at those eyes—they're huge," Natasha said.

"That beak looks sharp. Its head is as long as its legs," Meat said.

"Look out!" Suge cried.

The head poked through the roots, and the beak's tip sliced Meat's left side as he twisted his body to avoid it. The toothless jaws opened to catch its prey, but Meat found a passage that led to safety.

The roots became thicker toward the tree. So the six-foot head nearly reached the length of the space they had to maneuver around. If not for the roots in the way, they would have been easy pickings.

"Clint, you're bleeding," Natasha said.

"I'm fine. It just nicked me a bit," Meat said. "It's coming in another direction. Get as far back as you can."

The beak came forward and stopped right about the point where its head reached the roots.

Meat stepped to the side of the beak and whacked it with the rock in his hand. It bounced harmlessly off.

SKEER-AK!

In the confines of the tree sanctuary, the reptile's cry had Meat thinking his ears might bleed. He was close to the head, but there was too much tree material in the way to make an attempt to bash in the creature's skull.

"You're really pissing it off now," Suge said.

The Quetzalcoatlus increased its effort to shove its head through, spreading the roots farther apart. This gave Meat and idea.

"Suge, get on the other side and pull the root away from its head. I'll do the same on my side," Meat said.

"But its head will come through...oh, okay," Suge said.

Meat dropped the rock and grabbed the root, pulling backward with all his might.

Suge grabbed his root, and soon the head popped past the defense.

Now that the head was through, Meat and Suge let go, and the roots snapped back into their original position—pressing tightly around the reptile's neck.

SKEER-AK!

"Damn, that thing's loud," Suge said.

The Quetzalcoatlus tried in vain to pull back and free its head. It was trapped tightly between the two roots, though, and had no chance of escape.

Its ear-piercing squawk had the humans snaking their way through the root maze and to the outside of the open skies of Patagonia. Suge and Natasha had exited by one side of the Quetzalcoatlus and Meat the other. The three met up by the backside of the trapped reptile.

"We did it," Meat said.

"That was some quick thinking," Suge said. "At first I thought you were nuts, but then saw the plan."

Meat turned his head. "I'd like to kick that thing in the ass, but I might hurt my foot."

"Should we try to kill and eat it?" Natasha asked.

"Kill it with what? That thing's still dangerous. We can't wait around for it to die either. We need to head back south and hopefully find the others," Meat said.

Natasha abruptly turned her head, and said, "What's that? In the grass—coming this way."

Something brownish in color scurried toward the struggling reptile. It might have been three foot in length, and as it approached, it showed itself to be of the theropod variety.

"It's another one of those two-legged dinosaurs," Suge said.

"Does it look hungry?" Meat asked.

With half-open eyes and a smirk, Suge looked over at him.

"It was a joke. Every fucking thing in Patagonia is hungry, and that includes me," Meat said.

"I don't think we've seen one of these before," Natasha said. "Look how it runs. It reminds me of a roadrunner."

"The cartoon?" Meat asked.

"No, silly. The actual bird the cartoon borrowed from. Roadrunners can run almost thirty miles an hour,' Natasha said.

"That means it can outrun us. Thank goodness it's small," Suge said.

"It's probably drawn here by the pterosaur's struggle. I bet it's a scavenger," Natasha said.

"We're in no position to deal with it now. Plus, it's not going to be the only guest to this all-you-can-eat buffet. Let's go," Suge said.

Meat and Natasha turned and followed.

***

The three walked through the jungle at a slow but steady pace—more from fatigue than caution. The trees had grown thicker and the foliage denser. So far they had caught glimpses of small bipedal theropods here and there. None were curious enough to check out the larger interlopers.

Each had picked up short pieces of wood to use as clubs or beat back brush and tall grass to ease travel.

"I didn't know my mouth could get this dry," Natasha said.

"Something I never thought about," Meat said, "does it rain in Patagonia?"

"It must. Look at all these trees and jungle plants. They're getting water from somewhere," Suge said.

"I know we haven't spent much more than a week here, but I've never seen anything resembling rain clouds. The sky always looks the same—just thick, white clouds," Meat said.

"Maybe the water table is high," Natasha said. "Maybe the veins of magma running under the ground keeping Patagonia warm also boils underground springs and pushes moisture toward the surface. Trees require a lot of ground water. It can rain in tropical rainforests every day, at least weekly, but more so in the rainy season. I don't know if Patagonia has a rainy season. But the weather pattern here is unique to any other place I know of on Earth."

"If the water table is close to the surface, we might be able to dig deep enough to find some. We just need to pick a likely spot," Meat said.

"I wish Coop was here. Being a geologist in a situation like this comes in handy. He might be able to point out a good spot to try," Suge said.

"Water may be more available where trees grow," Natasha said. "Although none of the ground here looks particularly different."

"Leaves have moisture in them. I'm tempted to chew a few," Meat said.

"That's a last resort type of thing. There's no telling what might be in there to hurt or even kill you," Suge said. "I'm not to that point yet."

"Hey, look at these," Natasha said. "Do you think we can eat them?" She reached her hand into a bush and brought forth a cluster of yellowish fruits about the size of tennis balls.

"There's really no good way to tell," Suge said. "If we saw something else around here eat it, it might mean it's safe. It would help though if we saw a mammal eat it instead of a dinosaur. No mammals around here that I can tell," Suge said. "Still, life here may have adapted to whatever it may have that could harm us."

Natasha plucked off one of the fruits with her free hand and gave it to Meat, who held his palm out. He squeezed it a little and sniffed it. The fruit felt firm but wasn't hard. He dug a thumbnail under the outer skin and peeled off a section. Juice streamed over Meat's fingers, and the peel held onto some of the insides. "Kinda looks like a lime—has a slight citrusy smell."

"I'll try it," Natasha said. "If it makes me sick, or worse, I'll be less of a burden to you two. If you or Suge are poisoned, it hurts our chances for moving on."

"You make a good point," Meat said, and then licked the juice on his fingers. "But I volunteer to be the food taster. I'm a big man, and my body can handle a small bit of nasties better than yours."

"So how's it taste?" Natasha said.

"Not bad. Not great, but not bad. Reminds me of an unripe orange," Meat said.

"How long are we going to wait before we think it's safe?" Natasha asked.

"I don't know…one, maybe two…minutes," Meat said, and stripped the fruit off the peel with his teeth.

"Meat!" Suge said.

"What? I don't care if it kills me. It tastes good and it's wet," Meat said.

"That's enough, though. At least give it fifteen minutes," Suge said.

"Okaaaaay," Meat said, and huffed in frustration.

During the wait, Natasha had Meat open his mouth, stick out his tongue, and fold over his bottom lip for inspection. So far everything appeared to remain normal. "Let's look one last time," she said.

"You know, when I made faces like this in grade school, I'd get detention," Meat said.

"I'll put you in detention if you don't do it," Natasha said.

Meat complied, and all three agreed chancing the fruit was worth the risk.

"I'm glad it's not too sour. I always hated sour candy," Suge said after finishing his first bite. "Hot candy—cinnamon, I liked though."

"Sour apple is one of my favorite flavors," Natasha said. "I'll even get a sour apple martini at a restaurant." She slowly bit down on the piece she had put in her mouth. "*Jooshie.*" Her lips remained tight to keep the liquid from escaping.

"I've eaten my share of candy, but I prefer fruit." Meat crammed the last piece of the lost world bounty into his mouth and stepped over to the bush to pluck out another. "Pineapple, mangos, bananas, papayas—They taste so much better fresh than the stuff you buy in the supermarkets. You two probably never had Lychees, rambutans, or dragon fruits. Hawaii has a lot of fruits you don't see in the states."

Suge finished his fruit and picked two from the bush. "You ready for another, Natasha?"

She ate the fruit's flesh from the last bit of peel and nodded. "Thanks." She took it and began peeling away. "You know, we ought to give this stuff a name."

As Meat peeled the fruit, a half slipped from his fingers. He bent over to pick it up, and escaping gas from his rear broke past his sphincter muscle—announcing itself to the world. "Uhh, excuse me…" His cheeks turned two shades redder, and the grin of embarrassment conquering his face had his eyes nearly shut.

Suge shrugged. "I guess we could call it *pooty fruity.*"

***

"Everybody still doing okay?" Natasha asked.

Suge led the way heading south. Meat maintained the rear. A good hour had passed since they'd eaten. They each held onto a makeshift club in one hand and a piece of fruit in the other. Trees and terrain had limited progress. Still, Meat wondered how long Natasha could keep up this pace.

"I might have a little bit of indigestion," Meat said.

"Not surprising. You must have eaten twenty of those things," Suge said.

"I feel kind of stupid for eating as much as we did. We should have taken in slower," Natasha said.

"That's easy to say now. You aren't dying of thirst. Funny how the regrets don't shine until after the deed is done," Suge said.

"Yeah. I ate a gallon of ice cream one time knowing I'm a bit lactose intolerant. An hour afterward, I was blowing out of both ends. I needed a seat belt to keep me from launching off the toilet seat, and I painted the bathroom wall with upchuck. That was nasty," Meat said.

"Gross," Natasha said.

Several minutes passed without anyone saying a word. The forest swayed with the breeze of rustling leaves, and far off pterosaurs called out on occasion. Something, though, had stirred Meat's sense of danger. It was more than a feeling. He just couldn't quite put his finger on it.

"Hey, you two, stop for a second," Meat said.

His Redwater teammate froze instantly. Natasha took a few additional steps before the request kicked in.

"What is it?" Suge said in a low voice.

"Not sure...I don't hear anything now. Let's keep walking...I'll tell you when to stop again," Meat said. He signaled with his right hand for them to move forward; after a minute, he told them to stop.

This time he distinctly heard footsteps crunching leaves and grasses following. "Hear that?" he whispered.

Suge nodded.

"Something's following," Meat said.

"What do we do?" Natasha asked.

"Let's move faster. See if we can find a high point and get a look at it," Suge said. He turned his head and scanned the landscape. "This way."

The race was on, and Meat heard the predator quicken its pace to the point he knew it had abandoned its stealth mode and was moving in for the attack.

"There's no way we can hide from it. The bottoms of my feet are bleeding. It will be able to track us anywhere we go," Natasha said, desperation weighed down her words.

"It's getting closer," Meat said.

"What is it?' Natasha cried.

"I don't know, but I'm not going to let it catch me from behind." With that, Meat put on the brakes. He let the fruit fall from his left hand to the ground and choked up on the club like a baseball bat.

"Meat!" Suge called and stopped. "Keep running, Natasha. Go up on that ridge and keep heading south."

"No!" Natasha said.

"I see it...son-of-a-bitch," Meat said.

"It's a Troodon," Natasha said.

"Troodon? That's what got Chief and the others before," Suge said. He positioned himself several feet to Meat's side and prepared for battle.

When the Troodon ran into view, it acted surprised to see its prey waiting to fight. A noise rumbled from its throat that sounded like a cross between a growl and a purr. Its mouth opened revealing rows of pointed teeth and jaws that looked like they could bend nails. When the beast reared up on its hind legs, it was still slightly shorter than an average man. The tail, though, added to the overall mass of the deadly creature. Its lizard-like head moved like an ostrich's on its long neck. The Troodon was green-yellow in color and had two short arms with sharp talons on the end of its claws.

"I think it wants to fight," Suge said.

"Let's get this over with then. The suspense is killing me," Meat said. "I'll distract it...see if you can get behind it and smash its head." He didn't wait for a response, as he had set the plan in action.

"Okay, you big pussy, come over here and get you some of this ass." Meat stepped away from Suge and poked his club toward the Troodon. "I'm over here...that's it."

Suge had moved behind the Troodon. Meat saw the tail presented an obstacle that had to be overcome. It was like a skipping rope, and Suge had to time it just right to step in and not trip.

When Suge sprang forward, the Troodon abruptly slung its tail against his body and sent him sprawling to the ground.

The distraction allowed Meat an opportunity of his own. He swung the club and smashed the Troodon on the side of the head.

A dull thump mixed with the bright snap of wood—half the club remained.

The Troodon swooned to the side.

Suge wasted no time. He picked himself off the ground and leaped on the Troodon's back—tightly wrapping his arms around its neck.

For a moment the wild ride reminded Meat of the one time he tried the mechanical bull. The bull won. The bull *always* won.

The Troodon was only at a disadvantage for a short time. It threw its body to the ground and twisted around until Suge was at the bottom of the heap. Its claws found the man's soft flesh.

"Ahh! Get it off!" he cried.

"Suge! Oh no!" Tears streamed down Natasha's face as she held her hands in front of her mouth.

There was no easy or safe way to do this. It was all or nothing. Meat jumped in the fray, and grabbed the Troodon by the throat, keeping the teeth from tearing into his buddy. He mashed his fingers into the slimy skin hoping to crush its windpipe.

Hand to hand combat proved to be a joke. Slinging its neck to the side, Meat tumbled to the ground. Before he could rise, the Troodon abandoned Suge and brought one its claws down his stomach. The talons ripped skin down his solar plexus until digging deep enough to spill his intestines onto his thighs.

Natasha gasped and collapsed unconscious to the ground.

Pain rolled in waves across Meat's body. Seeing his internal organs looked surreal. He futilely tried to sit up and pull his intestines back in—thinking that he would do whatever he could while still alive to save Suge and protect Natasha from a similar fate.

As Meat's reality shifted into a soft haze where colors bled into one another, Suge's last dying cry signified the Troodon's jaws had crushed his neck. At least his death was quick.

The Troodon turned and stared with its cold, reptilian eyes at Meat and snarled in what could only be a victory cry. The invaders were no match for a creature that evolution had hammered into a survival machine in this lost world.

Meat prepared himself as the Troodon left Suge's lifeless body and stepped over toward him. He hoped the theropod would end it quickly for him too and not feed on him while he was still conscious.

The Troodon turned away and headed for Natasha's unconscious form. It lowered its head and bit her forearm—twisting his head until it popped free from the body.

Natasha groaned and tried to roll on her side.

Meat hoped that she was running on some auto response and not conscious to feel the pain. But then Natasha screamed hysterically—inciting the Troodon's ire. It continued to mercilessly strip flesh from her body as she wailed in pain.

There was nothing he could do. He tried to call out her name, but his mouth wouldn't form the words. The air grew heavy, and it felt like a boulder weighed on his chest. He rode Natasha's dying cries into oblivion.

CHAPTER 9

"This way!" Chief yelled, and grabbed Susan Klasse by the wrist, pulling her to the side, and heading for the tree line. The giant pterosaur had blocked the path and split him, Susan, and Bats from the other six.

The whole scene had turned to chaos in a matter of seconds. Don screamed in the background as the first arriving Quetzalcoatlus held him under thick, taloned claws. Ron had abandoned his flight—there was no way he was leaving his brother's side—even though the beast he challenged was nearly four times his size.

As if there weren't enough pandemonium, a third Quetzalcoatlus flew in to divide the six others racing for the sanctuary of trees.

"Son-of-a-bitch! They're everywhere," Bats cried.

"You let him go you gooseneck bastard." Ron reared his right arm back and let one of the rocks fly. The anemic projectile hit the Quetzalcoatlus in the chest and bounced harmlessly off. The second and last rock wasn't any more effective.

Chief brought Susan and Bats to a halt after ducking behind a large tree. It was time to rein in emotions and collect his thoughts before the situation got completely out of hand. He wasn't sure what they could do to save Don, but with only rocks and bare hands as weapons, the pterosaurs were impossible to defeat.

"Ron! Run away!" Coop yelled, his voice distant.

At least others had made it to safety. How many, Chief didn't know. From his vantage point, he saw one Quetzalcoatlus chase after where Meat, Suge, and Natasha had entered the woods. He couldn't see Coop or his companions, but the Quetzalcoatlus who split the Geologist's group didn't follow them past the tree line. Instead, it walked on all fours—heading for Ron.

As Don wailed in pain, Ron jumped abruptly backward as the snaking head of his brother's captor snapped an open beak closed mere inches away. The poor man was grossly outmatched.

Chief watched in horrific amazement as the second Quetzalcoatlus walked giraffe-like toward his Redwater mate. The giant reptile shrieked its challenge and made a claim for the tiny human.

Ron barely had twisted around to face the new predator when its six-foot toothless beak scissored closed across his chest. "*Roll Tide!*" the man screamed out.

The battle wasn't over; in fact, a new one began. The Quetzalcoatlus holding Don wasn't content with its prize. Before its competition made off with Ron, it lowered its head and clamped its beak around Ron's legs. Chief's teammate howled in new pain.

For the first time in his life, Chief wished he were back in Iraq dodging enemy fire. At least the odds were better for survival. If a person or team could hunker down and hold their own, there was a chance of help arriving. In Patagonia, no SEAL team waited to parachute in. No bombs from 5,000 feet would find and destroy the enemy. This lost world was a harsh, cruel place. An environment not designed for human habitation.

He looked over at Susan. The woman had her head leaned back against the tree. Her eyes were closed and fear had contorted her soft, feminine features. No doubt she struggled to push the dying cries from Ron and Don from her mind.

At least Chief's emotions had been battle-hardened—this wasn't the first time he'd heard suffering in the throes of death. Not that it eased his conscience; two members of his team were dying, and he was doing nothing other than sit tight and preserve his own ass. If he had a gun it wouldn't have the firepower to do anything but grant final mercy to Ron and Don.

His thoughts returned to Susan. Would there come a time when death was imminent, where picking up a rock and smashing her head in would be more humane than giving her up to the hungry jaws of a dinosaur? Patagonia was a war with new rules. Chief would have to act as his own judge.

"Looks like the tug-of-war is over," Bats said. "They settled for one apiece."

"At least the screaming's stopped. Ron didn't have a chance to save his brother and he knew it. It just didn't matter," Chief said.

"They'll both end up back at the volcano. It's not like Ron didn't know that," Bats said.

"I doubt Ron was thinking that way. I believe the two have been together for so long that one couldn't live without the other very long. I don't think either wanted to find out what that would be like," Chief said.

"What's the plan?" Bats asked.

"We need to regroup. There's a pterosaur between us and Coop's group chasing after Suge, Meat, and Natasha. We all agreed to go south, so we head south," Chief said.

Bats shook his head and smirked. "I know, but I don't know what good it actually does us. Three, six, nine naked and unarmed people in this place—doesn't seem like numbers will make any difference. We can't outfight these things here. We can't outrun them—mostly because they're everywhere," Bats said.

"True. That's why we'll have to use our brain to keep alive—find some way to keep a step ahead of them. Alex and Matt stayed safe in the trees when we were attacked by Troodons. We could do the same—if the opportunity presents itself," Chief said.

"Yeah, *if* there're trees in the area, *if* the branches are low enough for us to reach, and *if* we can climb faster than they can catch us," Bats said. "Even if we get up a tree, what then? This ain't a Tarzan movie. We won't be swinging on vines from tree to tree. We'll be stuck up there with no food and no water. All the dinosaurs have to do is wait for us to drop and it's lights out."

"We have to keep moving and not give up if we want to leave here," Chief said.

"It's a long, long way on foot back to the Mule," Bats said.

The wheels were turning in the mercenary's mind. Bats usually wasn't one to beat around the bush with his opinion. What was he hiding? "If you've got something to say, say it," Chief said.

Bats turned his gaze to the ground and rubbed the back of his neck. He cocked his head to the side, and said, "I've had some time to think. Maybe we're going about this all wrong. We think we can escape this place. Maybe we can't. Every step we take into the jungle places our survival in uncertainty. We haven't been gone much more than a couple of hours, and Ron and Don are already dead. Some of the others may be dead, too. We don't know. How soon will the rest of us die? How many times are we going to play the stupid game of traveling to the Mule to call for help? Face it. We're *never* going to make it, Chief. We're all going to die one by one and wake up by that volcano all put back together to go out and do it again."

"Say we don't go searching for the Mule. What's your plan?" Chief asked.

"We find a safe location—away from the bigger dinosaurs—and set up camp. Some place near water where we live day to day. Sure, we may have to go through hell a few times until we find such a place. But I think it's better to spend our energy that way than running off on a journey hundreds of miles away. Ace Corp isn't going to leave this area until they map out all the natural resources. They'll find us one day. In the meantime…" Bats turned his head Susan's way, "we'll live our lives as normally as we can. We'll find or build shelter, hunt and fish, and we even have a couple of women to keep us company."

Lust had once again invaded paradise—threatening to fragment the group into warring factions. Chief looked over to read Susan's reaction to such a forward suggestion. Bats was already reducing the women to possessions, and Susan didn't seem like the type to keep her opinions to herself. She stared wide eyed ahead.

"Over there," Susan whispered and raised a finger. "There's something big coming our way."

At this point Chief didn't know if she had heard Bats' proposal, but at the moment it didn't matter. The theropod lurking in the jungle some twenty yards or so away had the potential to ruin their plans and much more.

"I don't know what that is, but I bet it's hungry," Chief said.

"I studied up on dinosaurs with Alex before the trip. It looks like a Dilophosaurus. See that pair of rounded crests on its skull?" Susan said.

"I was focused more so on all those teeth," Chief said. There was something unusual about the head—and not the double crest. It was difficult to see because of the distance, but the face had a series of deep scratches across it, and its eyes looked like opened wounds. "It's been hurt—maybe blinded. We'll have to make a break for it. I'm sure it can still hear and smell. Let's not do anything sudden."

"Shit. It has our scent," Bats said.

The theropod had frozen mid-step and pointed the tip of its nose on its pear-shaped head into the wind. The rounded red rose colored crests started past its nostrils and ran all the way past its eyes to the top of its head. The back, tail, and legs were gray-silver with faint black mixed in outlining a rough diamond pattern not unlike a rattlesnake. The underside was dull white like most other theropods.

Chief felt Susan's nails dig into his left forearm. There was no way to know how long she could maintain her composure. If she lost it, they'd all be in danger. His mind told him that if that happened, the correct decision would be to leave her and for him and Bats to seek safety—to continue the mission. But he didn't know if he could do that—leave Susan to die alone—leaving her with the dread of abandonment to go along with facing horrific death. Chief had feelings for Susan, and though his life would be wasted if he fought for her survival, she would at least know that he was there for her, and that he cared. If the two were going to have any future relationship and set him apart from the rest of the men, he had to be there for her when she needed him the most.

Chief moved his arm, breaking Susan's grasp. He then grabbed her hand with his and brought a finger on his other hand up to his lips. He narrowed his eyes toward Bats, signaling that he was taking the lead, and about to make a move.

Bats nodded, obeying the chain of command as any good soldier would.

How long would discipline rule? Hopefully until they found their way out of Patagonia. But if escape gave way to settling down, it would eventually turn to every man for himself. Chief thought it ironic how war turned men into animals but formed strong bonds between strangers—ties hardened by life and death situations. Sharing experiences that made a random group of men closer to each other than their own fathers and brothers. But take these same men out of war and put them back into civilization, every sacrifice of the past could be erased by the smile of a cute girl or the plunge of a blouse neckline.

It was impossible for them to take a path without leaves or other grasses calling attention to each step. Even though the adrenaline pumping through Chief's body had his legs ready to run as fast as they could, stealth would be the key to victory. He stepped lightly—trying to find the hardest ground and avoiding any brown, withered foliage. The sound of his own breathing amplified in his head, making it difficult to judge their success in being quiet. This wasn't like him. He had been in bad situations before but had managed to keep his shit together better than this. He was distracted—and it hit him why. *Susan*. His feelings for her had wormed its way into his unconscious and weakened him. Chief told himself to harden his resolve. This was a mission, a job; he needed to tune emotion out and achieve the objective.

A furtive glance back every now and then told him the Dilophosaurus had picked up their trail and followed. Perhaps it was only curious of the odd smell and questioned whether expending the energy to track down a potential food source would be worth it.

Several minutes went by, and Chief thought the dinosaur had picked up its pace a bit. A shuffle of leaves here and a twig cracking underfoot there might have inspired its pursuit. Breaking into an all-out run would certainly get one or all of them killed. There was a chance two could escape if one of them sacrificed their life. But it wasn't like he could order Bats to *take one for the team* and give him and Susan a chance. Maybe they could draw straws. Chief didn't want to leave Susan with Bats if he lost. At least he would give her a chance and perhaps spare her the pain of dinosaur teeth ripping flesh from bone.

Before he decided to put the offer up for discussion, an unusual mound of dirt a couple of feet high caught his attention. If it was what he thought it was, this might buy them a chance.

Chief pulled Susan from where he led for a detour a short distance to the side. When they reached the two-foot-high pile there wasn't any doubt as to what it was made of.

"Get a handful and rub this over your body—and make it quick," Chief whispered.

"It's shit," Bats said, disgust in his voice.

Chief was the first to plunge his hand past the dried crust and scoop out a gooey portion. "And if we smell like shit, baby Godzilla over there might stop following us." He smeared the feces across his chest and shoved some under his arms.

Susan looked at the pile like it was a serpent and reached in the crater, bringing a wad of the brownish-green organic material. She stuck her head out a bit and opened her mouth, gagging at the foul odors released into the air she breathed.

"I don't like the smell of shit," Bats said.

"Great. You go dance with the dinosaur then. It'll give Susan and me a chance to escape," Chief said.

The look Bats gave in return showed the man realized the suggestion might have been more than a prompt to motivate him into action. His expression turned to reflect that his feelings were slightly wounded. Still, though, he moved the rock from his right to his left hand and painted himself with a handful of dino dung.

Susan managed to keep whatever she had in her stomach down and went to work rubbing the feces on her body. Her disgust had her nose squinched and her bottom lip poking upward forming tiny dots on her chin.

By the time they had finished, the Dilophosaurus was too close for comfort. Chief led them away from the dung pile and stepped on over to a tree with a trunk at least six feet wide. He motioned for them to be still and wait.

The dinosaur had hurried its pursuit, and now the only chance the three had was hiding under the blanket of smell.

The theropod's footsteps crushed foliage on the ground. Its steps sounded surprisingly light. The animal itself stood slightly taller than an average man, but the way it was shaped made it appear much larger. From the head to the tail must have had it twenty feet in length. It amazed Chief that something that big could move so fast. Thinking of its crocodile-like mouth snapping closed on his soft flesh brought back haunted memories of the Troodon attack where he was dissected mouthful by mouthful while still alive. Cold sweat beaded across his brow, and a chill snaked down his back.

The Dilophosaurus was close enough for Chief to hear it snort the air. In a way it reminded him of a horse testing the breeze. The theropod uttered a slow hiss and moved into full view past the tree the three hid behind.

Susan kept her cool—thankfully. But Chief felt her flatten herself against the tree trunk next to him. Bats was on her other side, his eyes closed, and all emotion drained from his face.

The dinosaur moved slowly and headed away. So far so good, and with any luck, the camo-shit smell had it thinking a stinking pile of crap was by the tree—not three tasty humans.

Just as Chief thought the Dilophosaurus had lost interest, it abruptly turned around and hissed with a wide open mouth. His legs threatened to turn to water as the beast slowly moved toward him, its mouth open like a bear trap waiting to snare a victim.

Fear had him caged against the tree. He felt like a helpless mouse trapped by a cat in a corner. Where was his courage? Where was that last valiant effort where the warrior took on insurmountable odds and died in the glories of battle?

The theropod hesitated and turned its head from side to side. Maybe it hadn't discovered the human prey. Maybe it picked up the scent of a more familiar animal—one that didn't smell like shit and would taste better.

Chief's chest felt like the weight of the Earth rested upon it. He didn't know if he was lightheaded because of fear endorphins or because his breathing had become so shallow.

The dinosaur's curiosity won over whatever other options it entertained in its mind. It took two steps closer and slowly leaned its head forward.

The red crested head of death moved right toward Chief's face. The theropod's crocodile smile filled his field of vision. Its teeth loomed as harbingers of impending torture.

Bats still held a baseball sized rock in his left hand. He brought his arm up, and launched it over to the side.

The distraction stopped the Dilophosaurus cold. It jutted its head to the side and craned its neck in the noise's direction. But instead of taking the bait and leaving—it struck like a cobra. The theropod's head rocketed directly toward Bats, and the daggers of destruction in its maw chomped down between his shoulder and neck.

Chief reacted without thought. He had Susan's hand and had rolled off to the side dragging her with him. Bats' screams painted a horrible picture in his mind of the fate he had just barely escaped. His teammate had unintentionally sacrificed himself. For that, Chief was thankful. Oftentimes the saying *No good deed goes unpunished* proves itself to be true.

The two dashed away from the tree leaving the Dilophosaurus to eat uninterrupted and hopefully not notice their departure.

Bats stopped screaming, and though the attack hadn't lasted that long, Chief knew each agonizing second of being eaten alive felt like an hour. When the Troodons' had feasted on him, he remembered how time slowed. Each cut from teeth and every dig with taloned claw blossomed packets of excruciating pain.

Susan struggled to keep up—at times he pulled her along. They needed to get as far away as possible before the Dilophosaurus had time to decide if it was full after only one human.

A hiss mixed with a throaty baritone note told them the Dilophosaurus' gluttony had it abandon its meal for the chance of two more.

"Shit! It's following us," Chief said. He looked into Susan's eyes and saw any chance of hope dissipate. Death would soon be upon them.

"What's that up ahead?" Susan said between deep breaths.

Chief hadn't paid a lot of attention as to what lied before them, worrying more about what gained from behind. He turned his head and saw a gash in the earth traveling as far as he could see in either direction—cutting off forward escape.

They quickly arrived to the crack's edge. It was as if the land here had been pulled apart. The gap was some ten to fifteen feet wide. Both edges were sheer down the sides and dropped more than ten feet deep to a mostly flat bottom.

"Oh Chief, what do we do?" Susan asked. "The tree branches are too high for us to reach. If we jump down in the gully, we might break something. I don't know how we'd climb out. I'd rather just die quickly and get it over with."

Susan had given up, but Chief hadn't. Not just yet. The survival gears in his mind still turned. "Come this way." He pulled Susan to the side and hid her behind a tree.

"What are you going to do?" she asked.

"Stay here. I'm going to get it to chase me."

"But—"

Chief could delay no further. He ran and backtracked on their path a bit and waited—which wasn't long. The Dilophosaurus crashed through the jungle in the thrill of the hunt.

The dinosaur must have sensed Chief was nearby because it made that throaty bray as before, and brought its clawed feet up and down, propelling it forward at amazing speed.

Chief ran for his life—hoping he hadn't misjudged his ability to stay ahead of the dinosaur before reaching the gully. Each step of the pounding reptilian feet sounded closer. The large jaws snapped closed mere inches from his head. The gap in the earth neared. Chief stretched his leg out and leaped off his right foot—going airborne across the chasm.

The Dilophosaurus literally couldn't see the trap coming. It plunged off the edge, down into the gully's bottom.

Chief hadn't tried a running broad jump like this since high school. Even then he wasn't very good. At least his legs were longer now to better his chances. His adrenaline boost coupled with well-toned muscles sent him several feet past the edge. He landed on firm ground and fell to his hands and knees.

"Chief!" Susan called. She ran from her hiding spot, her right hand pressed against her chest.

"I'm okay," he said, taking in deep breaths as he tried to calm down. *They* were okay. His plan had worked. Everything had happened so fast that none of it seemed real now.

The Dilophosaurus made slight whimpering noises and moaned something that sounded like an elongated *fuck.*

Chief crawled to the edge and saw the dinosaur lift itself from the ground.

It wobbled slightly before gaining its balance and looked up at chief. It made an angry hiss.

"I love you too, buddy," Chief said. He looked over at Susan. "We did it."

"You did it. That was a smart plan. I…I first thought you were going to sacrifice yourself for me."

"It was only a smart plan because it worked. I really didn't know if I could clear the gap. If I wouldn't have, then it *would* have been a sacrifice for you."

"That's honorable and all that other bullshit. But Chief, you must know I'd have no chance out here on my own. Don't think you'd be doing me a favor by giving your life to save me, because you wouldn't."

Something crashed in the jungle. Chief and Susan looked over as a much larger theropod stepped past trees and thick jungle foliage.

"Son-of-a-bitch—it's a T-rex! Susan, you'll have to make the jump!" Chief cried.

Susan screamed and brought the back of her hand to her mouth.

"Susan! Run!"

The T-rex roared in ferocity unobtainable by the smaller Dilophosaurus.

Susan shook her head, but when the T-rex led with its head bounding toward her, she turned and ran.

All Chief could do was watch, thinking the whole time Susan was too close to the edge to gain enough speed and momentum to cross the gully. He was right.

Her jump took her near the other side—close enough for Chief to grab hold of her arm. Her body slammed against the gully's side, she let out a *whoosh* of air from her lungs, and a deep moan. He held tightly as grime and sweat threatened to let her slip from his grip.

"Hang on," he said, his voice straining as he tensed the muscles in his back, ready to lift her to freedom. The Dilophosaurus in the gully had other intentions and bit down on Susan's legs—thrashing its head about.

For a moment Chief was pulled downward and almost fell in head first, but then heard a loud *snap* and felt something stretch and give. His right hand came back with Susan's forearm—it had torn away at the elbow.

The T-rex towering on the other side of the gully lifted its head and cried out in frustration. Its short arms waved frantically in the air.

Chief jumped to his feet still holding on to the arm. All rational thought incinerated from his exploding range. "Fuck you!" he yelled at the T-rex right before he leaped off the edge headfirst.

Susan was being savagely eaten alive. Her cries pierced the air like sharp knives.

The Dilophosaurus' head came up after ripping off some of Susan's flesh. Chief landed on the back of its neck and locked his left arm around its throat. "Fuck you!" he yelled again and beat the side of the dinosaur's head with Susan's forearm. "I hate every goddamn one of you fucking lizards!"

The theropod whipped its body from side to side and had no trouble shaking free of the annoying human.

Chief hit the ground on his side, and his head bounced against the hard earth. Stunned, he tried to sit up and get his bearings, and then felt the dinosaur's foot smash his bottom legs into the ground. He was trapped, but it wouldn't last long, because the nasty rows of teeth that killed Bats, the teeth stained with Susan's blood, latched onto his throat.

He felt blood rush to his head as teeth skewered his neck and jaws crushed his esophagus. The crunch of cartilage crackled in his brain as pain and shock lit explosions of light blurring his vision. There he was again—trapped between seconds in time. The clock had frozen, and he suffered in unimaginable pain. Yearning for his life to end—begging, pleading to any God who would listen just to grant the bliss of oblivion.

A cool sensation spilled down the back of his head and chilled him to the bone. Darkness finally wrapped its gentle arms around him and carried him away on the winds of butterfly wings.

CHAPTER 10

The volcano belched its wicked breath into the mysterious Patagonian sky. The perpetual clouds filtered the warm rays of the rising sun.

Coop's synapses solidified consciousness one electrical signal at a time. It was as if random pieces of a jigsaw puzzle popped into his field of vision, slowly sharpening the distorted scene into reality. He was at the volcano—again. Even though he was suspended in time and couldn't move, he sensed all the others were with him.

Death by that huge theropod he didn't know the name of had been quicker than his death before by the Spinosaurus. Still, he winced at the harsh memory of those strong jaws and sharp teeth snapping down on his head. It was ironic how he had two memories of his death. *How many more deaths will I remember before I get out of here?*

His chest heaved as the rotten odor air filled his lungs, kick-starting the spirit, energizing his body much like a newborn's. A quick inspection with his fingers confirmed his head, neck, and shoulder were wound free. Coop was whole again, and no worse for the wear.

He moved his gaze around and saw the others in his group returning control over their bodies. Their facial expressions didn't show surprise as last time. In fact, they looked as if they had just come out of a deep slumber and were getting ready for a routine day at work.

Coop's gaze stopped when it came to rest on two men who were not part of the Redwater team or Alex's group. "Hawkins? Gerald, is that you?"

The other ten members of Coop's group all turned toward the two new arrivals.

Gerald raised an eyebrow. "Yeah…uh…who…Cooper? Vince Cooper? Damn, Coop. I almost didn't recognize you—standing here naked and all."

"You know these people?" Alex asked.

"I know Gerald Hawkins. The guy with him, if I had to guess, is probably none other than Will Prescott," Coop said.

"Quite right, sir. If I had a hat, I'd tip it your way," Will said.

"You two were the first to enter Patagonia—from the south," Chief said. "You know, I knew Prescott had been killed from the report, and I just assumed that you had been killed, too, Hawkins. But it never crossed my mind after my first resurrection that you two might have been brought back to life like us."

"I never considered that either," Coop said. "Is this your first rebirth or have there been others?" he asked Gerald.

"Second."

"Interesting," Alex said. "Any idea how long ago the first was?"

Gerald rotated his left shoulder and stretched. "Don't know how much time passed from the time we died until we awoke. Will had been killed first. I showed up here a few hours after he did. We made it on our own out there in the jungle for several weeks. Turned a cave, just east of here, into our home. Dinosaurs weren't much of concern where we lived except for the pterodactyls."

"Pterodactyls—pterosaurs aren't dinosaurs. Pterosaurs are winged reptiles," Alex corrected.

"Huh? Of course, they're dinosaurs. I learned that when I was a kid," Gerald said.

"Actually…" Alex stopped himself after looking at the faces of various members of the group glaring back at him. "Never mind. You can finish your story."

"As I was saying…" Gerald turned his head away from Alex. "Most of the dinosaurs in our area were the small type that walked on two legs. Will and I are pretty handy at surviving in the woods. We found flint rock and made fire. Sharpened stones and made weapons. It was a regular *Gilligan's Island*."

"What killed you to get you back here?" Coop asked.

"Curiosity," Will said, and then hung his head low.

"We were out to get water, and Will was feeling kind of big for his britches—wanted to deviate from the path and explore. I gave in. At first, I thought we had found something else to eat beside two-legged lizards. Found some trees growing dates. To make the story shorter, some big T-rex looking thing with a sail on its back showed up and chased us over the edge of a cliff."

"I'm assuming you all came to Patagonia to look for the diamonds. How much time had passed from when Gerald sent the drone out to when you crossed the mountains?" Will asked.

"The timeline's a little sketchy," Coop said. "At least two months. We had to get equipment in position and assemble a team."

"How about introducing us to the team," Gerald said.

Coop nodded and pointed at Chief. "I'll skip formal introductions. That's Chief. He's part of Redwater and in command of the six other members of his team. From left to right we have Meat, Suge, Bats, Caveman, and the two clones on the end are Ron and Don. Don't ask me right now which is which. It's harder to tell them apart now that they're naked."

"Roll Tide," the twins said in unison.

"The other three are part of a university group we used as cover to gain entrance into Patagonia. The official version of our business here was *to find and study prehistoric life*. We couldn't just say *we're here to steal your diamonds*. Anyway, the gentleman here," Coop pointed, "is Alex Klasse. He's a Professor of Zoology at Southwood University. His wife, Susan, is standing next to Chief. And over on the end is Natasha, a grad student from the university."

"You said these three are part of the university group. Where are the others?" Gerald asked.

"That's a good question. There were three others. Since they aren't here, we have to assume they're still alive. Where they are, we can't be sure. But if I had to bet, I'd bet they made it out of Patagonia safe and sound. Our main vehicle was an armor plated All-Terrain Tracked Carrier. That's what we used to cross the mountains. It was armed with enough firepower to kill a hundred T-rexes. They probably rode that thing back the same way we came."

"Do you think they'll come back with others?" Will asked.

"I'm sure Ace Corp will make every attempt it can to get the diamonds. I'm just not sure how and when. The carrier, we called it the *Warthog*, is too big to make it back to the cave with the diamonds. They'll have to send in smaller vehicles to make that trip. Of course, smaller vehicles might not pack enough fire power to get them there and back in one piece," Coop said.

"Gerald, Will," Chief said. "I think we need to concentrate on the immediate matters. We're back to square one—out here naked with no food or water. Obviously our plan to head south ended in our deaths."

"Yeah, and please note that we weren't resurrected until we all died—and that included Will and Gerald," Alex said.

"What does that mean?" Natasha asked.

"I don't know what it means. But it's a bit of information we should base any future decisions on," Alex said.

"Point taken," Coop said. "We need to determine who was the last to die and how much time had passed from our outing until that point. I can tell you that Alex, Caveman, and I didn't make it through the first day. Alex sacrificed himself to a group of Velociraptors, which kept Caveman and me alive long enough for some big theropod to kill us."

"We didn't last any longer," Meat said. "We tangoed with a Troodon—like the ones that attacked us the first time. Suge bought it when it chomped down on his neck. It tore my guts out with a foot claw and left me alive long enough to watch it eat Natasha while she was still alive." He looked over at her, closed his eyes, and shook his head.

Natasha stood next to Suge. She wrapped her arms across her chest and turned her gaze toward the ground. Suge's arm came up and rested across her shoulders.

"We died not long after reaching the tree line—less than an hour. Susan called it a Dilophosaurus. It was blind but still could smell well enough to track us. It had us cornered, and Bats did his best to save me by distracting it. The dinosaur got him instead of me," Chief said, and turned his gaze at Bats. "That was brave, buddy."

Bats responded with a slight nod.

"Anyway," Chief continued, "there was no way I could save Bats. So I grabbed Susan and ran. Without going into detail, not long after…" he shifted his gaze toward Susan, "the son-of-a-bitch won."

"I understand," Coop said. "Well, none of this has been very encouraging." He turned to Gerald and Will. "We have a nuclear powered Humvee variant back at the cave where you found the diamonds. Our plan was to hike over to it and use the radio to call for help. If we can't last a day out there, we're never going to accomplish that. Not in a thousand lifetimes."

"We'll have to go in a different direction," Suge said.

"Or split into two groups and go in different directions," Meat said.

"Why bother?" Bats said, and peeled away from the others. He came to a stop by Coop's side. "Coop's right. I don't think it matters if we go a different way or split into groups. The results are always going to be the same. We'll wind up back here."

"I know where you're going with this," Chief said. "And I for one don't think it's a good idea."

"Would you mind letting the rest of us in on the idea?" Coop asked.

"Sure. I saw this coming a mile away. People think *I'm* nuts, but it's you who don't have a grasp on reality. We're a bad-ass bunch when we're armed to the teeth. We can even hold our own in bare knuckle brawls. But if our only weapons are sticks and rocks, we don't have a snowball's chance in hell of ever making it back to the Mule. I don't know about you, but I'd like to avoid getting eaten by a dinosaur as much as possible. So what I'm saying is, we need to think about this in a different way. Let's set up a permanent camp where we can wait for someone to find us.

"Guys, the lid's off Patagonia. Ace Corp isn't going to have sole access to this place for very long. It's only a matter of time before other teams will come through here looking for whatever treasures can be found. Hell, I'll bet they'll keep sending up drones until they map the whole area. We can mark the land with rocks or wood to spell out S.O.S or something.

"Food, water, shelter," Bats had lifted a finger from a closed hand for each of the three things he named off, "that's all we need. Hawkins just told us they were able to live for weeks before things went bad. There's no reason to believe that we can't stay alive that long too. Hopefully we can stay alive much longer than that."

"I like that idea," Natasha said. "I know we can't stay here, but it just seems stupid to think any of us will survive a trip to the Mule that's hundreds of miles away."

"That's another vote for camp. Who else?" Bats asked.

"Who said we're taking votes?" Coop asked.

"I'm still in command here, Bats. I know we're in a difficult situation, but you need to slow it down a bit," Chief said.

"Chief, you know I have the utmost respect for you. Coop, you too," Bats said. "But there comes a point where rules and chains of command don't matter anymore. I've reached that point. I never volunteered for a suicide mission with Redwater. I always believed I was better than the enemy, and I always proved I was. The enemy we face now can't be defeated. I won't charge forward just because of orders. I'll fight to survive though. I'll fight for all of those who want to come away with me."

"Insubordination leaves a scar that never heals," Chief said to Bats.

"I've got other scars to go with it," Bats said.

"This scar cuts deeper than any and leaves no visible mark," Chief said.

"So be it," Bats said.

Coop knew that chaos would one day overtake order. He didn't believe it would come this soon, though, and he certainly didn't think Bats would be the one to rise up and challenge.

"Who wants to come with me? Hawkins, Prescott? You two can show us how it's done," Bats said.

Gerald looked over at Will and then back at Bats. "Hey, we just got here. Don't put us in the middle."

"I'll go with you, Bats," Meat said, and turned his gaze over to Natasha.

"Me too," Suge said.

"Not me," Caveman said. "I ain't figured out a way to beat these bastards, but I'm gonna."

"The Crimson Tide always rolls. Ain't that right, Don?" Ron asked.

"That it does, Ron. We're sticking with Chief," Don said.

"Guys, I don't think it's a good idea for us to take sides this quickly," Coop said. "There's still time—"

"How far is your cave from here?" Bats asked Gerald.

"Since it looks like it's morning, I'm pretty sure we can reach it before night time. We know where we're going, so it won't take as long to get there as it was to find it in the first place."

"See, if we waste any more time arguing over it, we'll miss out finding water and shelter for the night," Bats said.

"We found water heading south," Coop said.

"Water and killer dinosaurs," Bats said. "Our chances are better going back to Hawkins' cave."

There was nothing to dispute that fact. Coop had no intentions of going back south anyway. This truly was the moment of decision. And even though he agreed with Bats, he didn't like the way all of this was going down. He decided not to break ranks, mostly out of pride. "I'm sticking with Chief. I believe we'll find a way back to the Mule."

"Everyone. The situation is far more complicated than it used to be. Now that none of us are reborn until all have died, we're in a predicament. Let's say some of us reach the Mule—or just one of us, doesn't matter. We call for help, help comes, and…"

"And then you get them to come to our camp and rescue us. No big deal," Bats said.

"That's not what Alex was getting at," Coop said, realizing the situation. "Help comes, and we make it to your camp. How many are alive? Or rather how many of us have died? None can come back to life until we all die. So what happens? The survivors tell the rescuers to pick them up at the vortex by the volcano and then kill themselves?"

"What happens if just one of us makes it out of here, and the rest of us die? Do the dead stay trapped in some sort of suspended animation for all eternity?" Natasha asked.

"Which strengthens the point that we would be better off if we all stayed together," Alex said. "As much as I'd like to take another trip toward the Mule, I don't think it's the best plan."

"Susan, I don't think we've heard from you," Coop said.

She stood by Chief with the side of her face against his chest. "This is a horrible, horrible place. We've no chance making it back to the Mule." She loosened her embrace around the Redwater leader and gazed up into his eyes. "I'm sorry, Chief. I can't go back out there—it's suicide." She turned her head toward Bats. "I'd rather try to find some place safe and wait." Her arms wrapped around Chief's chest, and with her eyes closed and tears slowly rolling down her cheeks, she said, "But you can't leave me—you just can't."

Gerald stepped over to Coop's side, and whispered, "I thought you said that was the Professor's wife."

"I did. Long story for later," Coop said. *The fucking soap opera continues.*

Chief's face sagged like hooks with lead weights pulled it down. He had just drawn a line in the sand, and Susan had stomped all over it. His face reddened as he focused on Bats. Coop wondered who the man was madder at. Bats for dividing the group, or Susan making him choose between her or his command.

"I'm sorry, Susan," Chief said in a tone that sounded contrived to hide emotion. "I have to give it at least one more try."

She didn't hold her tears back and whimpered.

The man obviously had feelings for her. Coop watched Chief's stern expression melt as he tightly hugged Susan. "I'm sorry. I don't give up this quick. It's in my DNA. We're smarter now—learned some things. Every time we go out, we'll improve and increase our chances to make it."

"If you were fucking smart you would have learned you're nothing but dinosaur food out there," Bats said.

Chief tore his embrace away from Susan and stomped over to Bats. The two men faced off nose to nose. Chief said, "You're out of line, mister. And if you don't shut the fuck up right now, I'm going to do it for you."

Bats swelled his chest and brought a finger up. "I don't take to threats. There's nothing but air and opportunity between us. Take your best shot."

"Guys, stop this ri—" Coop began.

Lightning arced across the Patagonian sky, striking the volcano's mouth. The earth rumbled, quenching the situation. The swirling vortex that brought them back to life slowly darkened, turning the white smoke-like spiral gray. The blue, green, and red lights flashed in the time tunnel in a kaleidoscope of colors.

"What's happening?" Natasha yelled.

Suge pulled her closer. "I'm not sure, but it doesn't look good."

The winds picked up, bathing the survivors in hot air. Lightning spider-webbed behind the volcano and struck the vortex.

Coop had been in his share of firefights back in Vietnam, but that had been many years ago. He had been close to explosions as mining companies blasted the terrain in search of treasure. But never in his life had he ever experienced the brutal release of energy such as then. Everything had gone white and the noise so loud it deafened him.

He had collapsed to the ground but didn't lose consciousness. The sky above returned to focus, the familiar layer of clouds hiding them from the rest of the world. He turned his head and saw the others had met a similar fate—either flat on their back or on their side—slightly stirring.

"What the fuck was that?" Meat said.

"Did somebody shoot a nuke at us?" Caveman said.

"Doubtful, but something released a lot of energy," Alex said.

"Is everyone okay?" Coop sat up and surveyed the area.

Various voices answered, all indicating no one was hurt.

Chief was the first to stand. He looked over at Bats, who had fallen next to him, and offered him his hand.

Bats hesitated a second, and then reached out and accepted the kindly gesture. He rose to his feet. "Thanks." Then he turned his gaze away from Chief. His bottom jaw dropped, and he said, "Son-of-a-bitch."

"What?" Chief turned around, and said, "The vortex is gone. And look what's there!"

Pain shot through Coop's knees as he sprang from the ground. The spinning time tunnel had vanished, and what was left in its place was too good to be true. "I don't believe it."

"It's the Mule...and look, there's gear—supplies," Suge said.

"No fucking way," Meat said.

"Roll Tide," Ron said. "I bet the Bear heard two 'Bama fans were in need and sent us some help."

"You know he would if he could," Don said.

The Mule looked like it had seen some time in Patagonia, but it bore no damage from the earlier Spinosaurus attack. It was completely intact, .50 caliber machine gun and all. Backpacks, folded uniforms and clothing, and JNY-7 rifles and pistols lay neatly in front of the vehicle.

Caveman had made a beeline toward the equipment. "This better not one of thems mirage things."

Chief had gone and helped Susan up, and they and the others walked over to check the gifts.

"This is our old stuff. It's got our names on it and everything," Caveman said.

Natasha found her backpack and clothing. "Boots and socks, shirt and pants, I'm in heaven." She brushed the dust from her hands and the rest of her body. "I wonder—yep, panties!"

"I don't know what all this stuff is, but I bet it's a game changer," Gerald said. "Will, here's our stuff. Backpacks, food, nine millimeter pistols, and extra magazines."

Suge picked up his JNY-7. "Grenade launcher...RPG...full magazine." He pointed the barrel toward the volcano and squeezed off a shot. The caseless ammo left the barrel and made a small blast when the exploding bullet hit its target. "It's the real deal."

"Would everyone please turn around so I can put on my panties? A girl needs her privacy, you know," Natasha said.

Alex burst out in laughter. Ron and Don looked perplexed at each other. Meat chuckled. Apparently the gifts had elevated Natasha's spirits to where humor, though be it irony, found its way out.

Coop, too, felt renewed in spirit. Patagonia had put such a burden on everyone that the old civilized person had been lost. This equipment is just what they needed to bond the team back together. It had come at the perfect time.

"This changes everything, again," Alex said.

"You bet it does," Caveman said. "We's have a fightin' chance."

"Guys. The vortex is gone. The time machine is no longer here to bring us back to life. Now when we die, we won't be coming back," Alex said.

"We'll just have to make goddamn sure we don't die then," Bats said. He had his underwear on and his shirt, about to button it.

Staying alive was still going to be a challenge, but with weapons, the chances of surviving increased exponentially.

"Look, I even have my nut-free MREs," Susan said as she dug through her backpack.

Chief shot Alex an ugly look.

The Professor quickly averted his gaze and acted like he hadn't heard her comment.

"I've got six MREs and four bottles of water," Meat said.

"Don and I do too," Ron said.

"I'm going to check out the Mule. See if the satellite link is working," Bats said.

Coop probed his backpack and felt something hard and plastic. "Don't bother. Look what I have." He held up the satellite phone. "And it's got a full charge."

CHAPTER 11

"I don't know who this is or how you have Vincent Cooper's phone, but I must warn you that phone and anything else in Patagonia is the possession of, or solely permitted to be extracted by, Ace Corporation," Henry Lear said. The man's 11 lines between his eyebrows looked like rows in a garden.

An eerie warmth washed behind Matt's mind as his subconscious struggled to make sense of an impossible situation. The call couldn't be from Vince Cooper. From all indications, he had died not long after he had reached the cave with the diamonds. Meat had told them Coop had called, and all the big Samoan heard was gunfire, explosions, and dinosaur cries. Had the Geologist survived somehow? It sure sounded like Coop's voice coming over the satellite phone.

"Henry? Is that you?" Coop said.

Anger quickly melted from Lear's face, and the surprised expression, his mouth opening wider, threatened to let the cigar fall. It was obvious the CEO at least thought he recognized Coop's voice. "Who is this? Vincent Cooper is dead."

"Henry, I'd know your voice anywhere. There's a long story I could tell you—and I will later. Right now, we're just looking for a way out of this place," Coop said.

"Vince Cooper died in front of a cave. I watched a video taken by the Mule. He was eaten by a Spinosaurus. You *can't* be Vincent Cooper." It was hard to discern if Lear's words were an affirmation or said for the man to convince himself.

"*We*," Ben said. "He said *we*."

"Ben? Is that you?" a different voice said over the phone.

"Alex?" Matt said. "Alex, it's Matt." Nostalgic memories of his old friend clouded his reasoning. This couldn't be the Professor though. Matt had watched Alex get torn apart by Troodons. He had been the one who sent Alex plummeting to his death.

"Silence! Everyone," Lear yelled. He lowered his head into his shoulders and crossed his arms high on his chest. After lost in thought for a moment, he said, "I demand to know who this is and who you work for."

"I work for you, Henry H. Lear. CEO of Ace Corporation. We've known each other for over twenty years now. This is my sixth assignment. You paid me one hundred grand upfront, and I get a small percentage on the diamonds we bring back," Coop said.

"Cooper could have told someone that…or…or someone in my employment has that information, and they're fucking with me right now." Lear's eyes widened, as if he had figured out the ruse. "Where is this call coming from?" he demanded.

"Henry, goddammit man. Use the GPS on your phone and see for yourself," Coop said. The frustration in his voice sounded genuine.

"I don't know how to work this thing," Lear said.

"Here, let me." Ben balanced on his crutches for the short travel to the desk. He picked up the phone, pushed the screen a few times, and then turned the screen for Lear to see. "It's coming from inside the mountain range. From Patagonia, all right. The location is in the north—see right there on the map? They're near one of the major landmarks—the volcano."

"The volcano? That's nowhere near the cave," Lear said.

"You're right, it's not," Coop said. "Henry, the story we have to tell is totally unbelievable. Yet, as evident by my voice, is true. Me, Chief, Bats, Suge, Meat, Caveman, Ron and Don…the Professor and his wife, Natasha—even Hawkins and Prescott. We're all alive, and we want nothing more than getting the hell out of here."

"Coop, if this is Cooper, you know how I am. I don't want to hear the whole birth. Just give me the baby," Lear said.

"Okay, this is it. I'll give you the facts and the speculation," Coop said and then took a deep breath. "Sometime after we all died, we woke up by the volcano. There is—or *there was*, some phenomena that looked like a vortex. We believe it to be a time machine of sorts. This vortex brought us into the future, meaning now, from a time before we were killed. We weren't actually brought back to life, although it seems that way to us. So the man you're talking to hasn't truly died. We all just stepped from a time where we lived, to the present, avoiding the hazard that killed us."

"Fascinating," Lear said. "What kind of machine is it? Can you control it? Do you think it's something we can disassemble and ship back to the states?" Lear asked.

Lear's greed showed no boundaries. Learning of nothing short of a miracle wasn't enough to restrain his consuming desire for profit. He just couldn't rest in the comfort that his friend and the others were actually alive.

"Henry, we had no control over the time machine. It really wasn't a *machine*, per se. But that's all moot now. Whatever that thing was that brought us from the past to the present is gone. It just disappeared. An equally unbelievable story is what appeared in its place," Coop said.

"I can't imagine anything topping a time travel story," Lear said.

"Well, the vortex disappeared but did leave us gifts. All of our gear—clothes, food, weapons, all laid out nice and neat for us like we were about to start a new mission. And...and the Mule is here."

"What?" Lear said.

"I'm looking right at it. Bats has the engine rolling, and he just gave me a thumbs-up. We're all good to go, but we're going to need some help," Coop said. "I take it the Warthog made it back with Ben and Matt there. Is Logan with them?"

Matt turned toward Logan.

The young man had his gaze glued to the ground. With some effort, he said, "I'm here."

Matt's mind was racing ninety to nothing. Alex was alive. Transported from a time before he was killed? What the hell? Could this be true? If so, did Alex have a memory of him kicking the Professor to his death? And what was up with Logan? It'd seemed to Matt that Logan would be ecstatic to hear Natasha and the others were alive. Something was eating at Logan. What was it? Did it have something to do with the way Natasha and Meat had died? Did the two deaths go down a different way? What was Logan hiding?

Coop continued, "We have the Mule, and though it's going to be cramped, we can all fit on it and make better time escaping. I'm not sure how far we are from Lear's River, but I know the Mule won't be able to cross that. We'll need the Warthog to meet us on the other side—or as close as it can get to it—and get us back over the mountains. How soon do you think you can hire a crew and bring the Warthog this way?"

"I have a six man Brazilian force that I can send over now," Lear said.

"Hold on," Matt said. "The earthquake dumped a bunch of rubble on the path through the mountains. I don't know if it's possible to go back the way we came."

"Shit," Coop said.

"I've got some heavy equipment in place ready to clear the path," Lear said. "I had the bulldozers delivered in case we had to extract the Warthog. But now, we can use them to clear the path back."

"Any idea how long that might take?" Coop asked.

"Unfortunately, no," Lear said. "So, what's the plan?"

After some silence, Coop said, "We're going to load up and head southeast. You can track us and follow our progression. Send the Warthog our way as soon as possible. Maybe we can meetup in a few days. One thing is for certain, if any of us dies along the way, there will be no coming back. The time machine's gone."

"Not the most unusual of circumstances," Lear said. "I expect a full report, Coop. You're still leading this mission. I want you to bring everyone back alive. It's bad enough we're losing the Mule. Now we won't have any way to get back to the cave and get the diamonds until I can get another shipped in—and that may take months."

"Well, then, I have some news for you that just might brighten your day," Coop said.

"What's that?" Lear said.

"Bats just handed me a pouch he found inside the Mule," Coop said. "A pouch filled with red diamonds."

"Red diamonds? In the Mule? What for the love of God is going on here?" Lear said.

Coop laughed so strangely Matt thought the geologist might break down and cry. "I don't know...I just fucking don't know. It's...it's like there's some game going on, and we're all just pawns."

"Let's hope the game is stacked in our favor then," Lear said. "You get your team together and head toward the river. I'll get the bulldozers clearing the path. Waterman will contact you later for updates and a rendezvous point. Don't forget about that report. And don't let those diamonds leave your sight for one second. Are we clear?"

"Yes, Henry, we're clear. I won't let anything happen to your precious motherfucking, cock sucking, ass licking, goddam pieces of colored glass," Coop said, and then the call terminated.

Lear's eyebrows lifted. "What got into him?"

"Your compassion," Ben said. "Meaning, lack thereof."

***

"Greedy-ass bastard," Coop mumbled after his ended the call. He looked up and saw the faces of his crew ready to receive orders. He needed some time to look at the map and plot a course to Lear's River. The Mule was a versatile vehicle, and having tracks instead of wheels enabled it to travel on almost any surface. It was designed to carry four people comfortably. Coop figured one more in the front and one in the back could be crammed in. Two could ride the rear bumper; two could ride flat on the roof with the .50 caliber gun between them; the other three could sit on the bulldozer-like blade in front when turning it horizontally. It wouldn't quite look like a clown car, but it would be pretty damn close to it.

"Everyone finish dressing and go through your personal items. If you find anything unusual let me know. We have no way of knowing where all this stuff came from. I don't want us to let our guard down. It wouldn't make sense for whoever provided our gear to do something malicious but we can't be sure. Inspect food and water before eating it. Look for signs of tampering," Coop said. "Chief, after I dress, come over, and we'll plot our course."

The crowd around Coop broke ranks and everyone left to follow orders. There was a slight *spring* in everyone's step that had been missing. They wouldn't be heading into the unknown with rocks, sticks, and bare fist. The dangers they faced still might end lives, but that was true in any war. The key to survival was to outmaneuver the opponent and kill them before they killed you.

Natasha finished tying her bootlace and stood upright. Her brown cotton shirt was buttoned, but the bottom hung past the waist of her shorts. She grabbed her shirt tails and tied them in a knot, exposing her midsection and navel.

Suge had his boots and pants on. He picked up his shirt and shoved a muscular arm in. "You know, that outfit looks really good on you." The other arm went in, and he began buttoning his shirt.

"Thank you. I spent a lot of time picking it out. I wanted to dress practical, but I didn't want to give up fashion," Natasha said. "Funny, though. When we were naked, it was like we didn't notice. Wearing clothes certainly adds distinction."

"Oh, I noticed that you were naked. It just wouldn't have been appropriate for me to comment at the time," Suge said. His tone had matched a noticeable desire in his eyes.

Natasha must have noticed it too. An embarrassed smile crept across her lips. She said, "Maybe they'll be an appropriate time in the future."

Okay, things we're really getting closer to normal now, Coop thought. Not even a half hour had passed since some semblance of civilization had returned and stirred the attractions between men and women.

"What about Logan? You know, what he did to you. Have you thought much how you would act if you met him again?" Suge asked.

Natasha sighed and closed her eyes. "I have." She opened her eyes back. "And I can't think of one good way to handle it. He killed me—pushed me over the edge of a cliff. I can't forgive him just because I returned from an earlier time before it happened. He meant to kill me. He had no way of knowing I'd be back. And *why*? What reason did he have to kill me? We had been close friends."

"You heard what Bats said. He thinks Logan had a *thing* for Matt and wanted you out of the way. I'll say this, I don't know much about gay people, but I did notice how Logan acted differently to Matt. Logan went out of his way to do little things— checking on him like a mother would do a child. He wouldn't overdo it. And anytime Matt asked him to do something, he hopped right to it and always did something extra. The man would look so self-conscious when Matt thanked him. It was like Logan searched for approval. I guess it could have very well been Logan trying to win Matt's affection."

"I guess...that's the only reason I could think Logan would want me dead. He never talked about Matt, you know—in that way. And we talked a lot about his relationships. I don't know how I'm going to react when we meet again. There's nothing either of us can do to change the past."

"No, but thank God something changed the past. You're here now. You were given a second chance," Suge said.

"Third, if you want to get technical. I don't know if I can be as gracious as whoever or whatever has us alive right now," Natasha said.

Coop had finished dressing and looked about for Chief. The mercenary leader was in the passenger's side of the Mule. Coop walked over and tapped on the window.

Chief opened the door but kept his gaze fixed on the GPS screen on the dash. "I'm checking things out now. We're close to two hundred miles away as a crow flies from Lear's River. From the satellite information we have stored, we should be able make it on this route." Chief pointed to the screen, which had the route marked in small dashes. The path was far from a straight shot but looked like it didn't add an excessive amount of miles to the journey.

Will and Gerald showed up by Coop's side.

Gerald said, "This is some wicked piece of machinery."

"You should see the Warthog. It's a beefed-up version of this," Coop said.

"Tell us about it," Gerald said.

"The Mule's nuclear powered. The rods are good for three months of continuous use before they have to be replaced. The tracks allow us to go just about anywhere—including on sand, snow, and mud. The fifty caliber machine gun can be operated from the cab. We sent the Mule ahead of the Warthog to clear tight paths for the larger vehicle. The blade in front comes in real handy at clearing the path of debris and foliage."

"Is it hard to drive?" Will asked.

"No, we could teach you how in five minutes," Coop said.

"We noticed the Redwater team has some sophisticated rifles. Can you show us how to use them? You know…in case we have a man down. I don't think Gerald's or my nine millimeter are going to do much good against dinosaurs," Will said.

Coop saw the logic in the request. It was a morbid thought of sorts. But in war, whoever had the best weapons usually won. Will and Gerald would need to learn how to use the best weapons. He looked around and saw Meat inspecting his rifle. "Meat, can you come over here and show Will and Gerald how the JNY-Seven works?"

"Sure thing, boss," Meat said, and stepped over carrying the rifle across his chest. "What we have here is the baddest-ass rifle created by man not in a video game. It's called the JNY-Seven, but we just call it a Seven. The rifle holds one hundred rounds of custom ammunition. The bullets are caseless, so we don't dump brass everywhere. The projectile in the bullets are small, but it's made of a compound that explodes on impact. It's an exploding bullet." Meat held the rifle in one hand and pointed with the other. "Right on top, we have a grenade launcher used for blowing up shit a short distance away. There are three grenades in reserve. On the side here, is a version of a RPG—rocket-propelled grenade— for distance. Blows up Troodons pretty good. Too bad the Seven only carries one rocket. The gun shoots single shots, three round bursts, or can go fully automatic. The trigger mechanism is itself a pistol." Meat pushed in a button, the hand-grip-trigger mechanism and a short section of gun barrel detached as a single piece—a handgun. "The rifle still can be used to fire grenades. This pistol is exactly like the sidearms the Redwater's carry and is interchangeable with the one in the rifle. If you two will step over to the side, I'll let you handle it yourself, and squeeze off a round or two."

As the three men left, Suge arrived with Natasha leading the way in front.

Caveman, who had been unusually quiet, stumbled up next as he struggled to put on his belt. The man had a small ass to support such a rotund gut, and his pants would have had a better fit had they been a size or two larger.

Ron and Don arrived with Susan in tow.

Alex was last and the one who Coop wanted to speak to. The Professor first stopped next to Susan, who turned her head, shooting daggers his way. He casually sidestepped over by Suge and Natasha. The young ex-lover crossed her arms, and her laser stare warned him he wasn't wanted.

"Come over here, Alex. I'd like to go over a few things, and I'd like your input," Coop said, trying to diffuse the situation. This really wasn't the time for the women to hold grudges, though he understood why they did. He wished all the distractions could be pushed aside until all of this was over.

Alex stood next to Coop. Chief had the window down in the Mule and waited to hear the discussion. Bats exited the driver's side, stood on a track, and looked over the roof.

"Did anybody find anything noteworthy in their gear?" Coop asked

A few people said *no,* and the rest shook their heads.

"Anyone else have a phone?" Coop asked.

Again, all negative responses.

"Not that it matters. The Mule has a satellite connection. Now, I don't mean to look a gift horse in the mouth," Coop started, "but I feel foolish for just taking all this stuff and hitting the road without asking a few questions."

"I know what you mean," Alex said. "Aliens, or someone from our future, keeps pulling us from our past and placing us back in the normal timeline. We are being used for a specific purpose. If the purpose is for us to leave Patagonia and reintroduce dinosaurs to the present world, why not just awaken us back at the camp on the other side of the mountains? That's not happening. Instead, we're outfitted with basically the same gear we had when we entered. Why would a *higher power* do that?"

"Well, if it's God who's doing this to us as Meat had suggested, then it might be to teach us a lesson," Natasha said.

"Cut the God stuff," Coop said.

"I'll stick with science whether it's alien or manmade," Alex said.

"Cut the alien stuff," Coop said.

Alex continued, "We've been given the means to make our way back, but we'll have to fight our way. There's no free ride here. And since we've been given the tools to leave, then I have to believe whoever gave them to us is also observing us."

"Oh, Alex. You're making our situation sound like some bad episode of *The Twilight Zone*," Susan said. "The fact is we don't belong here, and we're given the means to leave the same way we came. There's no reason to overthink any of this. We have this chance, and we have no other choice than to take it."

The Professor's wife had a point, Coop thought, when you cut the situation down to the basics. Still, Alex had made a good point too. "Alex, Susan, I think you're both right. We have a chance, and we're going to take it. If we're observed along the way, then this was somehow a test. And whoever lives past the test might have an opportunity to discover more truth. So, that's our goal. All of us make it out of here alive."

"Let's get this show on the road," Caveman said.

"You heard the man," Coop said. "Let's load up and head on out."

***

"Compassion?" Henry Lear said. "Coop is in no need of my compassion. Do you know the literal meaning of the word *compassion*?" Lear asked.

"I know what compassion means, Lear," Ben said and slightly rolled his eyes.

"To have *compassion* means to *suffer with*. You heard Coop. He's a man in fine health. He has food, weapons, and a means of transportation. He's not suffering. The fact remains that he and the rest of the Redwater members are in my employment. I'm paying them, and their job is not complete. As a businessman, it behooves me to keep all business deals in perspective."

"Death usually terminates all business contracts," Ben said.

"Did Cooper sound like a dead man to you? As far as I know, the dead can't speak. The contract is binding. In fact, because you three have prematurely abandoned the mission, you're all in breach of contract," Lear said.

"Excuse me, Mr. Lear, but you can't be serious," Matt said. He had wanted nothing more than to run out of the tent and hop aboard the Chinook. Now, the situation had spun into a whirlpool threatening to suck all three of them in. "We stayed in touch with Waterman the entire way back. Ace Corp was fully aware and in full compliance with our return. Our commitment to you is done."

"But the information you gave us turns out to be incorrect. Isn't that right? The others aren't dead, as you reported. Let's look at the facts: the mission is ongoing, and you're outside the mountains surrounding Patagonia."

Matt's shoulders slumped. "Mr. Lear, you said a few minutes ago we could leave, and—"

"I'm not convinced that's really Cooper you spoke to. Time machine, are you serious? I watched Clint Perry and Natasha Kamdar fall to their deaths," Logan said. "There's nothing the three of us can do to help get out whoever's in there. We're not military. You should let us go home. I hope to goodness that they really are alive. We can wait for them back in the States."

Matt didn't want to be any part of a rescue team going back into Patagonia either. He felt the three of them would just get in the way. There was something in Logan's voice again that was a bit off-note. The young man was hiding something.

Matt knew he had reservations about meeting Alex again face to face. And for some reason, Logan acted like he had reservations too. Was there something about Clint's and Natasha's death Logan was hiding? Then it dawned on him, something Logan had said right when everyone believed there was only one bullet left in the revolver that Lear had pointed at Matt's head. *I love you, Matt*, Logan had said. At the time, Matt categorized the statement as an emotional farewell. But now that he thought about it, and the way Logan had been acting toward him over the last few months, maybe the young man was reaching out for something more than favor from a friend and teacher. Logan had been so loyal and dutiful, concerned and caring...dare he think it? *Loving*? Did Logan do something to Natasha? Alex was dead, and Matt's plan had been to be there for Natasha. Did Logan see this, too, and decided to remove Natasha from the picture?

Lear had been patient. Perhaps waiting for Ben to protest too. A few moments passed, and he said, "Mr. King, you said your commitment to me was done. How about your commitment to

Alex Klasse? Hmmm? Or Susan Klasse and Natasha Kamdar. If there's one chance in a million you could aid in the rescue of your companions, don't you owe it to them to take it?"

So now Lear had resorted to the guilt trip game. Of course, it was easy for a person to ask someone else to risk the ultimate sacrifice. Why was it so important to Lear for them to go? Was there a plot within a plot? Before Matt had the chance to sidestep the question and ask again to leave and go home, Ben interrupted, and said:

"He's right, Matt. We have an obligation to go back."

Logan showed the internal conflict on his face. Matt thought it looked like the young man had aged ten years.

"If I thought we could be of some use, I might feel more of an obligation. Look at us. You can't even walk without crutches. What happens if we get in a tight spot and have to leave the Warthog? We can't carry you. Logan and I aren't warriors," Matt said.

"You don't have to worry about me. I'm willing to take the risk. If I have to be left behind, then so be it. But I don't think that way. Never have and never will," Ben said, the words couldn't have sounded more heartfelt.

Which made Matt feel like someone had just cut off his testicles and thrown them in the trash saying he didn't deserve the pair. "Mr. Lear. What can we possibly do out there other than get in the way? I guess you could use us as dinosaur food. Are those diamonds more important to you than human life?"

"I think you and I have different philosophies concerning *life*. Life without risks is a life not worth living, in my opinion. I've lived an opulent life, but I've lived a hard and dangerous life too. Do I push others to risk their life? Yes, I do. But I ask of them no more than I ask from myself. Getting back to the question of *what can you do*, you three can do a lot. First off, none of the six-man team here is familiar with the Warthog and how it operates. You are. I need you to navigate the ATTC for the rescue mission. Also, you are scientists. I believe your counsel is invaluable. Captain Diaz is a very capable military commander. The best commanders have a well-rounded team at their disposal. You three have made it across the mountains twice and have some feel for the Patagonian landscape. Time is a factor here too. I don't have time to get another experienced Redwater crew over here. The quicker we can make the rendezvous point with Coop and the rest, the more lives can be saved. Wouldn't you agree, Mr. King?" Lear said.

There were no gaping holes in Lear's argument for him to try and crawl out of. Matt looked over at Logan, and the young student looked like he had just swallowed bitter medicine.

Ben had locked a gaze on Matt that demanded for him to commit or get the fuck out of his way.

"Logan, I'm not going to lie and say I don't have reservations. But I feel like I need to do this for Alex and the rest. I…" Matt felt his conscience threaten to betray his secret, but this was not the time or place to confess his sins. "I need to go back and do this for me too." The more he thought about carrying the burden of killing another man for the rest of his life, there had grown a monster he never thought would arise. Who knew how the consuming guilt would alter his future? This was a chance to right a wrong. A great weight lifted from his shoulders.

"That's great, Matt," Ben said. "Logan, you with us?"

The blond haired student lifted his nose slightly in the air and breathed out. "I feel just like Matt. I want to do this for the others, and I want to do this for myself too."

"Admirable," Lear said. He turned to Diaz. "Captain, would you please have your men assist in loading the Warthog? Get the heavy equipment operators on the bulldozers, and start clearing the path. I want everyone ready to head out one minute after the way is clear."

"*Sim, Senhor* Lear." Diaz commanded, "*Nós temos nossos pedidos. Vamos lá.*"

The Brazilian mercenaries snapped to attention and headed out the tent with Diaz on their heels.

"What now?" Ben asked.

"I'll have your quarters prepared. You can use your free time to each fill out a report. Waterman will be in charge here, as I'll be leaving soon and heading back to the U.S. Get some rest and try to make friends with the Brazilians. Each one understands English but to varying degrees. It wouldn't hurt to learn a bit about their culture. You can search the internet with your phones which I will return to you. Don't try and contact anyone in Patagonia. We have access to all lines. You'll take orders from Diaz once on the Warthog. You'll find your chances of success depends greatly on your cooperation," Lear said.

"Understood," Ben said. He was either the best soldier or the biggest pain in the ass.

Matt was committed now. He doubted that he or the other two would be able to change their mind. Lear was one strange character. Something inside told Matt that had they refused to cooperate, the situation may have gone south for them. Feeling like he had nothing to lose, he gazed at Lear, and asked, "What would you have done if we had refused to go back?"

Lear looked a bit surprised at the question. He said, "Had you decided to leave, I would have put you aboard the Chinook, and sent you on your merry way. I'm a man of my word."

"That's great to know, Mr. Lear."

"And somewhere over the South American jungle, each of you would have been tossed out to plunge to your deaths. Your friends and loved ones would be told the story of how the plane carrying you to safety met its untimely demise in a thunderstorm. No one will know the precise location, so there's no fear of investigation. We'll use that same story if all of your companions don't make it back alive from Patagonia," Lear said.

A lump formed in Matt's throat. Lear was a functioning lunatic. He looked over at Ben and saw the athletic man throw up a steel-like gaze at Lear's growing smirk.

"I don't like loose endings," Lear said. "Either you all come back alive, and we all live happily ever after, or you all die. Accidental deaths are a tragedy. There will be few questions for us to answer, and insurance payments to your families will dry many tears. I don't want to worry with any survivors calling my business activities into question."

CHAPTER 12

The Mule rode the desolate land toward the east. Coop was at the wheel with Natasha sitting between him and Suge. Bats and Chief sat in the backseat with Susan in the middle. Susan noticeably leaned in toward Chief, which wasn't surprising. Coop wondered, though, if Susan's objective was to get as far away as possible from Bats rather than getting closer to Chief.

Ron and Don stood on the back bumper, and after only three breaks over the six-hour ride, Coop figured their old leg muscles must be getting tired. The two refused to rotate out of position, saying the *spirit of The Bear made them good.*

Caveman, Meat, and Will Prescott sat on the blade. Thank goodness for beefed-up front suspension. The three did partially block Coop's driver's view, but fortunately the roof camera gave him a far and wide picture of things to come. Which so far hadn't been much more than scrubby grass on a mostly flat landscape.

Alex and Gerald Hawkins lay flat on the roof on their stomachs, the fifty available for a hand hold, or sat with their legs hanging down by the passenger side windows. Coop felt bad that some got to ride in relative comfort while others had to endure the constant bumps and jiggles against an unforgiving surface.

For safety's sake, he didn't drive over 20 mph. The odometer read they had traveled ninety miles so far.

"The map shows it won't be long before we reach jungle," Suge said.

"Think I can see some trees in the distance. It's funny how the terrain can change so quickly around here," Coop said.

"Must have something to do with soil conditions and underground water. Natasha thinks the water table may be above the magma veins. The hot magma might be pushing the underground streams toward the surface providing water for all the jungle foliage," Suge said.

Interesting theory, Coop thought. Patagonia was an anomaly in every sense. For dinosaurs to exist for all these centuries, the living conditions had to be kept within certain parameters—of which variations had to remain minimal. The more he thought about it, the more it seemed like the entire ecosystem had been engineered for the specific purpose of preserving dinosaurs. Technology to pull something like that off was well beyond anything mankind could do in the next one hundred years—maybe the next five hundred years. It boggled his mind to think of the enormity of such an engineering feat.

As the jungle neared, the ride became softer. The ground underneath the tracks turned from reddish clay-like earth to rich brown soil. Smaller palms and other types of trees sparsely outlined the perimeter. Taller Trees and lush green foliage loomed before them.

Coop sat up in his seat. "We're about to get into the thick of things. How far is the river from here?"

"A little over a hundred miles straight shot. But we're going to have to take a few detours along the way. Might add twenty to thirty miles," Suge said.

"That's not too bad. We made pretty good time in the open. Now that we're in the jungle, we're going to have to cut our speed way back," Coop said.

"We also have to worry about arriving at Lear's River too soon. The area's sure to be hot. We don't need to get there before the Warthog's in place. Waterman said the satellite photos showed the path through the mountains didn't look as bad as they feared. They estimated it would take at least thirty-six hours to clear it. But you know how things could change once the job gets started. It might take longer," Chief said.

"Yeah. We don't know how long it's going to take us to get to the rendezvous point either. Neither one of us can afford to just sit around and wait for the other to arrive," Coop said.

"At least they'll have the Warthog around them for protection. We're basically wide-ass open in the Mule," Bats said.

"We never opened up the big gun on the Warthog on any dinosaurs. I'd bet it could turn a T-rex into ground meat in thirty seconds," Suge said.

"Okay, this is where we slow things down. Suge, I'll need you to be my navigator as I negotiate the terrain," Coop said. "I'll get a headache if I keep looking at the GPS and back out the windshield."

"Sure thing, boss," Suge said. "Just keep going left until you pass those two trees and edge to the right."

The Mule traveled now slightly above 5 mph. The dense foliage did more than present driving hazards. The thick brush and huge plants walled off the living dangers lurking in the jungle.

"We've got a problem," Coop said. "The guys riding the blade are going to have to get off and walk. Things are too thick ahead, and I'll have to use the blade to clear a path for us." He slowed the Mule to a stop and called out the window, "Hey, you guys are going to have to get off the blade. It's either that, or you'll be eating jungle as I plow through it."

"Yeah, I saw that coming," Meat said.

"Y'all can start calling me *Cavemanasaurus*," Caveman said as he slid to the ground.

"Why's that?" Coop asked.

"'Cause my *ass is sore*. Get it? Saurus…sore ass."

"Yeah, I should have picked up on that, knowing you," Coop said.

Caveman cackled at his joke, and he and the other two walked to the rear of the Mule.

Ron and Don stepped off the bumper and joined them. "Hold on, we want to stretch our legs a bit."

"Aren't you guys tired of standing?" Will asked.

"Not so much. Knees' getting a might stiff though," Ron said. "Don and I can sleep standing up. We joke sometimes that we're part horse."

"Roll Tide," Don said.

Alex slapped the roof, and said, "Hold on, I'm getting down."

"Me too," Gerald said.

"Should we stop here for a while?" Coop asked.

Chief said, "Hasn't been two hours since our last break. Plus, it'll be getting dark soon. I'd rather find a better place to spend the night than out here in the middle of everything. Let's go farther and be on the lookout."

"Okay," Coop said.

"Suge, check the GPS and see if there are rock structures nearby where we can camp," Chief said.

"Will do."

The blade's hydraulics hummed as the implement pivoted vertically. The fern-like plants stood a few feet taller than the vehicle. Coop put the Mule into gear and cleared a swath effortlessly through the jungle. The others followed on foot with rifles at the ready.

Walls of foliage folded and opened to partially clear parcels. Coop hoped this was an exceptionally dense area. He doubted they could travel more than 5 mph at this rate—which was faster than an average person's walking speed. He didn't want the men on foot any longer than they had to be.

"Guys, if this keeps up much longer, we're going to trades place with some of the men back there," Coop said. "I don't want to wear anyone out. Plus, I'm feeling guilty sitting here soaking up air condition."

"We can swap out now, if you'd like," Suge said. "I know Ron and Don would never admit it, but I bet those old joints of theirs are feeling their age."

The blade met the next obstacle, and after a few feet in, hit something solid—jarring everyone forward. Coop immediately let off the accelerator.

The bray of an unknown creature cut through the gentle song of the jungle—sending chills down Coop's back. "Oh shit…"

"What is it?" Natasha said.

"We're about to find out," Chief said leaning forward.

"Get ready, men," Meat called out.

Brush rustled, and something much bigger than the Mule scraped against the driver's side. A creature with orange and black markings on its body lumbered by braying like an angry bull. Coop recognized the skin coloration from the video the drone took at Lear's River. It was a Stegosaurus. A *pissed-off*, Stegosaurus.

The men behind the Mule fell back as the dinosaur stomped past the vehicle and into the open pathway, with the Mule's rear camera blocked from viewing the scene by its large mass.

"Get the fifty zeroed in on it," Bats said.

"Can't right now," Suge said. "It's too close. Plus, the guys are on the other side of it."

"Let's hold our fire. Alex, Will, Gerald—scatter," Meat called out. "Fall back, men. I don't want to start shooting unless we have to."

The Stegosaurs stood over twelve feet tall and nearly thirty feet long. Its head was small on a short neck, with short front legs that kept its head naturally low to the ground. Its rounded back had spade-shaped plates sticking out. As it continued toward Meat and the others, its stiffened tail, which loomed about the height of an average man above the ground, came into view—deadly looking spikes jutted from the end. Black perforated bands circled the orange colored skin.

As the dinosaur moved farther from the Mule, Coop and his crew watched the Redwater team back down the path.

Suge moved the .50 caliber with the remote control and pointed it at the dinosaur's body. "I can't see its head or chest. I can't shoot at it with the guys in the line of fire."

"Let's wait this out and hope it leaves without giving us any trouble." No sooner than the words had left Coop's mouth than the beast moved with uncanny speed—twisting its body sideways and slinging its tail at the men.

Meat and Caveman flattened to the ground as the meaty part of the tail whooshed above their heads.

Ron and Don weren't as fortunate. The spikes caught them waist high, and sent them careening into the jungle.

"It got Ron and Don!" Chief said. He pushed the door open and hit the ground running, his Seven at the ready.

Bats opened his door.

"See if you can find the twins," Coop said.

Bats left without saying a word.

"Get ready, Suge. If it gives an opening to the vitals, take a shot."

Meat and Caveman opened fire while lying flat to the ground. The suppressed shots mixed with the *bangs* of exploding bullets.

The Stegosaurs didn't like getting the business end of the rifle. It backed away and roared a defiant cry.

Chief had made it past the dinosaur and dropped to one knee. The JNY-7 came up, and he took aim—sending the RPG into its chest. The rocket exploded on target; the concussion hit the Mule like a solid object.

Flesh and red blood flew out like a meteor hitting mud. The Stegosaurus heaved in pain. Meat and Caveman continued to fire. Chunks of flesh and bone erupted from the dinosaur's head as exploding bullets whittled it away like a target in a shooting gallery.

One leg of the Stegosaurus buckled, sending it crashing on its side. Its tail rose and crashed to the ground—the deadly spikes missing the Mule by a few feet. What remained of its head listed over and thumped to the ground. It was dead.

Coop and the rest left the Mule. Susan ran by Chief and hugged his chest. Meat and Caveman were up and poking the Stegosaurus.

"Where's—" Coop began.

"Over here!" Alex called.

Everyone followed Alex's voice a few yards away and found him, Bats, Will, and Gerald all by Ron and Don's side. The twins' body were misshapen where it looked like their spines had been broken. The top halves of their bodies folded over at a weird angle. Gashes in their stomach and chest left gaping holes from the dinosaur's spikes.

Natasha gasped and started crying.

"My God..." Coop said, and heaved out a breath of air.

Meat lowered his head, sniffed, and cleared his throat.

Everyone remain silent for several moments.

Suge wiped his watery eyes. "You know, I used to get so tired of hearing *Roll Tide*. I never let them know I was a LSU Tigers fan. I didn't want them harassing me all the time. But man...I'd give *anything* if I could bring them back. I'd cherish every time they'd say it. I'd say *Roll Tide* along with them," his voice breaking at the end.

"They're gone," Susan said. "They're really gone this time."

The old reality was a harsh taskmaster. When you die, you're dead. Coop thought the finality of it all seemed such a shame. A person lives on this Earth for an infinitesimal amount time and then the light goes out as if it had never existed. What was the point of life in the first place? It now seemed to Coop that for life to have any purpose at all, there would have to be a chance of existence of some sorts when the body dies. He had never been a religious man, and he certainly didn't think he'd ever believe in some of the lamebrain things religious people adhered to. But if fate was kind enough to get him out of here alive, he would delve deeper into the spiritual side of life until he found truth.

"Dead is dead," Bats said as if he found some relief in the fact.

"What do we do with them?" Alex asked.

"We just can't leave them out in the open," Natasha said.

"Will and I both have folding shovels in our backpacks. We could bury them," Gerald said.

Coop looked over at Chief. The Redwater leader nodded.

"Make it quick. Night will be falling fast, and I want be out of the thick of things if possible," Coop said.

Gerald and Will dropped their backpacks and removed the shovels, stepping over to find a nearby gravesite.

"Everyone else be on the watch. At first sign of anything we leave," Coop said.

**

"There's a rock formation about a mile ahead. The satellite estimates show it to be about two hundred feet long and the highest point around forty feet," Suge said.

"I think I see it over there. Light's fading fast, but we'll be there in no time," Coop said. Everyone was aboard the Mule. The terrain still had a large number of trees but less jungle foliage. The area was hilly, though, so speed still had to be limited.

Coop had called in and reported the twins' deaths. Waterman sounded genuinely saddened. Coop was glad Lear hadn't been in on the conversation. Because if that man had asked one time about those goddamn diamonds, he was going to open the pouch and dump them on the ground. Waterman was a good man. Hell, most of Lear's employees were good people. That's what made Lear and Ace Corporation the success that they were. Henry Lear might be light on the humility side, but he'd admit it if you asked him that. The man had no illusions as to who and what he was. Coop had admired Lear for that and made certain exceptions for his harsh actions. Right now, Coop was in no mood to make excuses for anyone. In fact, if he made it out, things were going to be different. If nothing else, Patagonia had widened his worldview, and there were lots of wrongs in his life he needed to right.

"Uh, oh," Suge said. "Thermal camera shows something big over by the rocks."

"Stop the Mule, Coop," Chief said. "How big is it?"

"Let me zoom in…computer reads it at twelve feet tall and about twenty-five feet long. It's on two legs, so it's some type of badass theropod. Might be a T-rex."

"Why are we stopping?" Alex asked from the roof. "We're almost to the rocks, and it's getting so dark I can barely see."

"Dinosaur—big theropod," Coop said.

"Coop, let me take the driver's seat. The rest of you need to get out and wait. Suge and I will take care of the problem," Chief said. He put his hand out the window and tapped on the roof, and called out, "Everyone off the Mule."

Well, that is what Chief and the Redwater crew were best at— taking care of problems. Without any questions, Coop got out, and gave his seat over. The backseat emptied, and the Mule left the others to complete the mission.

Coop figured they were a half mile, away. They watched the Mule's headlights come to a stop. The fifty rattled off its ordnance. The Mule turned around and headed back to get them.

"That was quick," Coop said.

Caveman smacked his lips. "Hot damn! We's eating fresh meat tonight!"

CHAPTER 13

Patagonian nights made Coop feel like he was trapped in a cave. The cloud layer was so thick it filtered out all star and moon light. Surprisingly, he felt claustrophobic as he looked up into the open sky—as if a heavy hand weighed on his chest. He had felt more comfortable sleeping inside the Warthog in the beginning of the trip. Modern comforts had altered opinions which redefined *freedom.*

The pit in his stomach was from the result of losing two good men earlier, and the fear of who they might lose next. At least there was a chance for some of them to escape. Coop had forced himself to eat his MRE knowing that he would be a liability to himself and others if he didn't have the energy to keep thinking straight.

They had found a u-shaped indention in the rock formation. Chief had the Mule backed into position, so they were somewhat protected from the rear and sides.

Meat was in the passenger side of the vehicle, with the door open. He had his gaze glued to the thermal camera and hands ready to operate the fifty. The Mule's nuclear engine made little noise and provided him with cool air as he sat first watch.

The theropod they had killed turned out to be a Carnotaurus. Alex had pointed out some unique features of the dinosaur. It had a big roundish looking head on a thick neck. Horns jutted out right above its eyes. Whereas Coop had thought a T-rex's arms were short, they were NBA basketball players' length compared to the Carnotaurus. It had stood well over ten feet and was around twenty-five feet long. This dinosaur had scales and slick skin, showing no sign of feathers. As with any large theropod, it had massive jaws with teeth that looked like 20 penny sized cut-nails used to fasten wood flooring.

Caveman had a small fire going and roasted select parts of the animal. The meat cooking over wood smelled heavenly, but Coop had no desire to try any.

"Anybody want some?" Caveman asked, holding a strip of meat he had just carved from a tenderloin turning on a spit above the fire.

"Over here," Suge said. He caught the piece of meat Caveman had tossed his way. "Tastes pretty good," he said after taking a bite. "Needs some barbeque sauce—Sweet Baby Ray's."

"Anybody else?" Caveman asked after cutting off a piece and eating it. "Alex, you want to try a bite."

The Professor looked like he was about to let loose and caught himself. After a few moments of obvious internal conflict, he said, "Sure, why not."

Alex took the piece handed to him and brought it up to his nose. After an approving sniff, he nibbled on some. "Say, you know, this...this is actually good."

"I'm gonna make a hunter out of you yet," Caveman said, and hacked up his signature giggle.

That was a kind gesture for Alex to make, Coop thought. The earlier conflicts Alex and Caveman had over the dinosaur eggs early in the trip had put the two men at odds. If nothing else, Alex was still trying to make amends for his previous sins. So far though, time and lack of opportunity had kept Alex away from both Susan and Natasha.

"Hey, save me some," Meat said. "A big man's got room for more than one MRE can fill."

Chief and Susan had made a spot off to the side together. No one had sleeping bags, but at least the backpacks could be used for pillows.

Bats was off to the side keeping to himself. He had finished eating and was busy at his favorite pastime—sharpening his knife with a ceramic rod. There was a complex individual hiding within Bats' stone-like façade, Coop thought. Bats was *crazy like a fox* crazy; not an insane person who found killing as necessary as eating. Killing was a distraction from facing whatever demon he harbored inside. Killing gave him focus, then reward, then focus again—forever giving distraction from the real problem. Coop decided right then if they both made it out, he would try and spend some time with Bats and see if he could get the man to open up.

Gerald and Will made small talk with Suge and Natasha. Coop thought Gerald's lecherous stare toward Susan wouldn't go unnoticed and considered giving his old acquaintance a little advice before Chief bloodied his nose.

The fire crackled as Carnotaurus juices dripped on the glowing embers. When Coop looked at the burning wood, it transported him to different times in his life where he'd stare at the camp's fire. No matter where you were, when you watched a fire you were always *there*. The locations might as well have been all the same. The Congo in Africa, the jungles of Vietnam, the backyard of his parents' house. Watching a fire had the power to segregate him from the rest of the universe. He was alone within himself. Problems were outside of his walls. Right now he wished he could blink and find himself anywhere but here.

"Coop, you're not looking so good," Alex said.

Breaking from his reverie, Coop said, "Maybe not, but I look a lot better than Ron and Don right now." He realized he and Alex were out of earshot from the rest.

Alex dropped his gaze to the ground for a moment. "I figured losing two men had upset you. Coop, it wasn't your fault. You know that."

Yes, he did know it wasn't his fault. It didn't matter. He was in charge of this operation and was responsible to bring everyone back. Of course, he had failed miserably the first time around. And given this *third* chance, he had hoped to succeed. "You know, Alex, I faced a lot of adversity over the years. I could make hard, fast decision when pushed, and I had no problems living with the consequences. But something's happened to that man with the nerves of steel. I can feel it—in my inner core. I..." a sudden wave of emotion had him choking on his words. "I can't believe I'm even telling you this. It's not like me."

"We've been through a lot. You especially—carrying the weight of the expedition on your shoulders."

"It's not all on me. I have lots of help. I'm just getting...weak. Maybe I should put Chief in total control and just go along for the ride," the words poured out of him. He didn't recognize the man speaking.

"I don't think that's a good idea. People seeing you letting up a notch will plant a seed of uncertainty. We don't need any signs of weakness right now—if we can help it. You just need some rest. We're all tired—physically and emotionally. When tomorrow comes you'll have sounder perspective."

The Professor was over ten years his junior, and right now, sounded like his father giving him advice. He was tired—more so emotionally. In fact, he had never felt this way before in his life. "That's a good call, Alex. Thanks...I didn't mean to drop this on you. I didn't realize I felt this way until you came over to talk. I guess it was hiding inside looking for a door to exit."

"I volunteered to take next watch, but Meat pointed out I needed to learn how to use the remote on the fifty first. I offered to keep the next watch company, and Meat said he didn't think Bats would think too highly of that," Alex said.

"You know, we might be better off if we start letting people tell us how they feel, rather than letting others do it for them—to be fair to the person. When Bats starts his shift, ask him. You might be surprised with his answer. We all might be surprised with his answer."

***

Despite Coop's request to take last shift in the Mule, Caveman stopped Chief from waking Coop, and took his place. When Coop learned this, he realized his breakdown of sorts the night before wasn't a secret shared only between him and Alex. He doubted the Professor betrayed his confidence by telling others. Humans are creatures of the animal kingdom. Animals possess a certain ability to sense weakness. Caveman-John Jones was the most primitive man he had ever met. In fact, John had once said someone told him that humans contained a small percentage of Neanderthal DNA. After John heard that, he claimed to be the missing link between humans and Neanderthals, figuring his genetic ancestry had avoided major dilution of the weaker Homo Sapien species.

When Coop rose from bare earth under the orange-yellow glow illuminating the clouds in the east, every bone in his spine cried out in pain. As miserable as he felt, sleep had taken him down like a drug from the time his head hit the backpack pillow. He slept hard, so hard he didn't remember waking one time during the night. His dreams though had been unsettling. Coop found himself with a pile of metal parts on a table and an instruction manual. He opened the manual and began to read; the words were English, but he couldn't make sense of the instructions. Whole sentences seemed to be placed randomly fitting no logical pattern. Abandoning the manual, he spent the rest of the dream futilely trying to piece together the metal parts in hope to solve the mystery.

After stepping away to relieve himself, Coop saw that everyone was having breakfast and was dressed and packed to go. He guessed they were eager to get out of there, which was ironic in a way—knowing that they were about to put their lives on the line. But that was how life was. Fate deals the cards, and people play them to the best of their ability. Death was a possible outcome of any scenario. Might as well speed forward and face defeat or success.

"Did Waterman call?" Coop asked Chief as he stopped by his backpack and retrieved an MRE.

"No, we should touch bases with him before we leave. If there's been a major delay we might want to rethink leaving here," Chief said, and then finished his last bite of sausage. "This place," he swallowed and wiped his hand on the ground, "is well protected. We could hold our own here if we wanted to."

"True. What I'm afraid of is that dinosaur carcass over there is going to start stinking and attract scavengers. If we have to fight them off, we'll have less ammo for the rest of the trip. You know what to expect by the river." Coop opened his MRE and prepared his chili mac for heating, pouring the salt water from the packet into the plastic sleeve to start the chemical reaction.

"While my food is warming, I'll call." He fished his phone from the backpack, and made the call, making sure the speaker was on for everyone to hear.

"Hello, Mr. Cooper," Waterman answered.

"Hi. I'm pleased to report we had a good night. How's the roadwork coming along?" Coop asked.

"Better than expected. The operators are clearing the path in record time."

"Damn, I didn't expect that."

"Lear said he'd pay the operators double if they had it cleared in twenty-four hours."

"Lear knows how to inspire men."

Waterman chuckled. "You said last night you had over a hundred miles to cover. I doubt you can make that by sundown."

"No. I figure if we make sixty—eighty miles today, we'll be doing good. Problem is, we don't know how much we'll slow down once we make it to the river. We'll really have to be careful when we get there. Can't afford any mistakes."

"It would be great if you can make it that far. We figure the Warthog can leave here sometime after nightfall and be on the other side by morning. From there, they should be able to make the rendezvous point before night."

"Okay, sounds like a plan. Call if anything changes. We'll be pulling out in less than a half hour."

"Good luck, Mr. Cooper."

"Thanks, we'll need it." Cooper ended the call, put his phone away, and picked up his pack of chili mac.

"You *want* some meat?" Caveman asked. A roast size portion of Carnotaurus had gone uneaten from the night before, and the man had his fingers in it, stripping pieces away. Agitated, small insects clouded around the cooked flesh, unhappily disturbed from their current abode.

"John, I don't know if it's safe to eat that," Coop said.

"Hell, it ain't even green yet," Caveman said.

"You can have my share," Coop said, and dug his plastic spoon in the open bag of chili mac.

Natasha crunched her last strip of bacon. "You know, if we make it back—"

"*When*, we make it back," Suge interrupted. He had said the words with a confidence Coop was sure meant to give Natasha hope.

"Okay, *when* we get back, I'm going to have bacon with every meal for a month. Bacon sandwich, bacon and eggs, bacon wrapped shrimp, bacon ice cream, bacon wrapped bacon, bacon martinis—"

"I think we get the picture," Suge said and laughed. "Man, you sound like Bubba from *Forest Gump*."

"Was Forest Gump a movie or TV show? I don't think I've ever watched that," Natasha said. "Did he like bacon too?"

"No, he liked shrimp like you like bacon. I guess that movie came out before your time," Suge said, obviously noticing the fifteen years or so age difference between them.

Coop dug into his backpack and found only empty water bottles. He finished up the remainder of his breakfast and went by the Mule's water reservoir. Thank goodness the powers who brought them the Mule had filled the forty-gallon fresh water tank. There should be enough water for them to make it out before having to locate a natural source and use their water purifying pills to make it safe.

He filled his bottle and drank deeply. The cool water soothed his throat. The chili mac had contained a bit more black pepper than he would have preferred. "Gerald, Will, would you guys dig a hole so we can bury our trash?"

"Sure thing," Gerald called back. He and Will headed to find a suitable spot.

Chief walked up to him.

Susan remained off to herself and just gazed with blank eyes toward the ground.

"I think we're good. I pulled the guys off to the side earlier and gave them a pep-talk. Alex, Natasha, and Susan know their place. I don't think Prescott and Hawkins are going to be a problem, but I do want Hawkins to keep his distance from Susan," Chief said.

"I think Gerald will be too busy trying to stay alive than to bother Susan," Coop said.

"He better, or he won't stay alive long," Chief said. He turned around, and said, "Okay, we head out in ten. Get your shit together and stay alert. I don't care how big and mean those lizards are. We're going to come out of this alive."

As Alex walked by, Chief reached out and put a hand on his shoulder. "Alex, you've used rifles before, haven't you?"

"Sure. Mostly when I was younger, though. I used to hunt a lot."

"If I gave you Ron's Seven, would you be able to handle it?" Chief asked.

"I don't think I'd have any problems."

"Good. It's not a difficult weapon to use. The grenade launcher or RPG should be used as a last resort though," Chief said.

"I might need you to go over the basics again," Alex said.

"I'll do that," Caveman said as he stepped up by them. "Using a Seven is easier than buttonin' up your overalls."

"What about Don's rifle?" Alex asked. "Are you going to give it to Gerald or Will?"

"No," Chief said. "My trust has to be earned."

***

Coop had to remind himself to relax his shoulders and loosen his grip on the steering wheel enough to allow some color to return to his knuckles. He needed to react the moment danger would present itself and couldn't afford the luxury of letting his mind wander. The terrain was relatively flat, and though trees were numerous, the Mule kicked along near 20 mph. Meat rode the blade. Will and Gerald had the roof. Alex and Caveman stood on the back bumper.

Despite Coop's desire to rotate members out of the cab, he ultimately decided not to. Alex couldn't come in the cab—he'd have to sit next to Susan or Natasha. The last thing they needed was unnecessary tension and distraction. Meat or Caveman would make the seating too tight. Gerald and Will, well, the two men felt like outsiders, and Coop didn't want to give up Suge's or Chief's seat up to either of them.

Over the three hours, they had come across a variety of wildlife. Large amounts of pterosaurs of the smaller variety nested in trees. The Mule scattered them into the air as it passed by. Thank goodness none of the giant flying reptiles had swooped in for an attack. An aerial bombardment might take them by surprise. Alex and Caveman were supposed to keep an eye on the sky, but Coop knew how quickly things could change in the jungles of Patagonia.

There were all types of sauropods and theropods along the way. The Mule was such an oddity to them they treated it with curious looks or by slowly slinking out of eyesight. Coop had seen this phenomenon before when he and three others made the trip to the cave with the diamonds. The majority of dinosaurs didn't risk an encounter with the unknown. Coop also knew the cautious attitude was short lived. Humans and the Mule would become competition like any other animal the longer they stayed in Patagonia.

Coop had allowed Caveman to build a fire to cook the Carnotaurus because he knew fire would ward off curious predators. But if they stayed in one area, it wouldn't take long for dinosaurs to build up their courage enough to investigate the glowing flame.

Still, there always seemed to be one bad-ass who got its panties in a bunch over a track driven square hunk of metal filled with warm bags of flesh invading its territory. So far, Coop and company hadn't come across any dinosaur like that, until now.

"Fuck! It's a T-rex!" Coop yelled. The silver-gray colored theropod loomed directly ahead, with evil in its beady little eyes, and sharp teeth forming a wicked grin.

"Hit the brake! Everyone out. Suge and I will take care of this," Chief commanded.

Though seeing the T-rex had surprised him, Coop then realized the Mule was the one that surprised the dinosaur. He mashed in the Mule's horn, blaring a warning cry of a beast never heard before in Patagonia.

The T-rex raised its head and short arms in obvious alarm—a comical sight to behold.

Coop kept rolling the Mule at a steady speed toward it while engaging the horn.

As if its tail had caught fire, the theropod turned and ran out of sight, dodging trees, and crashing through branches.

"Son-of-a-bitch. You scared it," Suge said.

"That was risky," Chief said, disapproval in his tone.

"Yes it was," Coop said. "But I wanted a chance to try and scare it away. These creatures haven't seen man before or our inventions. They're afraid of the unknown—most anyway. I had a good feeling about this. It worked, we saved ammo, and we can continue without delay."

"Maybe you should let me drive," Chief said.

"I've thought about that, Chief. I'm sorry, but I can't do that. I'm still in charge of the mission, and I won't feel like I have control if I'm riding in the backseat. Not this time. You'll have to trust me. You all will just have to trust me."

"It's not about trust," Chief said.

"Everything is about trust. But I know where you're coming from. We're too much alike, Chief. It's better all the way around if we stick to our roles. It gives us the best chance of making it out of here alive."

CHAPTER 14

"Looks like Santos has got the feel for driving the Warthog. Who'd like to go next?" Ben asked as he sat in the Warthog's cab.

Santos left the driver's seat, wearing a proud smile.

Logan sat on one of the two long benches in the troop transport area as Ben gave the Brazilians' driving lessons. Matt went over details with Diaz and Alvarez on how to load the gun on the roof.

He had been unsettled the whole night long and could barely sleep. Who could blame him? Hell, he, Matt, and Ben had been brutalized mentally and physically by Henry Lear and the very same mercenaries who they now trained to operate the Warthog. Events had moved so fast from the time they had arrived at camp after escaping Patagonia, the last twenty-four hours seemed like a blur.

He couldn't just flip a switch in his mind and focus on the new mission and forget the turmoil of Lear's amusement and threats. Hearing the impossible news that Alex and the others killed in Patagonia were somehow alive opened another area of concern. Would Natasha remember him pushing her to her death? If so, how would he handle the situation? Say *I didn't mean to*? How fucking lame would that sound? Then what? Tell the others? He'd become a pariah and have to leave school. Matt would lose all respect for him. This was all one big mess.

The Warthog had been cleaned and loaded with a spare amount of supplies. This was a rescue mission, and there was no need for anything other than the basics. As for mechanical inspection of the ATTC, Ben was the most qualified. Ron and Don had trained him on what instruments to watch. There really wasn't much to do, though, other than drive the thing. The nuclear engine had no serviceable parts and had to be removed from the vehicle for any type of maintenance. There were enough safety trips built in that there was no danger of loss of radioactive containment. Ben had said the rubber treads on the tracks looked in good shape. If any of the treads had been damaged or missing there was a kit and instructions on how to replace them.

For this outing, the rear cabin had been uncoupled. Cramming the others in the troop carry area, if all survived the rescue, would be tight but manageable. Logan remembered Lear's threat: all the college crew had to return or none of them would be allowed to leave Patagonia alive. Was the man being truthful, or was this one of his eccentric mind games?

"For this trip, we're leaving the nonlethal projectiles behind. I've been told this is fifty caliber armor piercing ammunition. By itself it can punch a large hole. But this ammo has been modified to have explosive tips," Matt said to the Captain and Alvarez. He focused on Alvarez, and said, "Do you understand?"

Logan knew Matt was being patient with Alvarez. Of the six Brazilians, his English was the worse. Alvarez continued to look wide-eyed, nodding as if he understood.

"Not that I've seen the size hole a projectile can punch. We never used the Warthog's gun while we were out there. Never needed to. I think that won't be the case this time around," Matt said.

"The gun can be fired from on top of the roof or from the cab?" Captain Diaz said.

"Yes. Ben was trained by the Redwater team how to sight the gun in, fire manually and by using the remote. Ben showed me how to use it. The remote control is computer assisted, so it's easy to use. Captain Diaz, I think you should be trained along with one of your men."

"I will follow your suggestion," Diaz said. "How much ammunition are we carrying?"

"Nearly one hundred projectiles and around five tranquilizers. The tranquilizers are stored separately and aren't taking any room away from the lethal ammo, so I didn't remove it. Are you ready to go up and see how to fire it manually?" Matt asked.

"Yes, now would be a good time. Then you will show us how to use the remote," Diaz said.

Matt pointed to the four-step folding ladder hanging on a wall, and said to Alvarez, who was closest to it, "Can you go over there and get the ladder for us?"

Alvarez eagerly looked at the ladder and turned back to Matt, nodding his head with eyebrows held high.

Matt waited, and when Alvarez made no effort to get the ladder, Matt said, "The ladder, you get." He held his hands out and gripped open air.

The mercenary continued to smile and nod.

Diaz made no effort to step in and clarify the situation for his subordinate.

"You," Matt pointed again, "go," he pointed his index finger and middle finger toward the floor and moved them back and forth to indicate legs walking, "get," he grabbed empty air again with both hands, "the ladder." Bringing his thumb and forefinger together forming a circle, he said, "Okay?" Matt flipped his wrist back and forth a few times shaking the *okay* symbol at Alvarez.

The mercenary's pleasant, attentive expression melted into a scowl of indignation. He let a series of Portuguese profanities fly and shook his fist in Matt's face.

"Hey! Wha—" Matt stepped back. "Captain, call him off!"

Diaz bent over with laughter. The other mercenaries curiously looked over.

Matt had his hands by his shoulders with his palms pointing to the roof. "I don't know what I did, but I'm sorry."

The Captain finally composed himself, and said, "*Senhor*, Matt. You should have listened to *Senhor* Lear when he told you to learn some of the Brazilian customs. In our country, when you touch your thumb and forefinger together and shake it at another, you are calling that person an *asshole*." He turned to Alvarez. "*Ele não tinha a intenção de ofendê-lo. Em seu país, os dedos juntos significam bem.*"

Alvarez scrunched his forehead and nodded. He then shrugged his shoulders, and his eager smile returned.

"Thank goodness," Matt said. "We good?" Matt raised his right thumb in the air. As soon as he made the gesture, panic contorted his face, and he jerked both hands behind his back. "Wait! Was that bad? If it was, I didn't mean it."

Diaz chuckled. "No, *Senhor*. The thumb-up is a good sign."

Alvarez gave Matt a thumb-up in return.

"But I warn you, if you make that gesture in Iran, you might lose your hand," Diaz said.

"Guys, we really ought to get finished with the training. We'll be heading off sometime tonight, and we all need to rest before we go," Ben said.

Logan was glad Ben was there. The man had a sound head on his shoulders. He wished he could talk to Ben about his…predicament. Kind words from a friend, if he got them, would only ease his mind for a bit though. Whatever the future would bring, he would have to face it alone. He'd just have to own up to it and live with the consequences for the rest of his life.

***

The Mule rolled through the jungle, snaking its way between trees, and avoiding dinosaurs in the distance. This was the first time Coop had seen sauropods in the wild. The video the drone took by Lear's River didn't do the animals justice. The beasts were huge! They were so slow, at first sighting of a Brachiosaurus, he thought it was a statue. The damn thing looked like a mountain with a long neck and tail. And as far as fear of the Mule passing through its home, no fucks were given. Which was more than fine by Coop. As bad-ass as the Mule's fifty was, he figured taking one Brachiosaurus down would use most, if not all, of the ammo.

No one shared small talk inside the cab—too busy watching out the windows. Everyone but Susan. She had her cheek implanted to Chief's left arm and her eyes closed. This was a bad sign. Because if things got hot, and they would have to leave the Mule, she might become a liability. To make matters worse, she'd distract Chief from his duties. Chief was perhaps the most important person on this excursion, having him less than 100% might mean doom for them all.

A hand slapped wildly on the roof.

"Stop the Mule! Stop the Mule!" Gerald cried.

Coop hit the brake, glancing at the rear camera as they came to a stop. Caveman and Alex had jumped off the bumper and had their rifles up at the ready. A medium sized theropod bounded toward them.

"Something's attacking from the rear," Suge said. "Get off the roof so I can swing the gun around," he yelled.

Gerald and Will bailed off onto the ground, and the fifty swung into position.

Alex and Caveman fired their JNY-7s. The suppressed *pep-peps* made the weapons sound like an air rifle at a carnival, but when the bullets found the target, in this case the chest of a charging theropod, the exploding bullets announced its deadly power.

Gaping holes appeared on its pale white chest between and below the theropod's short arms. Its cry contained pain and surprise, surely to inspire primordial rage. Flesh and blood fireworks erupted from its chest. In no time it reached its two attackers, forcing Alex and Caveman to roll to the side on the ground.

"Do you want me to take the shot?" Suge cried out.

"Hold it!" Chief said.

The theropod stumbled as it ran past its two intended prey and fell flat to the earth, landing a few yards from the Mule's rear. Will and Gerald stood their positions by the side of the vehicle—their 9mm pistols aimed at the head.

Caveman was first off the ground and approached the dinosaur. Alex followed closely behind. Everyone in the Mule spilled out with weapons at the ready. Meat hopped off the blade.

"I think it's dead," Will said. He stepped cautiously toward it and gave it a quick kick to the head.

This was another dinosaur Coop hadn't seen before. This theropod was of a plainer variety, with brownish skin without any distinguishing marking. The color reminded him of an ordinary deer. It looked to be around twelve feet in length and upright might have been as tall as a man. Coop thought some theropods—like this one—looked off balanced. It surprised him how fast they could run. The legs seemed too far back as they leaned chest forward with their short arms hanging down. The head on this thing was round at the top and looked like a dome skullcap. It had large round eyes and rows of short spikes on the bridge of its snout. More spikes jutted from the back of its head. In a strange way, its face looked armadillo-ish, although he knew the two creatures weren't alike in any way.

"Good shooting, guys," Chief said.

"Weren't nothin'," Caveman said.

"It's a Pachycephalosaurus, I think," Alex said.

"I'm not even going to try to pronounce that," Meat said.

"I wonder what made it chase us? Why wasn't it scared like most of the other dinosaurs?" Natasha said.

"Because it's an *animal*," Caveman said. "Animals know fight or flight. We pissed this boy off for some reason, and he wanted a piece of that ass."

"We know nothing about dinosaurs. This species may be more aggressive than most. Size doesn't matter. I'm sure all of you have seen small dogs act as big as Great Danes," Alex said.

"I'm glad that was over quickly. We need to get out of here in case this guy has any friends," Coop said.

"Okay, everyone. Load up, and let's head out," Chief said.

*

Fate, fortune, whatever, had kept the eleven survivors alive in the wilds of savage Patagonia for the past nine hours. There was still more than an hour of light left. On one hand, Coop wanted to travel as much distance as he could before night. On the other hand, he knew dinosaur activity increased by the river. The smart thing might be to find a suitable spot for the night to make camp now. If they went too deep and found themselves in a den of dinosaurs while under darkness, there might be no chance of escape.

The odometer told him that they had traveled one hundred and ten miles for the day—a distance far greater than he had hoped to achieve. He was able to accomplish this by maximizing speed in the open, flat areas. Traveling 20 mph for fifteen minutes chewed up as much distance as 5 mph did in sixty minutes. They were traveling in an open area now, but the GPS imposed over the satellite map showed the area would soon turn to jungle and stay that way for the twenty-five miles or so journey to Lear's River. Coops eyes confirmed they'd be at the jungle line in a few minutes.

"We're making good time. I want to set up camp while it's still daylight. No need to push our luck," Coop said.

"Luck..." Susan said. "I've been thinking about our situation the whole day. On one hand we *do* seem incredibly lucky."

"Ron and Don don't feel so lucky," Bats said.

Susan turned with a narrow gaze Bats' way. "I'm making a point. I know the brothers were killed. We all know that. But I can't believe we haven't faced any more danger than what we have so far. Are we just lucky? Something returned us to life two different times. Maybe the same people responsible are watching out for us now."

"What did they have against Ron and Don?" Bats said sarcastically.

"I don't know. I would gladly trade you in for them," Susan's words seethed with contempt.

"Maybe it's true the good die first," Natasha said. "Maybe they're the lucky ones. They died in an instant…we might not be so…lucky."

"And maybe God's and Auburn Tigers football fan and was tired of hearing *Roll Tide*," Bats said.

Coop saw Chief's face redden as Bats instigated conflict. Before Chief upped the ante, he said, "Bats! Enough. Conflict is a distraction. We can't let our guard down now."

Fortunately, if anyone else had anything to add they kept it to themselves. The silence between them grew into a barrier pushing them farther apart. A situation just as harmful as out and out bickering.

"Everyone," Coop said. "We're tired, and the tension in this situation is eating us up from the inside. I'm sure Susan just wanted to talk some things out, and I know some of you probably would be better off if you didn't have to hear it. People are all different. We deal with things in our own way. Please try to be more understanding." Coop stopped as he felt a lump start to grow in his throat. It was happening again. This emotion welling inside threatening to boil out and turn him into a blubbering idiot. That's the last thing that needed to happen right now. He needed to lead, and he could only do that by sound, confident words. "So look, let's all take a deep breath, and make a special effort to be tolerant of one another. Let's not take out our frustrations on each other. We'll be setting up camp soon. We'll get something to eat and get some rest. With any," he hesitated, and said, "*luck*, we'll meet up with the Warthog some time tomorrow."

"Seems like our fate is always decided by luck. We're lucky if we live, but if we're killed quickly, we're lucky that we died. Luck brings both good and bad, and sometimes when luck is bad, it's good. I guess luck is the real God that controls our future," Bats said.

Coop thought it was funny how at times it seemed random events controlled the future, and at other times it seemed an omnipotent being moved the pieces. But then the arguments could be made from hindsight that the random events were specific moves by God, and that the *miracles* that seemed to come by the hand of God, could be attributed to random events. Fate? Who or what was fate? Random acts or intentional moves? Why were Coop and his companions still alive? Why were Ron and Don returned to life only to die again a final time?

"What the...Coop!" Suge said in surprise.

Less than a hundred yards away a herd of Triceratops poured from the thick of the jungle.

"They're heading right for us!" Natasha cried.

Even from that distance, the ceratopsids looked as big as school buses. They ran with incredible speed and agility for something that large. The bulls were pale green in color and the cows a dull brown—the same variety as they encountered on the way to the cave to find the diamonds. Coop wasn't sure of the number, but the line stretched out heading his way was so wide that he couldn't turn right or left and hope to outrun them. They'd be trampled before reaching safety.

Hoping that luck was still his co-pilot, he hit the Mule's horn, and pressed the accelerator.

Riding the blade, Meat popped his head up and looked at Coop, his eyes as wide as saucers. "Hey! Hey! Turnaround!"

"Coop..." Chief said, sounding like it was a threat.

"This is the best chance we have of all making it out," Coop said, sitting higher in his seat.

"Or all fucking dying!" Bats yelled.

This was it. Coop had committed his life and the others, and there was no turning back. Unfortunately, so far the Triceratops heading straight for them remained undeterred from their path. He let off of the horn and then pumped it, sending out pulses of warning. He had a burning urge to shout *Yah mule!*, but this wasn't a Western movie, and he wasn't a cowboy.

"Motherfucker! They're going to hit!" Meat yelled and disappeared from sight, flatting himself against the blade.

Susan gasped, and Coop felt everyone brace for impact.

At the last possible second two bulls in front of the blade parted, narrowly missing contact, and charged past the Mule on either side. Up ahead, the rest of the herd followed the lead and split, opening a clear space for them to drive through.

"Son-of-a-bitch…would you look at that," Suge said.

The back of Meat's head rose above the side of the convex-shaped blade. The Samoan turned around, wearing a large smile across his face, and pumped a fist in victory.

Chief breathed out a sigh of relief.

Coop loosened the muscles in his back and lowered his shoulders. He had been holding his breath, and he had just now realized it. His mouth fell open, and he breathed slowly in and out. They were entering the jungle, so he slowed the Mule to a safer speed.

"Good grief…there must have been fifty of them," Natasha said. She had sat up in her seat and turned around, looking out the window.

Coop wiped the inside corners of his eyes with his fingers, cleaning out bits of gunk. When he removed his hand from his face, a Spinosaurus appeared directly in his path. This was the reason the Triceratops herd fled for their lives. He gasped in surprise, and before he could hit the brake, something crashed into the driver's side of the Mule.

Will Prescott fell off the passenger's side of the roof and landed on the track as it turned pulling the Mule forward. The track moved him like groceries on a conveyor belt and carried him to the front—where he fell to the ground and met his death as the Mule's tracks rolled over him—crushing him like a grape.

Coop mashed the brake and the horn—inertia carried Meat's large frame forward, throwing him between the Mule and the sail-backed dinosaur.

He turned to see what had hit them. A second Spinosaurus loomed above as Coop looked out his window. The creature had a massive head, and its jaws were tightly clamped around Gerald Hawkins' midsection. Deep crimson spilled to the earth as the spike-like teeth dug deeply.

Gerald's scream assaulted Coop—he felt like glass shattered down the length of his spine. Seeing the massive beast devour another human exhumed memories of Coop's own death by the cave.

Suge hadn't waited for orders, and the fifty burst to life, throwing out massive amounts of jacketed lead into the Spinosaurus in front of them before it attacked. "Die, you motherfucker!"

Yells and discharging ordnance laced with the Spinosaurus' cries of pain electrified the air, gluing Coop to his seat.

Chief and Bats acted instinctually, and both bailed out the back seat with rifles in hand.

Meat was up and off the ground as fast as he could gain his footing. But even though the fifty punched holes in the Spinosaurus, its ire overcame whatever damage was being done to it, and lurched its crocodile-like head forward.

Suge let off the trigger as Meat's head and upper body disappeared in the dinosaur's mouth.

Coop watched Suge's eyes glaze over as if the mercenary fought to deny what he knew to be true.

The Spinosaurus thrashed its head about, and part of Meat's lower torso and legs flew off to the side.

Suge blinked his eyes twice, and the fifty fired again. The dinosaur's head exploded like a melon hit with a sledgehammer. What was left of the Spinosaurus collapsed to the ground.

Before Suge could swing the gun around to the other dinosaur, the theropod had finished with Gerald and attacked the noisy mechanism on the roof. The Spinosaurus grabbed the machine gun in its jaws and ripped it from its mount.

It wasn't until then that Coop heard the suppressed fire from the JNY-7s. The rear camera showed Caveman, Alex, Bats, and Chief in firing positions and rattling off ammo.

Coop saw Alex run to the side—was he turning cowardly and running for his life? Then Alex stopped, dropped to one knee, and took careful aim. The RPG launched from his JNY-7.

The rocket propelled grenade struck the Spinosaurus on its right leg—blowing it off, and leaving a bloody stump. The animal slung out a guttural hiss and collapsed, thrashing around on its side.

"Watch the tail!" Chief yelled. He aimed carefully and launched his RPG.

The grenade struck the Spinosaurus right under its bottom jaw—blowing it completely off and disfiguring the head.

The grenades going off so close rattled the Mule twice. A dull ringing filled Coop's ears, and he imagined the others were in the same shape.

Susan had her face buried in the backseat and had her hands over her head.

Suge opened his door and got out; Natasha followed.

Coop's still felt lightheaded—overwhelmed by the situation. Everything had happened so fast, and it was like his mind had problems processing it. He realized he was getting too old for this game. No matter how much effort he put into it, there was no way for him to *will* himself to become the man he was at an earlier age. There was nothing good about getting old.

He looked back at Susan and decided she'd have to deal with her problems on her own. He opened the driver's side door and got out. The others looked toward him as if waiting for instruction. Right now there was only one important goal—to get as many as possible to safety and meet up with the Warthog. Coop would just have to play his role the best he could. Someone else had dealt the cards; it was up to him how to play his hand.

"Is everyone okay?" Coop asked.

"We're alive," Chief said.

Coop had seen Gerald's and Meat's death, but he realized he hadn't checked to see if Will had somehow survived. "Did anyone see if Will—"

"I stepped on him when I jumped off the track. He was flatter than a doormat," Bats said.

"That's unfortunate. The whole situation is fucked up," Coop said. "Some good men died today."

Natasha had tears rolling down her cheeks and struggled to keep herself together. "Poor Clint."

"I'm gonna miss that big Samoan," Caveman said.

"We all will," Coop said. "Guys, I don't want to sound insensitive, but it'll be dark soon. We need to set camp."

"And the bodies?" Chief asked.

"We leave them where they are. See that over there," Coop said and pointed. "That's the lower half of Clint Perry's body. Clint Perry is gone. I don't remember Clint Perry being half a man. Clint will live in our memories from now on. He'll be whole again. He's part of us now, and we'll keep him alive in our thoughts until we die. I knew Hawkins better than any of you. His body is just a chewed up mess over there—but that's not Gerald. And Will—I don't even want to look at what happened to that poor man. He's gone. We're alive, and we need to do what's best for us to stay that way."

"What are we waiting for then?" Bats said.

Coop pointed to the fifty laying on the ground. Suge had knelt by it and was giving it a once-over. "Do you think we can fix the gun?"

"I don't think so," Suge said. "The mount's twisted, and the bolts are broken. We don't have any spare parts to make repairs. The gun still works, but regardless of what you've seen in the movies, it's impossible for a man to hold this thing and shoot and hit a target."

"As much as I'd like to still have it, at some point we're going to have to abandon the Mule and travel on foot anyway. At least it got us this far," Coop said. He licked his lips, and said, "Time to go."

"Alex, you or Caveman want to take my place in the Mule? I can ride the bumper for a while," Chief said.

Coop hesitated before jumping in and killing the offer. He didn't want to become a dictator, but he didn't want Susan sitting next to Alex. She had been in bad condition when he left her in the Mule, and figured she'd need support from Chief, not her ex-husband and killer.

"I'm good," Alex said.

"We ain't got long before we set camp. Plus, my ass takes up a lotta room. It'd be like four people riding in the back," Caveman said.

"Okay then, let's head out," Coop said. He looked one last time and the horrific theropods—memories of being eaten alive weakened his knees.

CHAPTER 15

The survivors had to settle for the protection of a fault escarpment to one side of the Mule. The earth wall wasn't much taller than the vehicle, which meant a constant fear that some long neck dinosaur might sneak up on them and play claw machine—with humans as the prize. Still, their rear was protected, and they could hide in and behind the Mule if something approached from the ground.

Coop thought that whatever inner fortitude the others had built the previous night had weakened greatly. There was less talking to one another—everyone caught up in their own thoughts. Even Caveman was quiet, and as aggravating as the large man could be, Coop missed his ridiculous banter.

There would be no fire tonight. Dinner would be MREs heated in their pouches and washed down with cool water from the Mule's reservoir. Coop had noticed that unlike the night before, where the others had carved out personal spaces, they now hung out in a loose cluster—even Bats. Today's tragedy had brought them with a need to be physically closer—consciously or not. So be it. Drawing closer would only increase their chances of survival.

Coop had already made the report to Waterman. Actually saying the words that Clint and the other two were killed was more of a challenge that he had imagined, but he was able to push his way through it.

Progress clearing the path between the mountains was ahead of schedule. Waterman believed the Warthog and nine-member crew would set off on the mission before midnight. With any *luck*, the Warthog should be inside of the lost world of Patagonia shortly after sunrise. If there was one word Coop hoped to remove from his vocabulary, it would be *luck*. If he survived this mess, he was going to make an effort to avoid using it ever again.

Coop opened his backpack and pulled out an MRE. The others were in one stage of preparing their own, with the exception of Caveman, who was eating. He had his spork deep in the pouch, and his mouth was chewing away. Another entrée pouch set next to him, steaming puffing out the cut end.

"John, what's for dinner?" Coop asked.

"Hog jowls and speckled butterbeans. Stewed squirrel in red gravy. Fried chicken and mustard greens. Big ole cathead biscuits with fig preserves." Caveman smacked his lips and wiped his mouth with the back of his hand.

"Really." Coop chuckled, and a few of the others did too. "I didn't have anything like that to choose from. Looks like I'm stuck with Salisbury steak."

"Yeah, I ain't got none of that either. I was just thinkin', if I was ahavin' my last meal, what I would get."

Coop sat next to Caveman and begin preparing his meal. "Do you think this is your last meal?" Instead of avoiding the 800-pound gorilla in the room, Coop thought it best if people did open up and express their fears.

"Don't know. I try not to think too far ahead with things. All I know is when I go out to face the enemy, its him or me. I take things one step at a time until I reach the end. Tomorrow ain't gonna be any different. But I'll say this, if I am takin' a dirt nap, I'll at least have a full belly."

"I wonder if they have soul food in Heaven," Suge said.

"Don't know, but I hope they have Jack Daniel's in Hell," Bats said.

The mood quieted as others begin to eat. Coop said as his MRE heated, "I'll take first watch. I've got the rear camera set up to keep a lookout overhead. After we eat, I'd like everyone to settle down and rest. Tomorrow is a big day—a moment of truth. We need to be at the top of our game to make it."

***

The Warthog traveled across the fissure cut through the mountains during the night. The headlights only illuminated a little more than three hundred feet ahead, but the low-level radar had Matt confident that nothing blocking the path would take them by surprise—unless, of course, there was another earthquake. That was something he didn't want to think about. If they did rescue Alex and his crew, they would still have to chance the ride back through. Wouldn't it be tragic to come so far only to be snuffed out on the way back? Again, it served no purpose to worry about such. He began to realize his situation was no different from those who took chances to do great things—like astronauts. Risking life heading into the great unknown, trusting men and technology for safety. Men and women like those were heroes. Matt wasn't a hero. He was making this trip to save his own life, not just the lives of others.

Ben had the wheel all night. Santos rode co-pilot with Diaz sitting to his left. The Captain was fascinated with the instruments, asking questions about the radar, and manipulating the thermal cameras.

The other four mercenaries sat on the floor and played a card game they called *Trucko*. The game was played only using certain cards, and score was kept by the number of *tentos* won. *Tentos* were seeds that looked a lot like dried black-eyed peas. The *pot* started with twenty-two seeds, but the first team (four people played, two to each team) to win twelve *tentos* won.

Logan was curious enough to watch, and occasionally Gomes would explain parts of the game.

Matt was too distracted to really give a damn. He was more curious about the Brazilian soldiers on the mission. Who were these people? They acted more like robots—following orders seemed to be their only concern. Seeing them play cards showed him a softer side he hadn't seen before; after all, Rodrigues had shoved the end of a rifle's barrel in his face two days ago. The next day the mercenary acted as if nothing life threatening had happened and treated Matt and the rest cordially. In fact, outside of Lear's mistreatment of them on arrival, the Brazilians proved to be polite—especially Diaz, their leader.

The team of Barbosa and Alvarez rambled off something in Portuguese, and team Gomes and Rodrigues fired back in loud voices.

Matt looked over at Logan, who shrugged his shoulders.

Gomes pulled himself from the fray, and said, "They are trying to raise the stakes. Don't worry, it's part of the game."

Grown men arguing over a game without money being a factor. There was some innocent beauty in that, Matt thought.

"We're almost out," Ben said.

Matt had been so wrapped up in his own thoughts, he realized he had lost track of time. The glow of day had emerged to where the headlights served no purpose. He walked up to the cab's open door and looked over Diaz's shoulder. "We made it. We really made it."

"Our job is just beginning," Diaz said. "We must be prepared for the worst."

Yep, it was all business all the time with the Captain. Matt couldn't blame him; the mercenaries were hired to do a job, and he was the commander.

The Warthog's tracks soon found purchase on flat land. The mountains now behind them slowly shrank in the distance.

"I'm going to stop for a break," Ben said.

"Now would be a good time to call Coop," Matt said. "Waterman gave us permission to speak directly with the others once we crossed over. Captain Diaz, can I make the call?"

"*Sim, Senhor* Matt," Diaz said. "I will connect your phone with the Warthog so we all can hear."

No conversation over an Ace Corporation phone was private anyway. Having everyone listening wouldn't matter.

Logan walked up behind him, and the four mercenaries had ended the card game and were ready for the next command.

Matt hit the fast-dial icon on his phone, it rang, and someone answered:

"This is Cooper."

"Coop, it's Matt. We made it."

"That's a relief to hear. You can imagine all the wild thoughts we had last night. Sometimes the *what-ifs* are more distracting than the dangers at hand."

"I trust you had a good night, then."

"We did. We're finishing up breakfast…waiting for your call."

"I'm—we were all sorry to hear about Ron and Don, Meat, and the others. We wanted everyone to come back. But I know what it's like out there."

"Yeah, it's bad. Just when you think you're in the clear all hell can break loose."

"For us the rendezvous is a little over two hundred miles away. According to the map, we can be there in five or six hours. There's two miles of thick jungle between the river and our location. You'll have to cross that on foot."

"We understand. At best we can be at the river in four hours. But if we have to abandon the Mule, it's going to take longer."

Diaz pressed a button on the communication system. "This is Diaz. It doesn't matter how long it takes you to reach us, *Senhor* Cooper. We will be safe in the Warthog waiting for you. You will contact us when you reach the river. We will provide assistance in getting you out safely."

"Thank you, Captain. We know the risks you and your men are taking, and we're all grateful," Coop said.

"My reward will be in bringing you all back and handing *Senhor* Lear the diamonds," Diaz said.

The phone went silent for an uncomfortably long time. "Diamonds? Oh, a T-rex ate the diamonds," Coop said.

Diaz stood, and shouted, "What?"

Coop giggled. "I was joking with you, Captain Diaz. I've got Lear's goddamn diamonds. In fact, I'd like nothing better than to take them and sho—" Coop's voice trailed away.

"Hello? This is, Chief. Coop had to leave to get the Mule ready to go."

"Hey, Chief," Matt said, realizing some of Coop's pent-up emotions were about to impede the mission. "We'll probably break here for another ten minutes and then be on our way."

"Trust me, we'll be glad to see you," Chief said.

"I'm praying for the best. Bye." Matt cleared his throat as his words started to stick. This was it. A defining moment in his life. The stakes were high, and it was all or nothing. Saving Alex and the others would be the first step toward his redemption.

***

"What the hell, Coop?" Chief said.

"I'm sorry, but every time I think of that son-of-a-bitch Lear I start to lose it," Coop said.

"We don't know anything about these mercenaries. If Diaz thinks you're making threats against his employer, you might not make it back alive even if you make it to the Warthog. Some mercenaries respect their employers as much as their own fathers. He could kill you after taking the diamonds."

"All right, I'll put a lid on it," Coop said, knowing Chief was right. Mouthing off to someone about Lear was a childish thing to do anyway. If Coop had a problem with Lear, he would take it up with the man face-to-face. That thought alone had him wanting to make it out alive, to settle a score with his *old friend*.

"Everyone, let's load up and head out," Chief commanded.

"Alex, I'm riding the bumper. You take my seat inside the Mule," Bats said.

"That's okay. My legs are sore—I'm not as in good of shape as you guys, but I'll make it," Alex said.

"I wasn't asking you. I was telling you," Bats said.

Chief was about to get involved, but Coop stepped in front of him. "Bats, what's this about? Why do you want to ride the bumper?"

"Look, Alex has proved he can handle a rifle. But he's not trained like we are. I don't give a goddamn about who sits next to who anymore. Get the fuck over it. I need to be ready for action—not trapped inside the Mule when the shit hits the fan. Caveman and I can hit the ground at the drop of a hat and draw first blood. We need every advantage we can get," Bats said.

There was nothing Bats said that didn't make sense. Coop turned to Susan, who looked over at Alex with contempt in her eyes.

"Alex doesn't concern me. He can sit anywhere he likes," Susan said.

Coop looked at Natasha.

"He's nobody to me, whatever," Natasha said.

The dejection on Alex's face had Coop glad the Professor wasn't holding a knife. He looked like a man who would cut his wrists.

CHAPTER 16

Maneuvering the Mule through the thick jungle took them on a path that was anything but straight. The satellite map had lost its usefulness; the detail far too coarse to plot the most efficient route. With the trees and other obstacles so close together, the GPS and low-level radar showed them as blobs on the computer screen.

Coop had to keep his eyes in front and depended on Suge to direct him to keep the Mule from veering away too far away from the rendezvous point. Dense brush and large leafy plants didn't help matters any. Although Coop figured the foliage kept them from being seen by predators as much as it hindered his view from seeing them. On more than one occasion his mind played tricks on him. A banana plant-like leaf poked past a tree as they rode by. At first he thought it was a T-rex coming in for the kill. Another time the Mule rolled over a fallen branch, and it somehow twisted underneath the tracks and a portion of it sprang up and hit his window. At the sound, he turned and thought he saw the deadly jaws and teeth of the Spinosaurus that took his life the first time.

They had seen their share of real dinosaurs, though. And motherfucking-*luck* had kept them safe so far. Small to man-sized theropods had fled whenever they drove through. A small group of Stegosauri simply stared at them, like cows looking at a new gate. The most frightening moment came when a large theropod—one of T-rex's cousins—Coop didn't know all of their names—and Alex didn't bother to comment on it, froze in position as they rode by. Coop turned his head and saw it just as they passed. The dinosaur was less than thirty feet away and stood as still as a statue, its head turned to the side as if it thought *if I'm not looking at you, you can't see me*. Of course, it did have one of its beady eyes focused on them. At that point there was really nothing Coop could do but continue without doing something stupid that would call more attention. He found himself holding his breath like he was walking past a hornet's nest until the theropod was out of sight.

Even though the Mule was air-conditioned with the interior at a pleasant 70 °F, the small of Coop's back was wet with sweat. His head moved like it was on a swivel, turning from side to side on constant watch and path plotting. Sometimes he stretched his neck forward as if he'd be able to see behind the trees.

"Coop, we're getting too far off course," Suge said.

"I know. But what do you want me to do? We've been at this for almost five hours, and God only knows how far out of the way we'll have to travel before we make it to the river," Coop said.

"Just looking at the map we're only three miles as a crow flies from the rendezvous point. You keep going this way we're going to have to double back three times that distance. What happens if we get too far away and have to abandon the Mule?" Suge asked.

"What are you suggesting?" Chief asked.

Suge scratched the back of his neck. "It seems to me at this point—being so close—we stop here and head out on foot. It's a three-mile hike from here. We might be able to make the river in an hour."

Coop let up on the accelerator and let the Mule come to a stop. He had been so focused on the objective, he had abandoned any further strategy—strategy that might save all of their lives. "Chief? What do you think?"

"I hate to expose ourselves any sooner than we have to. But Suge's got a good point."

"Don't get me wrong, it's been great riding in the Mule. But I'm afraid of being trapped in here in a surprise attack. A huge theropod might be able to crush the roof down on us. We'll all die. At least outside we have a chance to scatter. It's a morbid thought, but at least some will have a chance to live," Alex said.

"Back at the cave, a Spinosaurus had enough power in its tail to knock the Mule on its side," Coop said. "Without the fifty, the Mule becomes a liability in a fight."

"Susan, Natasha, are you ready for this?" Chief asked.

"I don't know if I'd ever say I'd be ready, but now is as good a time as any," Natasha said.

"I know we have to do this, and I know what might happen," Susan said. She took a deep breath. "I'm going to do my best not to get in the way."

"Okay then, let's go," Coop said. He killed the engine and opened his door, stepped onto the track, and hopped down to the ground. "Alex, start handing out the backpacks and rifles from behind the seat. I want to do an inventory before we leave." He checked his charge on his satellite phone. It was at one hundred percent. He called up the Map and GPS. The Warthog's beacon showed it minutes from the rendezvous point. Thank goodness for that.

"Here you go, Coop," Natasha said while handing him his backpack. The young woman was taking the equipment from Alex and distributing it. "And here's," she paused as Alex handed her a JNY-7, "your rifle."

Coop looked his rifle over. His gun was fully loaded and ready to go. He hadn't been in any position so far on this trip to use it.

Everyone gathered in front of Coop.

"Okay, there're eight of us and eight rifles. Looks like we've used three RPGs so far," Coop said.

"Yeah. I used mine and one from Ron's gun. Alex used his," Chief said.

"You can use Don's RPG. Alex, you'll have to do without," Coop said.

"Not a problem," Alex said.

"I'd love to bring all eight rifles, but I'm afraid they'd only slow Natasha and Susan down. Agreed?" Coop said.

"I could carry one across my back," Suge said.

"Me too," Caveman said.

"Guys, if we didn't have such a short distance to travel, I'd say go ahead. I think we'll be better off traveling lighter. We'll bring the ammunition, of course, but we'll leave the Sevens here," Coop said. "Okay, get some water in you, and make sure you have two bottles of water in your backpack. We have no idea how long it's going to take to reach the river."

***

Ben pushed the Warthog to maximum speed dictated by the terrain. The ATTC passed towering palms and flat grassy land along the way.

The Brazilian's *oohed* and *aahed* at a herd of Gallimimus running from the metal monster streaking through their land. A giant pterosaur or two, it was impossible to tell if it was the same one, dove in front of them on two occasions. Matt wasn't sure what the flying reptile had in mind. The Warthog was bigger than it. From what he knew of pterosaurs, they normally hunted much smaller animals. Must have been a territorial thing.

Ben only slowed to a stop once, at the request of Diaz. The Captain was totally captivated when they came upon a large sauropod. Matt thought it was a magnificent sight to behold, too. The beast's neck looked as long as its body and tail combined. Its skin was a beautiful green, and it had a creamy orange underbelly. If it knew the Warthog was there, it didn't show it. The dinosaur's only concern was munching on leaves from a tall tree.

"Trouble up ahead," Ben said.

Matt felt the Warthog slow. He looked out the window, and in the distance a T-rex slowly approached. "Can you go around it?"

"I can try, but I can't vary the path too much—jungle's too thick," Ben said. He veered to the left and sped on.

"There is another one joining it…and another!" Diaz said.

"Crap, if we keep going in this direction, we're going to run into a wall of trees." Logan had stepped up to see what was going on.

"Yeah, and the three T-rexes will pin us in," Matt said.

"The dinosaurs are coming for us. They are forcing us to fight," Diaz said. The Captain sat high in his seat and stiffened his back. "I'm am ready for the challenge."

Matt felt safe inside the Warthog. He didn't know, though, how much damage it would sustain from an attack by three massive theropods. With human lives on the line, it wasn't worth taking any chances. "Ben?"

"I'm going to stop here. Let them come to us. Maybe if we kill one, the other two will leave. I don't want any more to die than necessary."

"Maybe if we just fired a warning shot, then—" Logan cut his words as the Warthog's gun fired.

The lead Rex was at least fifty yards away. The projectile hit it in the right side of its chest and blew off its arm and part of its side. A sharp cry followed the boom of the explosion. The charging theropod listed to one side and fought to stay on its feet.

The two other T-rexes increased speed—their large, clawed feet pounding the earth to where Matt thought he could feel the vibrations.

"*Meu Deus*," Santos said softly.

"Captain?" Ben said, urgency in his voice.

Diaz sighted the next beast on the computer and fired. The projectile missed.

"Do you want me to—" Ben started.

"No!" Diaz fired again.

The blast sounded much louder now that the target was closer. This time Diaz hit the dinosaur square in the chest. He must have found its heart, because it dropped like a ragdoll. The earth shook, and it tumbled and slid face-first, shoving up dirt before it.

Matt couldn't see the wounded Rex but had no problem seeing the third of the bunch arrive at the Warthog. It threw its head back as it pranced from the Warthog's front to side. It was mad as hell, and slammed its tail into the passenger side tracks.

The Warthog shook, and excited cries went out.

"It's moving too fast for me to aim," Diaz said, flustered.

Ben hit the accelerator and headed for an open path before them. The Warthog quickly hit 40 mph on the speedometer. "Did we lose him?"

"No. He is following," Santos said, watching the rear camera's screen.

"*Isso é um lagarto louco,*" Alvarez said.

Matt and Logan both looked over to Gomez.

"He said *that's one crazy lizard.*"

"Ornery, too," Logan added.

"I can kill it now," Diaz said.

"Don't. It can't outrun us. Just leave it alone," Ben said.

Matt realized for Diaz to say he could kill the Rex and not just squeeze the trigger meant the man didn't wish to kill the dinosaur without reason. The man was a commander and didn't have to look to others when it came to decision making.

"There is the other one," Santos said, pointing to the left as they passed the wounded Rex. It had abandoned the fight to find a place to lick its wounds, but the deadly ammunition had taken its life.

"That takes the cake over passing a dead armadillo in the road," Ben said.

Santos and Diaz looked at each other with questioning expressions.

"Cake? What, cake?" Santos asked.

Matt raised open hands in front of his chest. In a bitter tone, he said, "It's…it's just an expression. Ben, you confused them. You explain it. I'm going to check in with Waterman."

Matt found himself too uptight to deal with Ben's sophomoric distractions, but then he felt like a little bit of an ass for losing patience with his friend.

Logan gave him a pat on the shoulder.

Matt turned and placed a hand on top of Logan's hand, returning an expression that said *thanks*.

CHAPTER 17

The expedition was a mile deep in the jungle before Chief signaled from the front for them to stop. Coop's job was to maintain the rear, with the Redwater bunch in the lead, and the college crew between them.

The air was moist and heavy, and the no-see-ums feasted on exposed skin. In his haste to leave, it never crossed Coop's mind to use the bug spray in his backpack. Riding in the Mule and enjoying the artificial environment had lulled him away from preparing for reality.

The journey stirred memories from his time in Vietnam. Tall trees grew thick choking out the sun's rays. If the rest of the jungle was as dense as this area, he was glad that they had decided to leave the vehicle. Staying in the Mule would have just put them further behind schedule.

The only life they had seen thus far was small to medium pterosaurs nesting in trees, who seemed content in allowing humans passage through their pristine abode. But Chief had stopped the group and then ventured on his own for several steps. Coop couldn't see what was going on, but did hear something rustling from up ahead.

Chief slipped silently back. He lowered his head, and whispered, "There're four Velociraptors not far—feeding on carrion. They're small—not like the ones we saw on the drone's video. We can try to go around them, but I don't know if that's the best plan. We're close to the river. At this point, it might make more sense to go for broke, and make a dash for it. If we go around, the raptors might catch our scent and sneak up on us. If we take them out, we can move forward without worrying about them."

"What about the noise?" Coop asked.

"I'm thinking the exploding bullets will have the same effect as the Mule's horn—an unfamiliar noise will scare most things around away. But there's no way to be one hundred percent sure we won't draw others to us," Chief said.

The Velociraptors Chief had described sounded like the kind that killed Alex. They weren't the most feared dinosaur in Patagonia, but ounce for ounce, they were just as vicious as a T-rex. Stealth had gotten them this far, but was it a reasonable risk for them blow their cover and try and make it to the river using *shock-and-awe* tactics?

Chief turned his gaze forward for a few moments, and then said, "Two of the raptors have stopped eating and are sniffing the air. They have our smell."

"That settles it for me," Caveman said.

Suge nodded.

Bats and the others turned and looked at Coop.

This was a war-like situation. Coop knew he was in danger of overthinking the matter. If they were going to make it, he had to let a warrior call the shots. "Chief, from now on, you're in charge of the mission."

"Dial 'em in your scopes, boys. The rest of you be ready to head out after we take them down," Chief said.

The four Redwater mercenaries moved cat-like into position. Rifles went to shoulders, and at some imperceptible command, simultaneously fired. The exploding bullets found their intended targets, and popped like loud fireworks.

Pterosaurs by the dozen cried out in surprise. The flying reptiles scared from tree limbs took to the air for safety. Their wings flapped in the air in such numbers it sounded like a Huey helicopter at takeoff.

The jungle was electrified now. Coop felt like someone had turned the lights on in a planetarium. There was no reason for them to hide any longer.

"Stay together!" Chief said loud enough for everyone to hear and led the way.

Pterosaurs continued to spill from tree limbs as boots crunched on Patagonian ground. Calls of surprise or warning from other creatures about the jungle had heads turning in all directions. They had attracted attention for sure. Coop could only hope none were curious enough to investigate.

Coop, with Alex's help, kept Natasha and Susan in front of them. The women were all business and continued without hesitation.

Reptilian hissing echoed through the trees, and a foghorn-like roar which sounded like a lion gargling water rumbled like it was right on their heels. Things were getting hot, fast, and now Coop questioned their decision.

His phone set to vibrate buzzed on his side. Coop brought a hand over and slapped it, momentarily thinking some insect had attacked. There was no way to know if the news from the Warthog was good or not, and no time for him to check. If they did make it across the river and the Warthog was stuck far away, all of this might just be for naught. *Motherfucking luck, don't fail us now*, he thought in half-prayer.

Everything was a blur. If there were creatures waiting to attack, the passing brush and adrenaline narrowing his vision hid them. They were all racing for their lives, and so far they were chewing up distance unimpeded.

Chief was pulling them forward, his body leading the line of survivors like a fullback leading the ball carrier to the end zone. His chest swayed from side to side, and his legs pumped like pistons. As he passed the trunk of a huge tree, an enormous head bigger than the warrior dipped down, and massive jaws with sharp teeth swallowed him in one bite.

Chief was there, then he was gone—almost without a sound.

Suge was next in line and hit the brake. He brought his JNY-7 up to his shoulder and hesitated. He lowered a hand to his side and signaled to move forward.

Suge had just lost a teammate, mentor, and friend, but his training had him in autopilot. He now assumed the role of leader.

Susan gasped and slowed as she stepped past the tree and looked up at the giant theropod. This dinosaur looked like T-rex on steroids.

Alex reached back and grabbed her by the hand, pulling Susan along. She jerked her hand free.

Coop couldn't allow her to give up now and ran by her side—snatching her left hand in his right. "Don't look! Keep moving!"

She gave in, and quickened her pace. Chief was gone, and they still had a chance. They were so close now. He had to keep Susan alive.

Her hand was sweaty, and when Coop relaxed his grip to get a firmer hold, she slipped free. He blindly reached back, and then he heard a muffled choke and a whimper.

He turned and saw Susan splayed on the jungle ground, a Troodon stood above her with its mouth clamped tightly around her neck. Without thinking, he stopped and fired his rifle.

The bullets exploded, scaring the predator away from its prey, but now the dinosaur came for him.

Caveman bounded past him, and said, "I got this. Go!" He fired his rifle until the Troodon dropped.

Just before Coop turned to run, he saw other Troodons in fast pursuit. "They're coming! Run!"

Seconds later grenades went off behind him. Caveman continued firing his rifle in short bursts and then sped on to catch the group.

A theropod with yellow-orange skin and stripes like a tiger attacked the group head on. It was several feet taller than a man and longer than a passenger van. The dinosaur had a single horn at the end of its snout.

Suge's chest met the full brunt of its charge—his body seemed to fold around the dinosaur's head, and the horn poked out from the center of Suge's back.

Bats let his RPG fly, striking the theropod on its left side. Blood and meat splattered on him and Natasha.

Now leading the group, apparently believing his missile had incapacitated the beast, Bats veered his path and ordered all to follow.

Caveman let another grenade go.

Coop looked back and saw a least a half dozen Troodons coming in for the kill.

"The river! It's just up ahead!" Bats called.

"John, hurry!" Coop yelled. The Troodons quickly filled the space between them and the rotund warrior.

Bats ran past Coop, and commanded, "Get to the river! Don't wait for us!"

Coop surprised himself by acting without delay. Normally his conscious would have him torn between saving himself or risking his life for others. He realized he didn't have what it took now to win the fight. Caveman had said it before, that animals knew only two things: *fight or flight*. Age had wormed its way into his body and mind—weakening him from a predator of fight to prey of flight.

The river was a short distance ahead. Alex had reached the edge and scanned up and down the slow flowing water.

Caveman yelled. It was his death call. The mighty warrior had met the enemy, and the enemy had won.

Alex waited with his hand out as Natasha watched her step as she traveled down the river's bank toward him.

"Swim for it. I'm right behind you," Coop hollered.

Bats' final cry cut through the air moments before what sounded like two grenades going off. Apparently the man fought to the death—waiting at the last moment to achieve the maximum kill.

Alex's rifle and two backpacks were by the shore. Coop tossed his JNY-7 aside and let his backpack fall off his shoulder. He tromped through the water until it came over his knees, and then began the swim. The other side was at least sixty feet away.

The last two survivors were a few yards ahead. Both appeared to struggle; no doubt fatigue had set in, and no one had taken the time to shed their boots.

Coop's hadn't given two thoughts of the dangers that might lurk in the water until now. They were nearly to the halfway point, and he had no clue how deep the river was. At least he hadn't seen any *logs* floating their way, remembering the huge crocodile the drone had taken video of.

Then, a theropod by the river's edge caught his gaze. It looked like it had four legs, but the front legs were shorter than what he thought legs should be. Its head was uniquely crest-shaped, and if Coop weren't swimming for his life, he would have loved to stop and take in the magnificent sight. As long as the creature remained where it was, it wouldn't pose a problem.

Right after that thought, Coop heard the survivors of the Troodon clan arrive by the river. Snarls and hisses were followed by splishes and splashes. The race was on.

The shore quickly approached. Coop saw Alex had made it where it was shallow enough to stand and trod through the water. The Professor stopped and waited for Natasha to arrive.

At this point Coop wished he had spent extra days at the gym. His arms started to feel like lead weights, and his chest muscles tightened and screamed with pain. But at least he was getting closer—almost there. His hand hit the muddy bottom, and he traveled a few more feet before planting a foot down and slogging his way to shore.

He turned and counted four Troodon heads speeding toward him like periscopes cutting above water. Dinosaur bodies seemed just as adept traveling under water as land.

Alex waited with his hand out, despite Coop motioning for the two to leave without him. He took the Professor's hand and stepped to dry land. Fortunately, the crest-headed dinosaur was content to watch from a distance, no doubt just as fearful of the four Troodons as he.

Climbing the bank took more time than Coop would have liked. At least the land on the other side was relatively flat. He looked around; if any trees had branches low enough for them to reach, they would take refuge and call the Warthog for help. The tall trees offered no hope, with the lowest branches well beyond any human's reach.

It was fight or flight. With bare hands as the only weapons, fight was out of the question.

Coop heaved for air, and so did Natasha and Alex. The two former lovers ran with panic-numbed expressions, fear frozen in their eyes. Coop imagined his face showed the same.

How long could he keep up this pace? His lungs burned, his breathing almost out of sync to where he swallowed air at times.

Coop heard clawed feet in pursuit pounding the ground behind him. He turned and saw the closest Troodon a few yards away—gaining fast.

Trees and foliage flew by, but there was no open area as far as he could see. No Warthog with its mighty gun ready to blast the dinosaurs to kingdom come. No mercenaries armed to the teeth ready to do battle to the death.

The nearest Troodon hissed. It sounded like it was so close it whispered in his ear. There was victory in its cry. It knew it would only be a matter of seconds before it had Coop and the two other tasty meat-bags to feast upon.

Coop's mind flashed back as the Spinosaurus ate him alive on his first death; how the other theropod he fought so valiantly crushed him to death with its jaws and teeth. He was about to be devoured by creatures of smaller stature. They would incapacitate him, hold him on the ground, pull flesh from bone one bite at a time, perhaps savoring the meal more as he screamed in pain, and begged for death to take him away a final time.

His foot hit uneven ground. Coop fell face-forward to the earth. "Run!" he screamed.

The Troodon yelped in delight.

Coop flipped to his back and saw his executioner loom over him. It brought its three clawed hands up in wicked delight, reared its head back on its long neck, and before it plugged down for the kill, its three companions arrived by its side—ready to share the spoils.

Machine guns rattled behind him.

Holes punched in the pale-white of the Troodons' chests and deep crimson poured out.

Reptilian screams interlaced with the bark of multiple rifles. Coop flipped over on his stomach and crawled away.

Six soldiers clad in black had emerged from around the trees. Their rifles spat fire and mercilessly slung lead into the hungry theropods.

Alex waited with Natasha, his arms loosely around her as she stood with her hands up to her mouth.

The moment reminded Coop of basic training—crawling on his belly while live ammo flew overhead. During the Vietnam war, it was said that an unusually large number of inductees caught in the draft died during this exercise. The Asian war had a terrifying reputation. Suicide was a quick ticket out. All one had to do was raise his head and catch a bullet that would send him home forever.

Today was nothing like days past. This wall of fire was his salvation—a gift he would not squander.

By the time Coop passed the last soldier and stood, the guns went silent. He turned and saw the four Troodons had succumbed to the barrage of bullets and had literally died on top of each other. The machine guns had fired conventional bullets and had no problem in killing the dinosaurs. This reminded Coop of the devastating power of any fire arm and how only those trained how to use them should be allowed to own one.

"*Senhor*, Cooper. I am Captain Diaz," Diaz said. The man was the only one of the six who wore a red beret instead of black. "Are you injured?"

Coop leaned over a bit with his hands on his knees—trying to catch his breath. After a moment, he shook his head, and said, "I'm fine...I'm fine."

Diaz turned his gaze over to Alex and Natasha.

"We're good," Alex said.

"The others?"

Standing upright, and leaning his head back with his eyes closed, Coop said, "They didn't make it."

"I am sorry, *Senhor* Cooper," Diaz said.

"Yeah, we're sorry too. They were good men. Really *good* men. You know what I mean, Captain Diaz, don't you? They were the kind of men who thought of the mission and the safety of others over their own well-being. They used fear as a platform to rise above the situation and do things beyond the ability of most mortals. They were good men, and now they're gone."

Diaz gazed intently at Coop. "I do indeed know of such men. I regret I never had the chance to meet them before their final reward. Your three friends have told us stories of the great men of the Redwater team on the trip here."

"The Warthog, where is it?" Alex asked.

"Three kilos from here," Diaz said.

"I can't believe we made it," Natasha said. "How did you know where to find us?"

"The beacon on *Senhor* Cooper's phone mapped your location. We brought the Warthog in as close as possible and hurried to assist."

"If you had been one minute later…well you weren't. I guess…I guess we were just *lucky* that way," Coop said, again his mind fought to find order in the universe outside of random chance.

"*Senhor* Cooper, *Senhor* Henry Lear gave me two sets of orders on this mission…to bring back the survivors and the diamonds. Do you have the diamonds?" Diaz asked, his tone dry and business like.

Coop chuckled to himself. The man leading the mission who saved his life now reached out to poke his last nerve. But he was just too exhausted to give a fuck anymore. He reached in a side pocket on his thigh and unbuttoned the flap. His hand brought out the leather pouch containing the priceless jewels. "Here you go, Captain Diaz." Coop tossed the pouch over to the leader, who caught it and brought it to his gaze for examination. "I never want to see these goddam things ever again."

CHAPTER 18

"Look! They're coming," Matt said. He, Logan, and Ben had their gazes glued to the camera waiting for Alex, Natasha, Coop, and the mercenaries to return.

"There's the Professor...Hot damn! Wow, he looks like shit," Ben said, the corners of his mouth stretching toward his ears.

"Natasha," Matt said, his tone showing relief.

"Natasha," Logan said, apprehensively.

Matt sensed something had gone on between Logan and Natasha before her death. He never confronted Logan about it, and now wasn't the time to ask questions either. "What are we waiting for?" He turned and headed for the door.

As Matt stepped down on the Warthog's track and then descended the ladder, his mind swirled with all the scenarios he had considered if he ever got the chance of meeting Alex again. Any prepackaged apology went out the window. Emotion took over, and he ran toward his good friend. "Alex! Natasha!"

Alex's and Natasha's haggard, dirt-smudged faces beamed with delight as Matt reached out and hugged them both. "I'm so glad...I'm so glad..." And that was it, he broke down. Tears streamed down his face, and he couldn't find his voice.

Logan stepped up and put his arms around Natasha and Matt. He began crying a waterfall.

Ben was on his crutches and was standing on the tracks. "Professor! Natasha! Yee-hah!" He raised one crutch in the air for victory.

Natasha and Alex waved to Ben.

Matt gained his composure, he let go of Natasha, and still in his embrace with Alex, he whispered in his ear, "There's something we need to talk about."

"Matt, whatever happened in the past doesn't matter," Alex said.

"No, that's not it. Susan didn't make it. Lear said—"

Lightning cracked above, and thunder rumbled like it announced Armageddon. A huge spiral of smoke churned like a slow moving pinwheel to the side of the Warthog, several yards away. Blue, green, and red ethereal lights flashed in the vortex.

Several of the Brazilians' screamed out *Meu Deus* and brought their weapons to the ready.

"Is that the time pool I read about in the report?" Diaz asked.

"It is," Coop said. "Look! Someone's coming out."

"It's not human," Diaz said.

A figure stepped from the spinning vortex—clearly a few feet taller than a normal man. It had an elongated head, which was bulbous on the crown. Its eyes were small and almond-shaped, above a nose that barely poked out over thin lips. A blue one-piece garment with a flared collar covered its body.

"What the hell..." Matt said.

Alex's hair was a wiry mess piled on top of his head. The exhaustion had him looking a bit punch-drunk. He lifted his eyebrows, spread his hands out in front of him a foot or so apart, and with a shit-eating smile on his face, said, "I'm not saying it's aliens, but...it's aliens."

Coop looked over at the Professor as if he were about to say something, but put himself in check.

"What does it want?" Diaz said.

"I don't know. It reminds me of a character from a Twilight Zone episode. The alien had a book with him titled *To Serve Man*," Alex said.

"That sounds promising," Coop said.

"No, not really. Turns out it was a cookbook," Alex said.

"Oh..." Coop took a step back.

The alien moved away from the mouth of the vortex. Ron and Don Bartel were the first to emerge. Both were fully dressed in freshly pressed fatigues. Every hair, what little was left, was neatly in place. "Roll Tide!" they said together as they ran toward Matt and the others.

Meat and Caveman followed, and then Bats and Suge. Chief and Susan were out next, and finally Will and Gerald exited the time pool.

The excitement of the returning members overshadowed the fact that an alien was standing not far from them. Slaps, hugs, giggles, and *Roll Tide* repeated by Suge, Ron, and Don occupied the group for several moments. Eventually everyone quieted down. Matt, Coop, and Alex stepped forward.

"Who are you?" Coop asked.

As opening questions to another life form go, Matt thought it was as an intelligent request as any.

The alien didn't open his mouth, but his words were clear—as if he spoke them directly in the ear, "Who I am is none of your concern. Though as you can see, I am not of this world."

"See, *aliens*," Alex said smugly.

The alien held a façade of indifference. He gave no indication he had the least bit of curiosity concerning humans.

"You are responsible for all of this?" Coop spread one hand away from him. "Patagonia? The dinosaurs living here well past their extinction over the rest of the Earth?"

"The answer is obvious," the alien said, his words frosty.

Coop started, "I...I'm sorry. I don't—"

"You're an alien. We don't mean to offend you. We want to establish communication and learn of your race," Alex said.

"It is not beneficial for my race to have ties with humans," the alien said.

"Will you at least tell us something? Where you're from? How old your race is? Why you're here now?" Matt asked.

"It serves no purpose for you to know my history. However, I am here because the Earth is a rare jewel even amongst the millions of planets in the galaxy that support life. It is our purpose to ensure that the Earth abides, despite its care by humans," the alien said.

Coop cast a wary eye toward Alex, and then asked, "Why did you preserve the dinosaurs?"

"Consider the dinosaurs as gifts. Gifts to humanity. Gifts to the Earth," the alien said.

"You have the power over time. You know everything. The end of all beginnings," Alex said, amazement in his tone.

"Very well put," the alien said.

"But this—all that you've gone through to save prehistoric life, all that we've gone through—dying and coming back again. Why? Why is it so important, and why now?" Coop asked.

"Humanity is at a crossroads. Now is the time for the world to marvel at evolution's greatest creations. Your scientists will study the ancient creatures and learn many things, including the destiny of mankind itself," the alien said.

"That's a vague answer," Coop said. "There has to be more."

The alien made no attempt to respond.

"You manipulated all of us—brought us here to find the dinosaurs so we can bring them back. Kept bringing us back to life so we could finish the mission. The way you did it…it could have been planned better. Why? Why did we have to go through all those horrible deaths? There had to be an easier way!" Alex said, anger rising in his voice.

"You are in no position to question," the alien said.

Alex raised his hands. "Okay, okay…I don't mean to try your patience. Please just tell me one thing…" He closed his eyes, and then opened them, and said, "I…I did something horrible—something I thought I would never do. I killed my wife. Those thoughts—I don't know where those thoughts came from. I can't even believe I was capable of carrying them out. You can manipulate time. Did you motivate me in some way that altered my thinking and led me to kill Susan?"

"And me, too, with Alex?" Matt asked.

Logan stepped by Matt's side, his body tense in anticipation.

"Time waves preserving Patagonia are an exotic band of electromagnetic radiation, which can impose negative effects on organic matter. Aberrations to the human psyche are a possibility and could give rise to irrational behavior. Search your hearts. Let your conscience judge your actions," the alien said.

At that, the alien slowly walked back into the time pool's mouth.

Lightning crashed; thunder rolled; the spinning vortex vanished.

Matt turned and looked at everyone's stunned expressions. His brain still processed the events of the past several minutes. He felt like a pawn in some grand theater—no—more like a puppet on a string.

"Let's get the hell out of Dodge," Bats called out.

"Roll Tide," Ron, Don, and Suge said in agreement.

Alex turned to Matt, leaned toward him, and said, "Matt, before the alien showed up, you were concerned with something. Something that Lear had said. What were you about to tell me?"

Matt smiled big enough to show teeth. "It doesn't matter now, Alex. We're all here and alive. Let's go home."

EPILOGUE

Five Years Later

The dim lighting in Henry Lear's office reflected his current state of affairs; of that of the United States of America; of the whole world.

A large TV on the wall gave constant updates of the turmoil brewing in the Eastern Hemisphere.

Another glass of Scotch wouldn't change anything, but he poured a tumbler half full anyway.

Ace Corporation's business had boomed after his expedition returned from Patagonia with rare diamonds and proof dinosaurs still lived. Lear knew who to bribe and who to coerce—finding more diamonds and rare minerals and farming out prehistoric creatures. Dinosaur parks had sprung up in thirty-three countries all over the world. Dinosaurs laid an abundance of eggs and incubator mortality neared one hundred percent. Being the middleman and a wise investor had netted Ace Corporation over twenty billion dollars over the past five years. Henry Lear had exceeded his personal goal of wealth over tenfold—with no end of future earnings in sight.

Except global war threatened to choke his business to death. Global war threatened the existence of mankind.

Russia had declared rule over Poland, Romania, and the Baltic States. Massive forces waited at the borders for the final order. NATO promised to defend the allied countries at any cost. With superior, modern tactical nukes in Russia's arsenal, they believed a quick and victorious war would be theirs by launching first-strike.

To make matters worse, a U.S. nuclear sub had gone missing in the South China Sea in waters claimed by the People's Republic of China. This happened directly after a final warning issued by the Communist government. China, too, believed NATO and the West were too weak to impose its limits on them any longer.

Lear had the TV's volume set on mute. The pretty blonde reading the news was in bad need of touching up her makeup. Apprehension showed on her face. A message scrolled across the bottom of the screen that the President of the United States had set the Defcon state to 2—Armed Forces ready to deploy and engage in less than 6 hours.

The intercom on his desk beeped, and a female's voice said, "Mr. Lear, you have a call from the research center."

With doomsday around the corner, Lear thought it stereotypical that the lab nerds kept working uninterrupted. But he knew Mark Johnson led the team and loved his work more so than the pay. If the man had something important enough for him to call directly, Lear at least should give him an ear for a few minutes.

"I'll take it," Lear said. The red light on the phone blinked, and he answered, "Lear."

"Mr. Lear, Mark Johnson."

"Hello, Mark. I'm used to reading your reports. I don't believe we've ever spoken on the phone before."

"We've made some important discoveries in the last seventy-two hours. Doing some random tests on a Compsognathus, we found an enzyme in its mucus membranes that has the biological ability to degrade radioactive isotopes—iodine-131, barium-140, strontium-90, caesium-137—essentially rendering them harmless."

"Really? How on Earth is that possible?" Lear asked.

"It's too early to say. The enzyme works on an atomic level. If we can learn how to mass produce this enzyme, then we can eliminate the world's nuclear waste. The nuclear energy industry will flourish, and Ace Corporation will hold the patents."

"The irony is palpable," Lear said. "The day we discover a solution to our nuclear waste problem we find ourselves on the eve of nuclear annihilation."

"It gets even stranger. We discovered the skin is made up of a strange array of biopolymers—unlike any other living creature on Earth. We subjected the skin of a test animal to a laser capable of reaching ten thousand degrees. Mr. Lear, the skin didn't sustain any recordable damage."

"That's not possible."

"Well, you wouldn't think so. But an inventor several years back created a plastic made up of organic material that proved in the lab it could withstand heat created in a nuclear blast. It's possible nature created a similar type material of its own."

"That doesn't make any sense, though. I'm no scientist, but I know how deadly radiation is to animal life."

"I admit, it's uncanny. If there is nuclear war tomorrow, I don't know what the fate of mankind will be. But the thousands of dinosaurs staged around the world will survive. They all have the same enzyme, and their skin is made up of the same biopolymers. It's like the dinosaurs were genetically engineered to survive a nuclear holocaust."

The phone line went dead. The TV picture went blank.

Lear stepped away from his massive oak desk. His twelve-hundred-dollar shoes carried him over by the window as he looked into the night sky.

The darkness cracked open in a blinding light that cut through his eyes like plasma from the sun. His world went dark. A growing vibration rose from the Earth and rattled his teeth. A force unimaginable ripped him apart, mixing his molecules with the debris of a failed species.

The Earth would heal, and the *terrible lizards* of eons past would once again have dominion over the planet.

THE END

CHECK OUT OTHER GREAT
DINOSAUR THRILLERS

THE VALLEY
by **Rick Jones**

In a dystopian future, a self-contained valley in Argentina serves as the 'far arena' for those convicted of a crime. Inside the Valley: carnivorous dinosaurs generated from preserved DNA. The goal: cross the Valley to get to the Gates of Freedom. The chance of survival: no one has ever completed the journey. Convicted of crimes with little or no merit, Ben Peyton and others must battle their way across fields filled with the world's deadliest apex predators in order to reach salvation. All the while the journey is caught on cameras and broadcast to the world as a reality show, the deaths and killings real, the macabre appetite of the audience needing to be satiated as Ben Peyton leads his team to escape not only from a legal system that's more interested in entertainment than in justice, but also from the predators of the Valley.

JURASSIC DEAD
by Rick Chesler & David Sakmyster

An Antarctic research team hoping to study microbial organisms in an underground lake discovers something far more amazing: perfectly preserved dinosaur corpses. After one thaws and wakes ravenously hungry, it becomes apparent that death, like life, will find a way.
Environmental activist Alex Ramirez, son of the expedition's paleontologist, came to Antarctica to defend the organisms from extinction, but soon learns that it is the human race that needs protecting.

CHECK OUT OTHER GREAT DINOSAUR THRILLERS

LOST WORLD OF PATAGONIA
by Dane Hatchell

An earthquake opens a path to a land hidden for millions of years. Under the guise of finding cryptid animals, Ace Corporation sends Alex Klasse, a Cryptozoologist and university professor, his associates, and a band of mercenaries to explore the Lost World of Patagonia. The crew boards a nuclear powered All-Terrain Tracked Carrier and takes a harrowing ride into the unknown.

The expedition soon discovers prehistoric creatures still exist. But the dangers won't prevent a sub-team from leaving the group in search of rare jewels. Tensions run high as personalities clash, and man proves to be just as deadly as the dinosaurs that roam the countryside.

Lost World of Patagonia is a prehistoric thriller filled with murder, mayhem, and savage dinosaur action.

SAVAGE ISLAND
by Alan Spencer

Somewhere in the Atlantic Ocean, an uncharted island has been used for the illegal dumping of chemicals and pollutants for years by Globo Corp's. Private investigator Pierce Range will learn plenty about the evil conglomerate when Susan Branch, an environmentalist from The Green Project, hires him to join the expedition to save her kidnapped father from Globo Corp's evil hands.

Things go to hell in a hurry once the team reaches the island. The bloodthirsty dinosaurs and voracious cannibals are only the beginning of the fight for survival. Pierce must unlock the mysteries surrounding the toxic operation and somehow remain in one piece to complete the rescue mission.

Ratchet up the body count, because this mission will leave the killing floor soaked in blood and chewed up corpses. When the insane battle ends, will there by anybody left alive to survive Savage Island?

www.ingramcontent.com/pod-product-compliance
Lightning Source LLC
Chambersburg PA
CBHW032005170626
46807CB00006B/2656